LAW OF THE JUNGLE

LAW OF THE JUNGLE

SANTANA SOKOLOV™ BOOK ONE

MICHAEL ANDERLE

LMBPN Publishing
PMB 196, 2540 South Maryland Pkwy
Las Vegas, NV 89109

First US Edition, October 2021
ebook ISBN: 978-1-68500-407-1
Print ISBN: 978-1-68500-408-8

THE LAW OF THE JUNGLE TEAM

Thanks to the JIT Readers

Rachel Beckford
Zacc Pelter
Deb Mader
Daryl McDaniel
Dave Hicks
John Ashmore
Diane L. Smith
Dorothy Lloyd
Jeff Goode

If I've missed anyone, please let me know!

Editor
The Skyhunter Editing Team

PROLOGUE

The temperature was unnaturally high, elevated by several kilns and furnaces located around the room. Steam and smoke created a carpet on the ceiling. A constant crackle popped in the air as the golden glow from molten metal channeled along preset paths.

Sasha Chechik folded her arms. Her dark skin glistened with pearls of sweat. She wore leather overalls, her hands hidden by oversized gloves. Nearby, the mountain of a man, Carlos Ariya, played with his toys, encouraging the molten metal along the track and into the mold.

"Doesn't look like much now, but soon this'll be one of the finest blades Atlantica has to offer." He grinned, a hypnotized stare on his face, the golden liquid reflected in the darks of his eyes. "I can't tell you how much something like this will fetch on the market."

"Does it matter?" Sasha replied sharply, only a little impressed by the molding. "What use are swords in today's world? You bring a sword to the house of your enemies, and you won't get an inch inside before they riddle your body with bullets. There's no place for swords or cutlasses when people wage war long-range now."

Carlos gave her a dirty look. He was large enough to crush her with a bearish squeeze, but Sasha sensed no threat from the smith. He rocked the bed where the molten metal was cooling, ensuring that the liquid moved into all the correct cracks and holes before stepping away. He took a cloth from his waist and wiped his forehead. "Then what the fuck are you doing here if not to purchase from my array of world-class *close-range* weaponry?"

Sasha's eyes lingered on the mesmerizing bed of gold. "You know why I'm here."

Carlos glanced at the shadowy space near the wooden door, where a set of four stone steps led to the only entrance in or out of his workshop. Resting against the wall was an ancient scythe, the handle black as obsidian, the blade a dull silver. "A tune-up?"

He wandered over to the scythe, then examined it. He rolled the handle over in his hands, then scrutinized the blade, running a thumb along the edge. "How long since your last sharpening?"

Sasha peeled her eyes from the metal, the golden gleam beginning to fade as the metal cooled. "Since its last owner handed it to me."

Carlos chuckled. "That much is clear. Why now?"

Sasha stalked closer, leaving a trailing scent of lilies mixed among the burning stench. Carlos retreated slightly, sensing the power she held. "Because my father saw the blade only as a symbolic item, a lingering relic of a time long past. It was never used to strike, attack, or mow down an enemy, only to make his dick look bigger in the rooms where they measured them. But now…"

An intensity crossed over Sasha's face that drew Carlos' unblinking gaze. "Now I intend to restore this to its former glory."

Carlos exhaled, turning his attention back to the dull blade. "So much for the woman mocking the man still making swords in a world of long-range combat."

Sasha smirked. "Indeed. Only, if an enemy comes into my domain, they will be stripped of their firearms and will face me fist-to-fist."

Carlos gave a firm nod. "Then I'd better get to work. No point letting a lady of your caliber wait longer than is necessary."

He shuffled past her, attending to stoking the fires of a nearby furnace. On a shelf by the wall were several stones and items used to sharpen and keen and hone.

"How much are you looking to pay for this service?" Carlos asked.

"Finance is not an issue. Whatever you deem worthy," Sasha replied.

Carlos nodded. "Friends and family discount it is."

Sasha wandered close behind him. She could barely see the fires past his broad shoulders. His black shirt was stained even darker with sweat. "You understand that's not the only reason for my visit, don't you?"

Carlos stiffened. She knew she had him where she wanted him.

"Oh?" Carlos replied. He stood straight, then turned to face her, having to look down to meet her eyes.

Sasha looked up. She knew the effect she had on men, her angular face and sharp jawline an attraction to the male gaze. Her eyes were the steely blue of an iceberg. "You know where it is, don't you?"

Carlos narrowed his eyes. "I'm sorry, you're going to have to be clearer—" He stopped, a great waft of air expelling from his lips. He glanced down at the blade stuck in his hip.

He doubled over, clutching his side. Now at eye level with Sasha, she drew closer, eyes inches from his, her demeanor still calm. "Don't toy with me, smith. You know why I've come, and I know you know where it is."

She twisted the blade a fraction to the left. Carlos grunted. "Now, either you tell me what you know, or I find one of your friends who will. One option leaves you with a small boo-boo on your side. The other leaves you melting facedown in your creations. Choose wisely."

Carlos groaned, squinting as sweat dripped into his eye. Sasha held his gaze awaiting the answer, the one she knew she would get.

"Say its name," Carlos replied weakly.

Sasha's lips peeled back into a menacing grimace. "La Daga de los Días Sin Fin."

Carlos gave a resigned sigh, his body jerking slightly at the pain of the blade. Sasha kept her hold firm.

"The Temple of the Summer Crown," Carlos replied at last. "A wanderer stumbled across it a few days ago. Almost lost his leg on a tumble down through the forest floor." He gasped for breath. "A rescue team brought him out. They'd never seen anything like it. Alerted the authorities. They're sending their teams down there now—if they haven't already got there…"

"Who's down there?" She twisted the blade again. It was unnecessary but brought her a certain joy to see the mammoth squirm.

"The Atlantican Historical Preservation Society." Carlos' breaths were shaky.

Sasha gave a steely nod. "Anyone else?"

"Not that I'm aware of."

She detected a hint of a lie in his eyes and twisted the knife again.

"Fine!" Carlos groaned. "Fine… The Albatross."

Sasha's heart dropped. In one fluid motion, she pulled the blade from Carlos' hip. "Thank you. You have proven most useful."

She turned and crossed the room. When she reached the door, she heard a *thump* as Carlos fell to his knees. He called, "Wait…your scythe…"

Sasha narrowed her eyes. "My price will be fair. Have it fixed up for me by the end of tomorrow. I'll have one of my people collect it."

Carlos glanced down at his side. Blood trickled between the cracks of his fingers. His lips parted, protestations ready on his tongue.

Before he had a chance to reply, Sasha was gone.

CHAPTER ONE

"So, are you going to tell me what's new with you?" Santana asked Terra Kris, the athletic woman who sat across the table. "Got a new fella in your life?"

Music played at a steady level, quieter than some of the other joints in this city. The club was sparsely populated, and of those patrons scattered around the place, a large number of the hot-blooded males kept their eyes fixed on Santana Sokolov.

Who could blame them? It wasn't often that they'd find a woman dressed as though she were ready for her next expedition into the tropics in a place like this. Santana's cargo shorts revealed long, muscular legs. Her tank top hugged her form. The long coil of a bullwhip hung at one hip.

Terra scoffed. "You could say that."

Santana's eyebrows raised. She studied the woman she'd known since they were both children. Santana, a young girl who had migrated to Atlantica from Russia in her formative years, found this woman fascinating.

Terra was born and bred on the island of Atlantica, had never seen the outside world, or knew of the ways of distant continents. Santana had seen plenty through her travels and knew that nowhere was supposed to be like Atlantica. Atlantica was a cesspool of wonder, crime, fortune, fame, and destruction. Even in the grand old year of 2027, injustice was allowed to reign supreme.

A modern metropolis in which the corrupt ruled the roost, and the authorities constantly swam upstream.

Terra was Atlantica Justice System talent through and through. Everything and anything she'd done in her life had paved the way forward for a career in law enforcement. So why the change in relationship status now?

"Well, I wasn't expecting that," Santana stated. "Terra Kris, the perpetually single, taking another into her life. What's his name?"

"APRIL," Terra replied.

There was a strange glint in Terra's eyes. "April?" She mused, a sudden realization dawning on her. "Oh… Have you…I mean… are you?"

"No, no," Terra interjected, a laugh playing on her lips. "Nothing like that. I've… Well… This is going to sound a little crazy."

Santana sipped her drink and crossed her legs. "I love crazy."

Terra sighed and leaned forward. "APRIL…it stands for Advanced Police Relationship Intelligence Liaison."

Santana cocked her head. "I'm not following you."

Terra tapped the side of her head. There was a series of puckered pink lines at the edges of her scalp, fading away into her hairline. Santana wondered if they were from Terra's recent accident.

"They…did something to me during my operation," Terra continued. "After salvaging what they could from what the blast had taken, they had no choice but to piece me together…manually."

Santana sipped her drink, her interest engaged.

Terra carried on. "They had been trialing a new AI system for the AJS, trying to find ways to increase the force's effectiveness.

Some donor was on the verge of integrating artificial intelligence with bio matter and…" She grinned and spread her arms wide to present herself. "The first successful example is sitting before you."

Santana's brow creased. She couldn't find the words.

"I told you it was crazy," Terra offered. She looked strange out of uniform. Santana tried to remember the last time she'd seen the officer out of her hexagonal-patterned blue fatigues that were standard among the Atlantica Justice System. Santana had begun to think that Terra lived, worked, and slept in the damned things.

Santana shook her head disbelievingly and waved dismissively. "Shut up."

"It's true." Terra's drink was nearly empty, a weight falling over her. "Ask me a question about you. Anything."

"What's my mother's name?" Santana teased.

Terra rolled her eyes. "A question you know I wouldn't know the answer to, please. Something you have on record that would be impossible for me to know."

"Fine…" Santana thought long and hard. "What's my social security number?"

She waited a moment while Terra's eyes narrowed. Something was going on inside her head that Santana wasn't privy to. Santana had seen a lot of examples of advanced tech in the city, but this one seemed to go too far.

Finally, Terra replied, "078-50-1120."

Santana's eyes widened. *Holy shit.* "Okay…That's impressive but could be coincidental."

"Coincidental, how?"

"You could've looked at my records on the AJS database before we met up," Santana replied. "Who were my last three clients to pay fees into my account?" She sat back and folded her arms with a smug grin. There was no way anyone but Santana and her clients would know the answer to this question.

She waited another couple of seconds while Terra calculated

and conferred with the so-called tech inside her head. Santana grew curious, wondering if Terra was speaking the truth and what that would mean to Atlantica going forward.

"Taylor Yungheim, Bonita Ung, and Charles Trevors," Terra replied.

The mirth left Santana's face, replaced with a deep fascination. She leaned closer to Terra, looking intently into her eyes. She honed in on the sclera, looking toward the pink corneas and wondering if that blinking light she could see behind Terra's eyes was imaginary or if it was there.

The light blinked again. A small LED tucked into the far reaches of Terra's eye socket. Santana gasped. "You weren't kidding."

"No," Terra confirmed. "Why would I kid about any of that?"

"I don't know." Santana sat back. "Sometimes people play pranks."

"About AIs sitting inside their minds? I don't think so."

"Fascinating," Santana breathed.

She reached for her glass and drained the last of the contents. Sitting across from her old school friend, trying to digest all that had happened to them in the years since they'd graduated and gone their separate ways was no small feat. Santana thought she and Terra were meeting up for a small catch-up, but this development was huge. This could spell massive disruption in the city.

Lucky that I don't spend much of my time in the city these days. At least out in the jungles I remain queen.

Finally, she managed, "It can do everything you say it can?"

"Everything and more," Terra replied. "Even now I'm still finding out things that it can do that I was unaware of." She nodded at Santana's glass. "Another?"

Santana thanked Terra. She returned a moment later with two of the same orders. "I'm surprised that you didn't go for a coffee again," Santana commented.

"Go big or go home."

Santana rolled her eyes and swallowed her mouthful. "Do you remember the guys that used to live by that as their mantra? I wonder what they're doing these days."

"Mostly rotting in prison cells or drug dens hooked on ink," Terra replied. "We caught Phillip Vaughn, by the way."

Santana nearly spat out her drink. "Little Pippin?"

"The very same," Terra replied. "Caught him a few months back dealing ink to a bunch of school kids. When we dove in further, there was…well, let's just say there were more kids where they came from."

"Damn." Santana's head filled with images of the vagrants who lined Atlantica's alleyways, their veins black and pronounced after injecting themselves with the latest narcotics craze the city had to offer. "This city hits their people hard, doesn't it?"

Terra nodded. "What about you, anyway? Any more trips back to the motherland recently?"

Santana shook her head. "Afraid not. It's been a few years since I've been back to see Papa. I have far too much to keep me busy here." She considered saying more but held it back. Terra knew better than most about the tragic and untimely death of Santana's mother after a rogue cave-in caught her underground and took the lives of her entire expedition team.

Her father had never truly been right after that. It barely took him a couple of weeks before announcing to a young Santana that they were migrating back to Russia. "Atlantica has a way of swallowing you and holding you here."

Terra smirked. "Tell me about it."

"I do miss the mountains, though," Santana continued. "Nothing like staring up at the canvas of stars from the top of Mount Elbrus. I can't describe it…it's like the gods birthed all their colors and swirls and slapped it on the black. You don't see that here. Only fog, fog, and more fog."

Terra looked down at the table. "I'd love to visit one day."

"You should," Santana replied. "If our days off ever cross, I'll take you there. I'll show the best trails to the top. We'll wrestle mountain lions and hug goats and…"

"Fall from the top?" Terra laughed. "Just the straight and up, please."

"You got it." Santana drained her drink in one. "You down for another?"

Santana smirked, seeing the slight glaze over Terra's eyes. She wobbled a touch in her chair. Terra had never been that great at holding her liquor, and Santana knew they always had more fun when the uptight, rigid, scheduled, lawful Terra allowed herself to have some fun.

Santana wondered if Terra had enough and was surprised when she rose from the table and took Santana's glass. "I'll get this round."

"Fine." Santana smiled. "I've got next." She watched Terra wander over to the bar, several nearby men shifting in their chairs and sensing Santana now sitting by herself. Santana caught one man's eyes and shook her head, clarifying that he shouldn't attempt what he was about to.

Terra returned with the next round. They both held up their glasses and *clinked* them together. "For one night only," Terra stated.

"For one night only." Santana closed her eyes and sipped, unaware of how much fun she and her old school friend were about to have.

CHAPTER TWO

The clock ticked past midnight, and still the two ladies of Atlantica strolled arm-in-arm down the street.

Santana's cheeks hurt from grinning. Terra had hooked her arm around Santana's. She'd lost count of how many drinks they'd both had, and she didn't mind one iota. Terra was having a whale of a time. She couldn't remember the last time she'd seen the justice officer let go and live in the moment.

That technology inside her noggin must be doing wonders for her.

Santana thought back, trying to track the number of drinks the pair had bought. They'd hit several of Atlantica's quieter clubs and bars and were now heading away from the place where they'd spent the last hour dancing. Together they had laughed and smiled and guarded each other against the advances of the predatory elite. With each step away from the club, the city grew quieter. Above them, the ever-present veil of fog that blanketed Atlantica obscured the full moon.

Set nearly a thousand miles off the East Coast of the United States, Atlantica had been an enigma for years. Although rumors flared around the existence of the isolated island cast adrift in the Atlantic Ocean, few knew of its location. The island maintained its sub-tropical climate, and sailors throughout the years simply missed the landmass due to the blanket fog cover.

It wasn't until the Second World War that the island was first "claimed" by soldiers from the Nazi party, using the island as an outpost for research and projects that were still a mystery. Toward the end of the war, US soldiers landed on the island's soil, and in a freak, unexplained event, no one ever saw a soldier from either side again.

Years passed with little story to tell. When the world officially launched satellites into the sky and showed the first full images of the Earth, countries were finally able to home in on the modest island.

Santana tried to recall the details, wondering where it all went wrong. In the seventies, the island grew in popularity. Arguments between territories broke out as nations tried to stake their claim and guide the island by their own rule. In a twisted fight for its identity, Atlantica finally settled on its rules and regulations. The main two being, shield the corrupt and taint the pure, and whatever happens on private property stays on private property. Santana had witnessed Terra's frustration throughout the years, knowing that as long as criminals hid inside their own four walls, even the AJS couldn't touch them.

What a place to live.

"Easy, now." Santana laughed, saving Terra from stumbling and falling on her face. "We should probably look at getting you home, shouldn't we?"

Terra waved it off. She slurred her words with a glazed look in her eye. "I'm fine. Fine, fine, fine. I could go all night!"

Santana chuckled. "Come on, pig. Let's drag you back to that house of yours. Your mama and papa still living there?"

A sudden fear passed over Terra's eyes. "No. Nope. Can't go there. They're not there. No…" She hiccupped, a dangerous burp following the sound. "Come on, one more, please."

Santana rolled her eyes. "Fine, where's good for you?"

Terra let out another hiccup. Her cheeks puffed out. Then she dribbled saliva to the ground.

"Charming," Santana stated.

Terra turned to her, a pained expression on her face. "I think I may have had a little too much."

"You think?" Santana replied, bringing her closer and supporting her as she veered Terra in the opposite direction. Terra didn't fight her.

"How come you're okay?" Terra asked, her neck seeming unable to support the weight of her head.

Santana gave a single reply. "Russian."

Terra nodded, then fell quiet. Santana led her across the street, heading through the forest of skyscrapers and magnificently eccentric buildings. As they walked, groups of young adults wandered between bars, cheery expressions on their faces, drinks in hand. Santana weaved through them, on one occasion slapping a man's hand away who had tried to squeeze her ass.

Finally, the streets quieted. Santana looked ahead, looking for the shortcut to her apartment. Terra had fallen silent, her eyes struggling to stay open as she stumbled. Her weight grew heavier on Santana's shoulder with every step.

They approached an alley. It was dark inside, but Santana knew the way even with several drinks in her system. She wasn't lying to Terra. Her Russian heritage—and her father's affinity for alcohol, particularly in the days since her mother's passing—had steeled her stomach to much of its effects. Although the edges of her vision were a little fuzzy, she navigated through the alley with ease, curving around dumpsters and bracing herself against the potent stink of the ventilation system behind the fast-food venue.

If Terra weren't still moving her legs, in the darkness, Santana would've believed she was sleeping. Halfway through the alley, she detected the soft sounds of movement.

She froze.

Over her years of jungle exploration, Santana's eyes had adjusted to the darkness. In the inky shadows, she saw the soft outline of trashcans, a rusted shell of a car, and something moving toward her.

Santana straightened up, eyes narrowing. A flame flared on the edge of a thick stick, and a gaunt face flickered into sight.

"Evening, ma'am," the man crooned. He looked skeletal in the frugal light. His beard was scraggly and brown. He'd combed his long hair back with only his fingers, leaving thick tracks on his head. "What's a pretty thing like you doing in a place like this?" He turned his head toward Terra, his tongue hopping out to play on his lips.

"Heading home," Santana stated briefly.

The man cocked his head, his eyes now drinking in Santana's legs and the small strip of flesh exposed around her midriff. He scratched his arm, bones pressing against his skin. She spotted the dark lines of his veins.

"Shame…" He sighed, then motioned behind him. "If you like, you can spend a little time with my friends and me. I'm certain the fellas would appreciate a pretty thing like you joining us, even for a little while."

Santana's skin crawled. His voice was soft, unthreatening, but she was wise to this city and knew what came next. Movement came from the shadows behind.

Santana unwrapped Terra's arm from around her shoulders and guided her to the nearest dumpster. She leaned Terra beside it. Terra slipped slowly, landing on her ass, head flopping to the side.

Santana strode nearer to the man, the firelight flickering on her face. His eyes strayed down to the coils of the bullwhip at her hip. "You can use that with the boys if you like. We ain't averse to a bit of kink."

Three other men appeared behind the first man, each one

with a dark glint in their eyes. Toothless grins and an overwhelming stink of sour alcohol wafted toward her.

"Oh, I plan to," Santana replied.

"Good girl." The man bit his lip. "Your friend can join if she likes?"

They both glanced toward Terra. She rolled her head back against the dumpster and gave a weak thumbs-up. Half a chuckle emerged from between her lips before a wave of vomit followed. She leaned to the side and expelled her insides onto the ground, the stream landing with a dull wet *smack*.

The man turned back to Santana. Santana grinned and shrugged. "Guess it's just me."

"I guess so." He took a step forward then lashed out toward her, grabbing Santana around her wrist. He closed in on her, his stench stinging her eyes.

Santana stepped aside, then tugged her arm away from the man. He kept his grip but stumbled forward. He landed on the ground with a *thud* and a moan, the torchlight sputtering in the cracks.

Another torch lit, then another. The other three men became five as more appeared from the shadows. Each of them sported the same dark veins as their comrade, which would work to Santana's advantage. While ink made its users feel a strong wave of euphoria, it slowed their reactions. She could work with that.

"Quick, stop her," one of the men shouted, lunging toward her. Santana threw a fist at his cheek, her knuckles and his cheekbone making a dull *pop* as they connected. She dodged around him, putting some space between herself and the others.

They ran at her.

Santana kept a watchful eye on each as she reached for her bullwhip. She flicked it, the lash and popper creating a powerful *snap*. She flicked again, and this time the whip coiled around one of the men's necks.

He gasped, hands clutching the tendril around his throat.

Santana ran to the right, sweeping past two more of the men. The whip pulled taut, creating a clothesline that caught the men's' foreheads and dragged them backward. They fell and hit their heads on the ground.

Using the momentum from the bullwhip, Santana jumped at the wall, using it to spring toward the fifth man. She kicked out, the sole of her foot catching him in the center of his chest. He attempted to grab her foot but was far too slow.

When she landed, two hands approached from behind, slipping beneath her armpits. They grabbed her chest and squeezed. Santana shuddered, feeling the man's greasy skin even through her clothes.

"Oh, hell no," she muttered. She held her grip on the whip, the man under its grasp turning purple as he fell to his knees, still clawing at the bond. Santana shuffled backward, pressing her ass into the man behind.

"There's a good girl," a voice crooned. "I knew I'd be your favorite."

Santana rolled her eyes, then doubled over. The man held on, now hovering on top of her back. Santana twisted, flipping the man onto the ground. He was light, no heavier than a grown child. Air expelled from his lips as he landed. "You bitch."

Santana shrugged. "You're right, there."

Turning her attention back toward the man coiled at the end of her whip, she snapped her wrist, and the lash unspooled. She drew it back toward her, leaving it to trail at her side.

The fallen torchlight harshly shadowed the man's face, yet Santana could still make out the vivid red lines around his neck. She cracked the whip, the popping sound echoing around the alley. "Have I made my point clear?" She didn't expect an answer.

"Hey… Go away," a voice came from nearby.

Santana turned to Terra, finding a man standing before her, working quickly to unzip his trousers. She batted weakly, a trail of thick phlegm down her lips. Santana's blood boiled, all the alcohol in her system evaporating as she reared back, then snapped her whip toward the man.

He let out a screech she'd never heard from a grown man. On the ground beside her, the others shuffled, pushing back, trying to get away from the woman they shouldn't have started a fight with. Santana flicked her wrist gently, pulling at the man's member. He stared down incredulously at his crotch, unaware of what to do. Any movement could make the pain worse.

Santana barked at the group, "Get the fuck out of here. Now. Don't ever let me catch you trying to prey on lone women in the darkness." The others were on their feet, sprinting from the pair. The man in Santana's grasp watched them run, a forlorn expression on his face.

Santana moved closer, coiling the slack on the whip to keep the tension. When she was nearer, she looked the man dead in the eye. "One flick of my wrist and your tallywhacker will be left on the ground for the worms to consume, you hear me?"

The man nodded rapidly.

Santana flicked her wrist. The man squealed. She drew the coil back in. The man glanced at his crotch, relief washing over him as he saw his parts intact.

"Go," Santana commanded.

The man ran. Without bothering to zip himself up, he hustled out of the alley, pursuing his friends. Santana watched until they were out of sight.

"Can't go one night in this city without some kind of incident," she muttered, the adrenaline shifting from her system.

"Ain't that the truth of it?" Terra asked, eyes glazed as she struggled to find which Santana to stare at through her blurred vision.

Santana chuckled. "When you go for it, you really go for it, don't you?"

"A job worth doing is a job worth doing well." Terra burped. "Shit."

Santana crouched, assisting Terra to her feet. "Come on, let's get you to somewhere safe where you can sleep off the worst of it." She chuckled. "You're going to have a hell of a hangover in the morning."

Terra hiccupped as one hand lazily tapped her temple. "Not with my secret weapon."

Santana laughed as they emerged onto the street and headed to her apartment building.

CHAPTER THREE

Santana strolled down the street, the morning sun doing its best to break the Atlantica fog.

The city was warm. Cars crowded the streets, and civilians bustled through, making their way to work. In the distance, Santana heard the blare of AJS sirens.

The air seemed thick with electricity. As Santana strolled down the blocks, making her way toward her favorite diner, she couldn't help but feel somehow claustrophobic in the big city. She was used to trees and bushes and foliage pressing in on her on all sides, but it was nothing compared to the towering metropolis that swallowed her now.

She watched the men and women around her, their eyes fixed to their phone screens or miserably pinned to the sidewalk, and felt a strong disdain for the world that humanity had built for itself. These people would likely never know the true freedom and peace that came with understanding and living alongside nature.

She sat in the booth she usually occupied on her rare trips into the city, tucked away in the corner, and ordered a breakfast of scrambled eggs on toast. A couple of AJS officers passed the glass window-front, and Santana smiled, remembering the officer she'd left to rest in her apartment.

Terra had been easy to put to bed. Santana had offered her the couch, but in her alcohol-fueled state, Terra had chosen the hard-wood floors. Santana couldn't help but laugh as she tiptoed past her friend that morning and wrote her a note, a string of drool connecting Terra's lips with the flooring.

Terra,

Thanks for a great night last night. Always fun to catch up. We say it a lot, but we should do this more often.

I have to head out and meet a client. Help yourself to whatever's in the fridge. Coffee is in the pot. I've activated the bare minimum of trip-wires and booby traps to ensure you can get out of the apartment.

Don't close the balcony door.

See you soon.

SS x

She had then proceeded to go around her apartment and set the usual protocols in place. Santana wasn't the suspicious type, but she also knew the city well enough to protect her things.

Her apartment featured an amalgam of tripwires, detectors, and other traps, which anyone trying to break in would set off. From her apartment at the top of the building, the balcony gave an amazing view of white fog, spiked and pierced with the rooftops and upper levels of the surrounding buildings. She hardly ever closed the balcony doors—one of her main traps set —but would also often step onto her balcony ledge to climb to the very top of the roof. Most of the time she still couldn't get a perfect picture of the sky, but on those rare few nights in summer she could see the stars and pretend she was far away from this place.

Setting the last trap, she glanced back at Terra, undisturbed on the floor. If the technology in Terra's head was as advanced as she said, surely she'd be able to detect everything and leave without a problem.

If it wasn't, well, then Santana would have to make a brief trip back, wouldn't she?

She left nothing on her plate and drank her coffee. Stomach full, she checked her watch and headed out of the diner. She hailed a driverless cab, stepped inside, and watched the city blur past.

The radio played gentle music, occasionally interspersed with updates about the latest criminal acts and murders within the city. Soon the close-packed buildings peeled back, the cab making its way to the outer limits where nature met metropolis and stood at a standstill.

Country roads led Santana away from the city proper. They passed fields of crops, small villages, and the occasional stately home set in the middle of nowhere. Soon they pulled toward an area of the island which could hardly be considered a village due to the collection of impressive houses and estates packed together. Each place was individual, each one a testament to modern architectural advancement.

Halfway down the street was a building painted in copper and decorated with large ornate gears on the walls. There was an observatory on the fourth floor with a hemispherical roof that opened at the back. The driverless cab pulled alongside the curb outside of the house.

"Thanks," Santana offered to no one, also sending a cursory glance at a tiny camera in the corner of the ceiling.

She tapped her cell phone against the contactless payment pad, then exited the cab. The air was fresher here. Not too far in the distance, she could make out the large green wall that fronted the Atlantican wilds. She could imagine the mountains, hills, rivers, and lost treasures deep in the fog that hid the impressive wilderness.

She drew a long breath, then walked up the broad stone steps to the front door.

There was no handle on the front door, merely a keypad and a scanner beside it. Santana took a fob from her belt and placed it against the scanner. When the *beep* came, she keyed in her pin, waiting for the hydraulic tracks to announce her entry.

The door slid open. She made her way inside.

The first two floors of the strange building contained the main bulk of the private museum's exhibits. "The Arch" was open during daylight hours and held some of the rarest finds discovered on the island. Since its first public discovery in 1941, Atlantica had been a constant mine for long-forgotten secrets. There was a mystery hidden beneath the surface. Santana could feel it. Each expedition she partook in yielded some new revelation. Each trip into the wild colored in some of the missing puzzle pieces.

She made her way past glass cases filled with rusting Nazi memorabilia from the Second World War. She crossed through rooms containing the taxidermied corpses of Atlantica's unique animal species. There were murals painted, telling stories of the early days of Atlantica when the battles raged, and the city struggled to establish its identity.

There was even a room for children to play in while their parents roamed.

When she reached the top of the third floor, she again scanned her fob, and the door opened to reveal a large glass capsule. She stepped inside.

Santana removed her bullwhip and dropped it into a receptacle in the floor. She felt the scanner's eye on her, so she made quick work of undoing her utility belt and holster, as well as three knives nestled in the belt. She also pulled off her boots, eyes lingering on the small slots that contained the hidden blades she could use in an urgent crisis.

Stripped bare of her weapons, she stood straight and waited, her eyes finding the tiny lens of the security camera.

A voice announced, "*Every* item, please."

Santana tapped her sides. "Done."

A mechanism *clicked* shut. The capsule started to rise. The room before her fell away, revealing the next floor of the building. Burgundy carpet unfolded before her, a cavernous room stretching in all directions, the walls lined with shelves packed tight with books. Tables held neatly arranged collections of books, maps, and assorted stationery of golds, silvers, and bronze.

The capsule stilled. The door *hissed* open.

The carpet felt strange beneath Santana's socks. She strode forward, unable to peel her eyes away from the majestic library. The air smelled of time, dust, and paper. Santana smiled.

An entrance at least twelve feet high waited at the room's opposite end. The large doors opened, drawing Santana's attention. An elderly gentleman in a motorized wheelchair drove toward her. In the center of the chair, a strange blue orb glowed and pulsed with power.

Santana recognized the Atlanticore as the one she'd personally fetched for the man when they started working together. The mysterious blue rock was a source of infinite clean energy and one of Atlantica's many unique discoveries that powered society on the island.

Taylor Yungheim had a gentle face with a groomed pair of mutton chops on his cheeks. He wore a satin burgundy robe that flew behind him in his chair. His pale white legs were thin. He sported a gleaming gold Rolex on his wrist.

He pulled up in front of Santana. She leaned forward and hugged him.

"Strange to see you at a regular hour." Taylor gave a chesty chuckle. "I'm used to you visiting in the middle of the night, crawling through my windows like a panther."

"Probably more likely a jaguar," Santana replied. "Or maybe an ape of some kind. You never were that great with animals."

"Depends on what animals you mean," Taylor shot back. "Not the kind you deal with in the jungle, but then, I have you for that.

However, give me the beasts that haunt Atlantica's elite, and I can crack my whip and have them eating out the palm of my hand."

"I have no doubt."

Taylor spun his chair and waved Santana after him.

"So much to tell you, so much to find." Bags hung under his eyes, yet the smile stayed on his face. "I can't even begin to tell you how exciting this all is. Your finds in the verboten zone have been incredibly illuminating. Each piece of the puzzle brings us one step closer to finding it."

Santana thought back to her most recent expedition. She'd spent over a week in the jungle hunting for a supposed ruin that would've acted as an outpost to the Nazis over eighty years ago. She'd almost given up her search until she followed the trickling of a tributary leading in the opposite direction of the main river. The water headed downhill, then underground, revealing a room filled with several items lost to time.

"I'm glad something good came out of it all. Nine days out in the wilds was no easy feat. You'd think I was sugar or something, the number of bug bites I got."

Taylor shook his head in disbelief. "Look at you, a solo adventurer working out in the verboten zone, and you talk about it as though it were a weekend camping in the hills. You know some say the wilds are haunted?"

Santana rolled her eyes. "You ask as though I don't do my research. Can we please stop calling it the verboten zone? Not every place I explore can be named the same thing. We said we'd start dissecting it, finding unique names for particular sections."

Taylor ignored her, answering her first point. "It astounds me how brazen you can be when you're out in the fields alone. This island has its secrets, and it has its ways to protect them. You should exercise more caution."

Santana laughed. "Just because the city slickers tell fireside stories of ghosts and skeletons and haunted dens, that doesn't mean there are any kernels of truth to them. Seriously, Taylor, I think you're getting senile sitting in that chair of yours all day. It's either that or the Atlanticore in the center is beginning to affect your brain. All that radiation…" She grinned. "Since when did children's stories give you such spooks?"

Taylor looked down at the stack of thick leather-bound books on his desk. Notes and clippings and open pages he had spent the last seventy-two hours combing through covered the desk's surface.

"This island has a short but rich history, Santana. You of all people should know that things happen out there. Unexplainable things. It's not always ghouls and monsters you have to consider. This island *speaks*, and it hates that people have discovered it. Why else do you think it stayed lost to the world for so long? It *chose* to be."

Santana pinched her brow, feeling a slight shove at the sudden memory of the pain she'd felt when her mother had passed. They had said it was a cave-in, a natural accident that could've happened to any group of explorers, but no one knew the truth of what happened out there. To this day, Santana remained convinced there was more the reports hadn't said. It wasn't the first time the island had purged its residents, claiming their ghosts without explanation.

Santana shrugged. "The Nazis deserved what they got. Even you, a man of German descent, would admit as much, wouldn't you?"

Taylor scratched his chin. "Hard to say. An entire population of German soldiers disappearing without a trace is nothing to wish on anyone." He laid a hand on the pile of books. "This is documented history, and still we have no sign. All we have are the ashes of the fires that destroyed their work. It might be the greatest mystery on Earth since…well…ever."

Santana pulled out the chair opposite Taylor and sat. She placed her feet on the desk and put her hands behind her head. "A mystery that we will one day solve, of that I'm sure. Until then,

I'm going to keep coming and bugging you with any update you can get on my private quest."

Taylor's mirth left his face. He spun in his chair and stared out of the floor-to-ceiling glass window behind him. The jungle stared back. "There's still been no word."

Santana let the news linger in silence. It wasn't even her mission initially, but still, the unresolved mystery of one of her most recent clients, Valentina Winters, weighed on her shoulders. She thought back to that time, to chasing down the man who had kidnapped Valentina's brother and vanished into the jungle.

If there was one place on the island where you could almost hide indefinitely, it was out in the wilds. With so much unexplored jungle remaining, they could be anywhere.

Santana had made a promise, and she planned to keep it. In the meantime, however, she still had coins to earn and mysteries to solve.

"Nothing at all?" Santana asked at last.

Taylor shook his head. "Every one of my expedition teams is aware of your hunt. I've spared the details but have informed everyone to report to me the moment they stumble across anything suspicious." He turned to face her, the daylight silhouetting him against the windows. "You'll get your answers, no doubt. You always do. Just remain patient."

"I can do that," Santana replied. "Provided the coin keeps coming."

Taylor returned to his desk, tucking the motorized chair beneath. He leaned down, then reached out of sight. A moment later, he placed a tiny wooden box on the desk. There was nothing extraordinary about the container. There were no markings or plaques to signify what might lie inside.

When he opened the lid, he revealed a smattering of German currency dating back to the late 1930s. One side of each coin had a large number embossed on its surface. On the other was an image of an eagle with a coin clutched between its talons. In the center of the coin was a swastika.

"The coins will keep coming, as long as you keep bringing the goods." His eyes lit with a fire behind them. "We're getting closer to something. I can feel it."

Taylor flicked through some pages on the desk and found his scrawling penmanship on one of the leaves. "This text reports a tectonic disturbance in the exact location you reportedly found the coin. You said yourself that you could hear something nearby, some kind of rumbling or *whooshing* sound beneath the surface."

"Likely a natural aqueduct of some kind or an underground cavern." She cocked her head. "Hardly a tectonic occurrence, more of a rumble. We're miles from the nearest tectonic boundary."

"Well, whatever it is, it's causing quite the ruckus on the grapevine," Taylor stated, pausing momentarily, a queer look in his eye. "Jakob Masque has sent his team out there to investigate further. There are whispers of a newly discovered temple, lost beneath the soil of the forest." His eyes flashed to Santana.

Santana's brow creased. "What are we talking, here?"

Taylor's gaze intensified. "They say they've found the Temple of the Summer Crown."

"Shit..." Santana breathed. "You're kidding?"

Taylor shook his head. "Jakob already has a several-hour head start. I shouldn't need to tell you that we have to get there before him. The Atlantican government funds his team. If they get their hands on what the temple has to offer, we're going to lose out on the chance to win the goods."

Santana smirked. "What you're saying is get there before them, before you have to take the back route and steal it from their heavily protected museums."

Taylor nodded. "You always could read between the lines."

Santana rose from her chair. "Consider it done."

"Before you go," Taylor interrupted, causing Santana to pause.

She knew what was going to come next. "I've assembled you a team. They'll be here by late afternoon to accompany you on your quest—"

Santana sighed. "This again? You know as well as I do that I work alone, Taylor. As long as the price is right, I'll get what you're after. The only reason I had to come back last time was because that goddamn jaguar sniffed the cheap-ass jerky you provided and wanted a nibble."

Taylor's eyebrows raised. "So *that's* what happened."

Santana shrugged. "What can I say? It's been a rough few weeks." Her mind flashed to a rogue detective named John Chambers and her request for him to help her find her mother's pendant, which someone had stolen within days of her receiving it. Images flashed of a stately home, tropical animals and plants, a *lot* of gunfire. Her hand moved to her neck, the ghost of the pendant still there when in truth, it was locked in a very safe location, away from prying eyes.

She felt Taylor's eyes on hers and regained her composure by sticking her tongue between her teeth.

Taylor surrendered. "Very well, keep your secrets." He reversed his chair and drove around to Santana, pausing at her side. "Your team will be here at 5:00 p.m."

Santana looked down her nose and placed a hand on her benefactor's wrist. "Well, I hope they enjoy their journey into the jungle without me. I'm Russian. I can survive on vodka and snakes if I need to." As an afterthought, she added, "The snakes are optional, though."

Taylor studied her closely. "You are *Atlantican*. Remember, that's why you get free access in and out of the country, as well as the privileges only the natives can harness."

She smirked. "You pick up a few things with a Russian father. Either I'll be back soon with the goods, or I'll be dead." Her voice went deep and thick. "Smert' ne posledneye prepyatstviye."

"What does that mean?" Taylor asked.

Santana grinned. "Death is not the last obstacle." She scoffed, musing, "Atlantican by nature, Russian by nurture... There is something to be said about the self-development opportunities of digging in the permafrost of Siberia, looking for animals preserved for thirty millennia. It's hard at first, the cold. Once your heart acclimates to sub-zero, nothing bothers you anymore."

She laughed at the serious expression that had come across Taylor's face. "Oh, wipe that look off your face. Have I failed you yet?"

Taylor held her gaze.

"Vodka?" Without waiting for an answer, Santana crossed the room to a mahogany sideboard. She poured two measures of vodka into crystal glasses and handed one to Taylor.

Santana raised a finger, stopping Taylor from automatically taking a sip. "One thing before we seal the deal. I want triple pay on this one."

"Double," Taylor returned.

Santana shook her head. "Triple. I'm doing the work of five men, remember?"

"By choice," Taylor reminded her.

Santana gave Taylor a stern look. "Triple."

Taylor held her gaze a moment, then relented. "Very well. Only because I've learned it's useless to argue with you.."

"Now you're getting it." She raised her glass. "Salut!"

"Salut." Taylor downed his shot, then winced at the burning alcohol trickling down his throat.

CHAPTER FOUR

The scent of the jungle mixed with the stench of fresh hotdogs. The *cheeps*, shrills, and cries of several critters jumping and dancing nearby filled the air, alerted and excited by Santana's presence.

Santana leaned closer to the nearest container where a bird with vibrant plumage nodded, its beak rhythmically tapping the glass. She clicked her tongue and held a finger toward the bird. The bird's excitement increased.

"Oi, don't wind the animals up," a cheery voice announced from behind. Emily Zayne spoke with a thick British accent, her khaki uniform neatly blending in with the jungle decor of the exotic animal store. "You of all people should know that."

"I'm not winding her up," Santana replied. "She wants to play. I can't say I blame her. Do you know how it feels to find yourself trapped in a cage for most of your life?"

Emily tapped on a digital tablet, the screen harshly under-lighting her face. She had almond eyes, her hair neatly cropped at the shoulders. "These guys were born into captivity. They don't know any better. If anything, by selling them to new owners, they'll find their new freedom there."

Santana studied the bird, a small hooked beak, the colors of her feathering hypnotizing. She had seen several of these out in the wilds, flying overhead, startled at the roar of a jaguar or the heavy footsteps of the less-experienced explorers.

She had mixed feelings about selling animals as pets but knew that many of the critters sold through Zayne's Exotic Emporium found much better lives with their owners. Not only was Emily's vetting process intense for the clientele who walked through the door, but most of her customers were the insanely wealthy who made a point of creating entire exhibits and "roam rooms" for their creatures.

Santana stepped back from the glass, her eyes caught by a pangolin on a shelved container over Emily's shoulder. Beneath the pangolin was a raccoon happily nibbling on a tasty treat.

"Each to their own," Santana replied.

"At some point, you'll be buying from me." Emily smirked.

"Maybe," Santana returned. "The day I decide to settle, I'll come to you for something, I'm sure."

"So…never?" Emily winked. She started back toward the counter at the far end of the store. Santana followed. "I'm guessing this isn't a social visit?"

"Is it ever?" Santana replied.

Emily turned to a young woman who was unpacking boxes and littering foam peanuts all over the floor as she stocked the shelves of animal feed and various items. "Can you watch the floor for a few minutes, Chelle?"

Chelle nodded, taking her place at the counter.

Emily led Santana through a set of bead curtains into the back. The chaos didn't stop back here, with boxes stacked precariously, trails of birdseed on the floor, and a couple of stray cats roaming around.

Emily thumbed a code into a locked door, then took Santana up a set of stairs. Santana closed the door behind them.

The smell was fresher up here, the A/C blasting and bringing a chill to Santana's skin. Her flesh prickled. They took a right toward a room that leaked bright light.

Inside was a series of steel counters and shelves. There were several vials stacked neatly in rows, each one filled with a strange and different liquid. Some were clear, others black, some tinged with pinks and greens and blues. A mist hung in the air, the temperature low to preserve the fluids inside. On another wall was a series of metal lockers.

"What you in the market for?" Emily strode over toward one of the back lockers. She used a key hanging around her neck to unlock it. Inside was a stack of tranquilizer darts. "What's your poison?"

"Literally," Santana replied. "Just the usual, please. Unless you have anything particularly spicy?"

"Cytotoxic, hemotoxic, or neurotoxic?" Emily asked.

Santana waved. "Yes."

Emily laughed. "Still can't retain the information?"

Santana shrugged. "I have a lot going on."

Emily crossed to the collections of vials by the wall. "These are your cytotoxins. If you're looking for something that will damage your target's cells and cause severe destruction in particular cellular groups, this is your poison."

She moved along the wall. "Hemotoxins. These will severely fuck up your target's cardiovascular systems, playing around with red blood cell levels, disrupting blood clotting, etc."

Emily moved to the final selection. "These are your neurotoxins." A dark smile appeared on her lips. "These can fuck up your target's nervous system."

Santana scanned the selection. "What did I go for last time?"

"This." Emily plucked at a vial that looked like it contained a sample of urine. "Paralysis. Krait venom. Get this in the victim's bloodstream, and they'll be incapacitated until you've long fled from the scene."

Santana examined the vial, the off-yellow liquid splashing

around inside. She found it strange how something so innocent could do so much damage to humans and animals alike. "More of the same, please."

"Gotcha." Emily took a handful of the vials and busied herself with dropping small quantities into the tranquilizer darts. As she worked, Santana crossed to another wall that displayed many dangerous-looking creatures. Snakes, spiders, scorpions, and several brightly colored frogs occupied the exhibits. Santana recognized most of them as creatures she'd encountered in the wilds and, thankfully, avoided on her treks.

After a short while, Emily placed a small leather pouch on the counter. Inside were the fresh tranquilizer darts, neatly wrapped. "Pistol?" held out a hand to Santana.

Santana handed over a small pistol she kept tucked into her belt. Emily gave the firearm a once-over, examining all the nooks and crannies before returning it to Santana. "Seems to be all in order. Anything else you need?"

Santana considered this. "You got any of those protein bars left over?"

Emily laughed. "I'll go get them."

She swept out of the room, leaving Santana alone. Santana's skin prickled, but she didn't feel the cold internally. Her thick skin had gotten her used to handling extreme temperature changes throughout her life. She moved closer to the glass case that contained the tree frogs. A piece of damp bark was leaning at an angle, the floor littered in dirt and wood chips. A small purple frog, no larger than her thumbnail, hopped eagerly around, landing in a tiny puddle of dirty water. Nearby a vibrant red frog leaped away. Santana put a hand to the glass and grinned.

The door opened. Emily returned with a cardboard tray lined with silver-wrapped protein bars. She chuckled. "Don't get that close in the wild. Those things will have you dead in seconds."

"You don't need to tell me." Santana pointed at her face. "Remember who you're talking to here."

"There's no reward in hell for bravery around toxic animals," Emily commented. "You're one of my highest-paying customers. I don't want to lose you."

Santana laughed. "That's all I am to you? Currency in your account."

Emily winked.

Santana filled a small leather backpack with enough bars to last her a few days. Satisfied, she offered her cell phone to Emily. The other woman presented hers, and they tapped screens. A chime rang as money transferred through the Satiata Cash App.

"Pleasure doing business with you," Emily stated.

Santana pocketed her phone. "And you." She slipped the leather pouch into her pocket, then returned her pistol to its hiding place in her utility belt. "See you on the other side."

"As always," Emily shot back.

Santana's phone vibrated. She checked the screen and let out a soft sigh.

Emily smirked. "Boyfriend of yours?"

Santana looked up from her screen. "Something like that. Catch you later."

Santana stopped outside the Emporium and hit "Dial" on her phone.

A man answered.

"John Chambers, as I live and breathe…" Santana mused, her eyes straying across the road to where a group of excited teens had gathered outside a futuristic-looking comic book store. Digital screens took the place of windows, advertising the latest superhero cult phenomenon to sweep the island.

"It's Dick," he replied.

"You can keep protesting that all you like. I won't be an enabler to your sick fantasies."

Santana heard Dick's smile in his voice. "It's not a fantasy. It's my nickname. You think I chose this?"

"You're clearly reinforcing it now," Santana retorted. "Where did it come from anyway? I'm guessing there's a great story behind the name."

One of the teens squealed excitedly as another emerged from the store, drawing a sealed comic book from a paper bag. Santana smirked. *Oh, to be that innocent again.*

Dick paused. "Yeah, I'll save that one for our next date."

"Date?" Santana blew air between her lips. "Haven't we already covered this? You might think you're God's gift to women, but this is one girl you won't be netting."

"We'll see," Dick replied.

Santana rolled her eyes. She'd seen John Chambers in action. She'd specifically sought out Atlantica's number one private investigator to reclaim her mother's pendant, which had been gifted to her by a stranger declaring that they knew her mother. In a strange set of circumstances, that stranger was declared dead the next day, the pendant also missing.

John had been the perfect hire and had managed to trace Santana's pendant and put it back in her possession. Although his methods were unorthodox, he got the job done. His grizzly appearance, grim-set face, and constant stench of stale whiskey affected the ladies that encountered Chambers.

As much as he'd tried to put the moves on Santana, she'd firmly stood her ground and declined. Not only did Santana never mix business with pleasure, but she also had no interest in finding a boy-toy to play with when she had bigger fish to fry.

"What do you want, John?" Santana asked.

"Dick," Dick replied.

Santana remained silent.

Dick chuckled. "You free to meet? I have some questions for you that pertain to a current investigation."

Santana's eyebrow arched. The group of teens started scuffling. The group shoved the kid with the comic. He went to the ground, and they piled on. A moment later, an AJS officer ran toward them, uniform gleaming blue. Several of the teens ran. The officer dispersed the crowd, helping the bruised and beaten kid to his feet.

Not one passerby spared a glance.

"I hardly believe that I'm going to be a suspect in any of your cases," Santana offered. "Unless I've somehow pissed off the wilds."

"I never said anything about a suspect. How about it? Carlos' at four?"

Santana checked her watch. That was an hour away. She glanced toward the jungle—not that she could see the greens past the towering metropolis—remembering her obligation to Taylor. If she timed it right, she could quickly meet with Dick, then carry on toward the jungle to be there by nightfall. Her sleuthing would work better in the darkness, anyhow.

"Sure thing. See you at three-thirty," Santana answered.

Before Dick could protest, Santana hung up.

CHAPTER FIVE

Santana wasn't surprised to discover that Dick wasn't waiting for her at 3:30.

She sat at a table for two, the air filled with the scent of tomato, pasta, and herbs. Carlos' was well-renowned for its premium Italian dishes. Wines and crystal glasses immaculately decorated the tables. Servers roamed between tables in perfectly pressed uniforms, paying attention to each customer's needs.

Santana poured herself a glass of water and waited. On her way in, the servers had given her a strange look as she flouted all dress conventions and strolled through the room in her climbing boots and shorts. She examined the menu, then tossed it back on the table. She had never been one for fine dining and wondered why Dick had chosen here of all places.

"Sorry I'm late," a deep voice announced from behind her.

Dick laid a hand on her shoulder, then took his seat across from her. She was glad to see that he also flouted the dress code, sitting in his long leather jacket, a crinkled dark top showing beneath the lapels. His stubble was dark and grizzled, peppered with white flecks, and his hair had only had the minimum attention paid to it.

"I told you this wasn't a date," Santana stated.

Dick grinned. "Of course." He picked up his menu and scanned down the list of items. "You understand this isn't the kind of date that I'd take a lady on."

"Then why bring me here?" Santana asked.

Dick shrugged. "A change? Isn't life too short to experience the same day in and day out?"

Santana rolled her eyes. The server stood by the table. "Can I take your order, please?"

Dick studied Santana through narrowed eyes. Before she could open her mouth, he offered, "Actually, nothing for us both. Thank you." He closed his menu. "We'll be dining elsewhere."

He rose from the table, motioning for Santana to do the same. She grinned, then followed Dick as he swept out of the restaurant and into the street, leaving behind a flummoxed and slightly perturbed server.

"What was that?" Santana checked the time. "I have things to do."

"Me, too." He didn't look Santana in the eye. He glanced up and down the street, then walked across the road, weaving between stationary traffic.

Santana moved briskly to keep up with him. "John…"

"Dick."

Santana caught up with him on the sidewalk and grabbed his arm. He turned to face her. "Where are you taking me?"

"For food," Dick replied. "Come on."

Santana pulled him back again. "I'm not fucking around and wasting time. Tell me what you wanted to tell me."

Dick glanced up and down the street. "Not here." When Santana raised her eyebrows, he added, "You'll thank me. Trust me. Haven't I earned that much at least?"

Santana sighed. "Fine."

Dick led Santana into a darkened little Irish pub on the corner. The inside was foggy with cigarette smoke. Neon signs *crackled* and fizzed out. At the back of the pub were several pool tables with grizzled men and women lining up their shots to clear the balls.

Dick took a table by the wall on the right. Santana sat across from him, sensing the gazing eyes of the older men in the bar.

"Drink?" Dick asked.

"Water," Santana replied.

"Suit yourself." Dick crossed to the bar and gave the order. A moment later he returned with a glass of water topped with ice and a lemon and a tumbler of whiskey.

"No Blue Moon?" Santana's mind cast back to her first meeting with Dick and the premium beer he favored.

"Not today. Blue Moon is more of a social drink. This is business."

Santana picked at the lemon slice on her drink. "I asked for water."

"You have water."

"I have lemon water," Santana shot back. "Lemon flavors water. I didn't ask for lemon."

Dick smirked. "You're impossible."

"You have no idea." She sipped her drink. "Whenever you're ready to get to the point, I'd be happy to know what it is you're after. I'm sure I didn't fuck around this much with my instructions when we first met."

Dick glanced toward the pool table. A woman with broad shoulders and a severe crop of red hair was bent over the table, lining up a shot with the black ball. Her eyes caught Dick's. He held her gaze for a moment, then turned back to Santana. "It was a pub like this one."

"The Armada." Santana remembered it well, a swinging sign with a wooden ship. "Surprised you didn't invite me to meet you there."

"I'm not welcome there anymore."

Santana laughed. "You mean you can't get into a bar brawl

with their patrons and expect a welcome return? Shocking news, that."

Dick nodded. "It happens."

"Often?" Santana asked.

"More often than I care to admit. I'll wait until management changes hands and I can resume my privileges."

Santana shook her head. "Seems a sound strategy." She narrowed her eyes. "Dick."

"Dick?" Dick repeated.

"John," Santana clarified. "Your point?"

Dick nodded, then took a long sip of his whiskey. His upper lip peeled back as the heat of the liquid burned his throat. "Have you ever heard of the Temple of the Summer Crown?"

Santana's ears pricked up.

"I'll take that as a yes," Dick confirmed.

Santana nodded and waited for Dick to continue.

"My client has discovered the temple, Santana," Dick informed her. "They're heading after some ancient artifact that's supposedly linked to…" he drew a deep breath and waved a hand dismissively, "…some kind of sun…thing. I don't know."

Santana cocked her head. "La Daga de los Días Sin Fin?"

Dick grinned. "Bingo."

"What do you have to do with that, though? Isn't your entire jurisdiction city-bound? Why would you be tied up with relic hunting?"

Dick shrugged. "I go where the money is. My skills lend to finding things, and in this example, my client wants to find the things."

"Who's your client?" Santana asked.

Dick shook his head. "You know better than to ask."

Santana nodded. "So if your client found the temple, what do you need me for?"

"Because my client is shit at finding things," Dick replied. "His team has spent the last two days scouring the temple and looking for the dagger, and they've turned up empty-handed. Now the Atlantican Historical Society have turned up with their numbers, and my client is concerned that the item is going to end up in the wrong hands."

"Depends who you think the 'right' hands are," Santana muttered.

Dick sipped his drink. "They contacted me to do some digging and see if I could use my keen eye to find it. I'll be the first to admit that relic hunting isn't my forte, so I thought I'd come to the queen of the jungle."

He held Santana's gaze, studying her closely.

Santana gave nothing away. "Do you understand what it is they seek?"

Dick frowned. "Somewhat. An ancient dagger that's supposed to provide the location of another place lost in the jungle."

He waved. "There's always some kind of ridiculous myth tied behind these things that you treasure hunters are after. Only, the myths never become truth, do they? You end up seeing paintings of some sun god or raging fires and the death of armies, but it's all bullshit at the end of the day. Atlantica was founded upon a search of the lost city of Atlantis, and where did that search lead?"

Santana glanced at the pool table area where the grim-set woman was resting against the wall, eyes locked onto the back of Dick's head. "It didn't go anywhere. We found Atlanticore, and that was it."

"Exactly. Despite our advances in modern technology, we haven't found a trace. Myth. Legend. Kid's stories. That's all it is."

"Then why get involved?" Santana asked. When she saw Dick's expression, she grinned. "Right. Cash."

"Man's got to make a living," Dick offered. "Plus, it seemed a fun exercise and meant I could have the chance to work with you."

Santana scoffed. "Say I do help. How much of that money makes it my way?"

"Fifty-fifty," Dick offered.

"Eighty-twenty."

Dick scratched his chin. "Fine. I mean, if you only want twenty…"

Santana laughed. "Eighty. Twenty."

Dick shrugged. "Sixty-forty."

"Seventy-thirty."

"Sixty-five, thirty-five," Dick shot back.

"Done." Santana took Dick's hand. It was a win-win for her. Getting paid by two clients for the same work. What could go wrong? "When do we begin?"

"Right away," Dick replied. "I'll sort us a cab to the jungle if you're happy to set sail and go?"

Santana nodded. "Sounds perfect."

Dick tapped on his cell phone, ordering a driverless cab through the app. "Says it'll be eight minutes." He glanced longingly at the bar. "Time for another?"

"For you," Santana answered.

Dick grinned. He left his chair and crossed to the bar. While waiting for the barman to return with his drink, Dick glanced at the woman in the shadows. She screwed the chalk onto the tip of her cue. Dick offered a cursory wave.

The woman grimaced, then strode toward him.

Dick glanced at Santana, then turned his body toward the woman. Her sour expression could have wilted the mirth off any man's face, but Dick held his ground. "Meredith."

"Dick," Meredith crooned.

The pair faced off for a moment in silence. Santana watched closely, the air pregnant with tension. The barman placed Dick's drink on the counter.

Dick reached for the drink without taking his eyes from the woman's. She was a strange fashion concoction, with a crocheted scarf wrapped around her neck and a long suede jacket. Her skirt was pleated and covered in zigzag patterns, and a small tuft of hair sprouted from a large mole on her chin.

Dick sipped his whiskey. Meredith's grip adjusted on the pool cue. As Dick lowered his drink, she slapped the glass from his hand.

The tumbler shattered on the floor, amber liquid pooling by Dick's feet. The barman was in the middle of serving another customer but now stared back over at the pair.

"That was a mistake," Dick stated.

The woman growled. Behind her, another man appeared from the shadowed pool area, watching them closely.

Santana sipped her water.

"You're an asshole," Meredith stated. She spat at Dick's feet. "Turner is in for fifteen years because of you."

"Because of *him*," Dick clarified. "I didn't make him stab three innocent Atlanticans in your apartment."

The woman broke. She shoved Dick backward, rage filling her features. She adjusted the cue into two hands, then swung it like a baseball bat. As it passed the bar, its tip smashed through several glasses that were hanging upside down. Dick raised a hand, just managing to stop the worst of the impact on the side of his head.

She roared, then swung again. This time, before the cue reached Dick's body, a great cracking sounded. Santana strained and pulled the bullwhip taut, holding back the cue from doing any further damage.

Dick took a moment to turn to the barman and apologize. The woman turned to Santana, eyes filled with rage. She strained against the whip's hold, then decided to let go of the cue and lunge for her.

She leaped into the air. She crashed onto the table. Santana moved out of the way.

Dick came to her side, looking down at the brutish woman. "Let's get out of here."

Santana was about to reply when the man from the shadows steamrolled toward them. He slammed into Dick, tackling him to the floor.

Santana turned to help, but a hand gripped her ankle. She kicked out as the woman used the chair as support to bring herself back to her feet. She grabbed Santana's shirt and tugged.

Santana braced against her. She punched the woman's face, her fist connecting with her chin. The woman roared again. A gun was cocked. Santana turned to the bar to find the barman aiming a shotgun at the group.

This is all too eerily familiar.

Dick rolled around on the floor with the second brute. He took a fist to the face, then twisted out of the way of a second blow. The man punched the floor, yowling as he shook his fist. Dick brought a knee up and caught the man in the groin. He shuffled out from beneath him, then pushed himself to his feet.

He straightened his jacket, then kicked the man in the side of the head. Santana stepped toward him and opened her mouth to talk.

"I know," Dick stated, waving toward the barman. He walked closer to the bar, not withering under the glare of the shotgun. "In all fairness, I didn't start it." He tossed a couple of crisp blue Atlantican bills on the counter. "Keep the change."

Dick strode toward the door with a minor limp. Santana followed as a series of stunned patrons watched in silence.

The barman snarled. "Don't bother…"

"I know," Dick replied, opening the door and holding it for Santana to leave ahead of him. "I know…"

Outside, the cab was waiting.

CHAPTER SIX

The cab rumbled quietly through the city. Santana had turned the music off, leaving them both with only the ambiance of the surrounding traffic and bustle.

Dick massaged his jaw. There was a red mark where the brute's hand had connected. He stared out the window, eyes narrowed, though Santana couldn't tell if it was because of thought or pain.

"You okay?" She broke the silence at last.

"Mmhmm," Dick muttered.

Santana watched him closely. "I'm trying to remember the last time I've been in a bar or pub with you, and it hasn't resulted in violence."

"I have a lot of enemies," Dick replied. "Some of them not directly involved in my work, others… Well, you heard the woman."

Santana nodded. "You put away her husband."

Dick scoffed.

"You didn't?" Santana asked.

Dick turned to her, fixing her with a curious gaze. "I don't put anyone behind bars. It's not my responsibility to stop people from doing the bad shit they do. If anyone is responsible for her husband going to jail, it's her husband. I didn't make him commit three murders in forty-eight hours. That was all his doing."

Santana nodded. "I get it."

"Do you?" Dick asked.

"I do," Santana confirmed. "Morality is a personal choice. People don't like taking responsibility for the shit they do."

Dick nodded, then turned back to the window.

The city faded into farmland. Soon the great green wall of trees and forest pressed up toward them, looming ahead like a great wall of sentinels. The cab pulled to a stop a short walk from the trees, the road ending abruptly at a rickety gate with a sign reading, "Danger. Enter at own risk." Above them, the moon attempted to break through the fog veil.

Dick exited the cab and lit a cigarette. "I'm a long way from home."

Santana laughed. "It's only trees, John. You're not scared of an itty bit of nature, are you?"

Dick shook his head, eyes narrowed. The tip of his cigarette glowed brightly. "Not at all. I'm afraid of the monsters who lurk within."

"They're only animals."

"Not on this island." Dick didn't elaborate.

Santana led the way, confidently striding toward the break in the trees. There was a narrow dirt path that wound between the trunks and faded into the shadows. She reached into her bag, pulled out a headlamp, and strapped it to her forehead as she trundled on.

Within moments the world behind was forgotten and a thick quiet pressed in on all sides. Santana loved the blanket of the jungle, how nature shut out all the bullshit and artificiality the city brought to the island. In here, the world was as it should be. Trees spoke an ancient language long forgotten in urban environments. Birds called in the darkness, insects shrilled and vibrated, strange mammals prowled in the shadows.

Dick kept closely behind Santana, treading over the same roots and fallen logs she passed over. Soon the path came to a small clearing where a wooden hut sat quietly in the darkness.

"This must be the gingerbread house," Dick offered. "Is the witch inside?"

Santana chuckled. "It's a check-in point for travelers. A place for explorers to camp and wait for sunrise if they need to. Sometimes explorers leave provisions for others based on an honor system. Often there's nothing there but water and wrappers from previous meals."

"I knew there was no honor among thieves," Dick stated, "but no honor among explorers either? That's sad."

"That's Atlantica," Santana replied.

Santana reached the front door. The sound of trickling water reached their ears. She entered the hut, the smell of dirt and wood reaching their nostrils. Inside was empty, though signs of previous life were left behind. A crumpled sleeping bag occupied one corner, a trashcan with a pile of moldering food was near the other. Another door stood at the far end, and as Santana crossed and opened it, the trickle of water grew louder.

She pulled a lighter from her bag and lit a torch fixed to the outside wall. A sphere of soft orange light illuminated a small stream passing the back of the hut. A series of wheels and cogs trailed pipes into the stream. Santana wound a handle and fresh water trickled from a nearby tube.

She splashed the water on her face. Even in the middle of the night, the humidity from the day remained. She topped up her water bottle, then offered to fill Dick's. He washed his face, eyes widening at the cool water.

"Better?" Santana asked.

"I suppose," Dick replied.

"Good." Santana stared over the river and into the place

where the trees grew thicker and darker. "Because things are about to get a whole lot trickier." She grinned, then held out a hand.

Dick took it.

She slapped it away.

"Okay. I'm getting mixed signals."

"Your map," Santana clarified.

"Oh, yeah." Dick handed over his cell phone, showing a map on the screen with a pin dropped at the location.

"That's not too far from Nureguard Valley. I've been past that way so many times. There's a long ribbon of stable pathway leading through the valley on the other side, but I never thought to cross and explore the far bank." She handed the phone back. "We should get going. We have a long trek ahead of us."

"How long is it going to take?" Dick asked.

Santana considered this. "On a good run? We should be there within twenty-four hours."

Dick's lip curled. "On a bad run?"

"We die en route." She held his gaze for a moment, then clapped once. "Shall we?"

They trekked on through the night.

Santana strode ahead, utilizing the checkpoints she had built up over years of exploration of Atlantica's wilds. Fallen trees, odd clearings, strange rock structures, as well as the occasional ruin acted as navigation markers as she homed in on the Nureguard Valley.

For the most part, Dick was the perfect companion. He trudged on in relative quiet, only occasionally complaining about the swarms of flying insects that clouded them. Drawn by Santana's light, the moths and midges found their way to Dick, attracted to the stale scent of his sweat. Halfway along their journey, he had removed his jacket, feeling the need to let his skin breathe. Now he'd put the jacket on and grew more and more irritable with every step.

Santana shook her head, her mind filled with memories of the journeys she'd made through the jungle with others over the last few weeks and months. It was rare she took on a passenger, but it was memorable when she did. She thought back to a crimson assassin, out of her comfort zone yet still fighting for dominance in a world that had been Santana's. Valentina Winters had been an interesting companion, though her constant dick-measuring contests had grown tiresome. At least Dick had the grace to let Santana own her domain.

They stopped on a little plateau among ruins as the sun was rising. Ivy, moss, and weeds covered the flat hilltop, but the trees hadn't yet closed back in.

Santana was starting a fire in the center of the crown of ruins when Dick finally emerged through the trees. His hair fell over his eyes, and dark bags showed beneath them. "You know, I wouldn't have taken this job had I known how much travel it involved."

He shrugged off his jacket and let it fall to the ground. A series of angry red welts covered his arms. "All these years on Atlantica, and no one has created a train line through the center of the jungle."

"Protected ground," Santana replied. "One of the founding rules of the place. The founders believed that magic lay beneath the jungle. Only problem is no one ever found it, and no one has since bothered to overturn the ruling."

Dick sat by the fire. He swatted at the last stragglers of insect hordes and drew a few long breaths. "How come they haven't bitten you?"

Santana smirked but didn't answer. She prodded the fire with a stick, encouraging the flames to swell. When the fire was at a satisfactory size, she used vines to lash together a series of branches to create a structure over the fire that supported food.

Dick watched Santana closely as she took fruits and berries from her backpack. She swiftly field dressed a 'possum, tied it to a stick, and suspended it over the fire.

Dick frowned. "When did you catch that?"

Santana smiled. "En route. Amazing what you can do when you're not worrying about tripping over roots and slapping away midges."

Dick gave an impressed nod. "Gives me something to aspire to."

Santana gave him a strange look. "Mr. Chambers… Is that a compliment coming from your mouth?"

Dick grinned. "I could shower you with compliments, you know. We're out here, in the middle of the jungle." He held his hands out either side. "No one around. Me and you. In nature…"

Santana rolled her eyes. "For a moment, I thought you could be charming without the underlying intent."

"What did I say?" Dick protested with a smirk. "I only suggested that I could treat you well."

"You wouldn't know the first thing about what a lady truly wants," Santana replied.

"And you would?"

Santana was caught off-guard. Her mouth flapped.

"Thought so," Dick stated triumphantly. "You're different from the usual Atlantican women. They're tied up in status and appearance. All you need to do is soothe them with the right words and dangle the right carrot, and they're putty in your hands. But you…" Dick studied Santana closely. She rotated the possum. "You're a different kind of lady."

"I am," Santana replied. "You know what we call that in Russia?"

"What?" Dick asked.

"Unobtainable." She removed the 'possum and cut the meat with a small but keen blade.

They ate in silence, the sun slowly rising over the tops of the trees. A ribbon of smoke curled into the air from the fire, losing itself in the Atlantican fog. Peaches and oranges colored the sky.

"You don't get that in the city," Dick offered.

Santana agreed, picking pieces of meat from her teeth.

"What is this place, anyway?" Dick motioned to the ruins around them. There were carved rocks with decorations scratched into their fronts and the remains of a small stone hut now half-eaten by plants.

"An outpost," Santana replied. "When the Nazis occupied this space during the Second World War, they created several check-points and outposts to spy on the surrounding world."

"Why?" Dick asked. "From what I know, the Nazis discovered this place in the forties. The Americans came years later. What were they defending themselves from?"

Santana shrugged. "No one knows. It might have been for their peace of mind, or it could've been from an enemy that historians have yet to identify. Really, it's lost to history. All we have left are these structures and the occasional relic of Nazi memorabilia left inside."

"Shame."

"I didn't have you down for a history buff."

"You don't know much about me."

Santana couldn't argue.

"Where are we sleeping?" Dick asked.

Santana nodded toward the trees where a large rock jutted out of the green. "There's a stone shelter on the other side there. We can set our sleeping bags down and hunker down for a few hours."

Dick looked around himself. "Er..."

Santana laughed. "I wondered how long it would take you to

realize." She reached into her pack and took out a bundle of wrapped-up material. "Here, take this."

Dick took the sleeping sheet. "What are you going to sleep on?" A thought crossed behind his eyes. He grinned.

"Before you say a word," Santana interjected, holding up a hand, "I'll keep watch by the fire. I'm too awake to sleep, anyway. Don't want to miss the full sunrise."

Dick rose to his feet. "Fine." He moved to the rock. "Thank you."

"You're welcome," Santana replied as Dick disappeared into the trees.

She waited until she could hear nothing more from Dick, then got to her feet. Nearby was a series of stacked stones. Santana climbed atop them. There, she drew her bullwhip and snapped the coil toward the upper branches of the nearest tree. When it was taut, she scaled the trunk until she was at the top.

She found a comfy spot to sit, high above the leafy forest canopy. Around her was a sea of green, rising and falling in vast waves. Here the air was fresh, not a single hum of a car engine or an AJS siren audible. Above her, the sky melted in pastel watercolors, the sun slowly rising on the horizon.

Gladness filled her heart. She rested her head on her hands and watched the sunrise.

CHAPTER SEVEN

Dick Chambers awoke to the sound of gunfire.

He sat bolt upright, confused for a moment as to where he was. Around him, the walls were rough stone, peppered with moss and lichen. Light streamed in through a nearby entryway. He rose to his feet and ran for the outside world, heart thumping as he thought of Santana out there by herself.

Light flooded his vision. He blinked to adjust, looking wildly around the clearing. Their fire stood in the center, now turned to ash. Santana was nowhere in sight.

He drew his gun and spun on the spot, looking for the gunfire's source. A few more *pops* and he realized that the reports were coming from a distance.

He moved to the edge of the clearing, looking out over the canopy of trees below. Birds took wing somewhere in the distance. Another few *pops* and all fell silent.

Dick shaded his eyes and tried to see signs of life out there. All that returned was green.

"What the…"

Someone moved behind him. Dick whirled, aiming his pistol at Santana's face.

They held each other's gaze. Santana had her hands on her hips and wore an intense expression.

Dick lowered his weapon.

"Thank you," Santana stated.

"What was that?"

"Gunfire."

Dick sighed. "Out there."

"Gunfire," Santana repeated. She moved past him, staring out into the canopy. "Hard to tell without getting nearer. There's always something popping off somewhere. Could be raiders, could be a gang, could be hunters. All we know is that's the way we're heading, so we need to watch our backs today."

She returned to the center of the clearing then rubbed out the ashes with her boot. Satisfied, she beelined toward the shelter. She emerged a moment later with her sleeping sheet.

"Where were you?" Dick asked.

"Hmm?"

Dick tracked her with his gaze. "Where were you?"

"In the trees," Santana replied as if it were the most obvious answer in the world.

"Did you sleep?" he asked.

"I did." She placed her items in her bag. "Did you?"

"I did." Dick turned back to the forest. "You sure we're going to be okay heading in that direction?"

Santana shrugged on her backpack. "Nope. I'm never sure. Life is a funny thing to take for granted."

Dick chuckled. "You have a way of making your clients feel comfortable."

"I'm not here to make you feel comfortable," Santana replied dryly, making her way toward the other side of the clearing. "I'm here to recover a relic and get you your money."

Roars sounded in the jungle. Birds called, and unknown creatures moved in the underbrush.

Dick trudged on behind Santana. They made great time, only stopping on the odd occasion to ingest their power bars and stop to pee. Once again, Dick remained silent for most of the trek, although as Santana turned, she was sure she caught him staring at her ass on more than one occasion.

Primitive structures popped up here and there on their route, further evidence of the island's Nazi occupation. Halfway to their destination, they stumbled across the remains of a pathway.

They followed it for a short way, thankful for the patch of smoother ground where they didn't have to stretch their legs to tread over debris and large, snaking roots. Soon they encountered a building, no larger than a garden shed, the roof all but caved in. Ivy penetrated the brickwork, and a family of marsh rats had nested in the corner. In the center of the outpost was a hole that Santana had recently dug to retrieve the coins that now sat in Taylor's chest. She'd quite literally stumbled on the find during her last exploration.

Santana brushed a hand against the wall and cleared some of the ivy. She read the words scratched into the remaining brick.

"You speak German?" Dick asked. "Keiner wird passieren…"

Santana took a picture with her cell phone and allowed the Silver Tongue app to translate the words. "None shall pass? Huh… No kidding. I bet they believed it at the time, too."

"Haunting," Dick offered.

Santana shrugged. "Only if you're still living in the 1940s."

She took a step back and glanced around. Something moved in the bushes nearby. Crouching slowly, she grasped a rock and hurled it at the shrubs, breathing a sigh of relief when a red brocket darted into sight and dashed away into the darkness.

"What was that?" Dick asked.

"Jungle reindeer," Santana informed him. "This is where Santa comes on his vacation." She grinned, catching Dick's eye. "At least it wasn't another jaguar."

"Jaguar?" Dick looked up at the trees.

"Don't worry about it. We're not in jaguar territory. They're closer to the center. We're still very much in the south." She returned her attention to the writing on the wall. "So, if there's writing to say none shall pass, that will mean something is nearby that's worth protecting, won't it? Where was that rumbling sound I heard before?"

Santana stepped out of the outpost and onto the path. She quieted herself and closed her eyes. She could make out the faint whispering of running water but wondered where it was coming from.

Dick stepped near her, disturbing the quiet with the crunch of his boots. "I feel like you're getting distracted."

"Shhh," Santana replied. "A girl can multitask, can't she?"

She lowered herself to her stomach and pressed her ear flat against the stone and earth. A gentle vibration caressed her face, and the whispering grew louder. There was certainly running water beneath her, but did that mean the treasure-laden caverns that Taylor thought might exist there?

"Only one way to find out," Santana mumbled as Dick sat nearby and drank from his canteen.

Santana unzipped her pack and drew out a coil of tough, yellow rope. She anchored the end to a hollow in the outpost's brickwork and held the loop in her hand as she continued her trajectory. The line created a trail she could follow back to where she'd been if she ever got lost. "Wait here," she instructed.

Dick raised his canteen in reply.

As Santana walked, she would occasionally stop and press her ear to the ground, encouraged by the increase in volume of the rushing water.

She passed through an archway with dropping vines, waving a hand to break through a smattering of spider webs. An angry assortment of colored arachnids scurried away as their homes split, with one of the spiders finding themselves unlucky enough to have found its way onto Santana's shoulder.

It crept toward her neck. Without turning to look, Santana flicked the creature away.

After a few hundred meters of walking, the path abruptly stopped. A great wall of dirt, roots, and bushes towered over her. Santana craned her neck upward, measuring the wall to be at least thirty feet high.

She checked out the stone paving once more. *There's no way this leads nowhere. Why would a path suddenly stop? This is a goddamn blockade. The good ol' Nazis didn't think anyone would bother to scale this.* Santana plucked one of her knives from her belt and dug into the dirt. She only had to go a few inches before the earth subsided to reveal stone.

"Camouflaging your hideout… Clever."

She touched the cool stone of the wall, excitement welling inside of her.

"Found something useful?" Dick asked.

Santana turned with a grin. "Looks that way."

"I'm not paying you to get distracted," Dick stated. "I'm paying you to help me find what my client is after."

Santana nodded. "Lucky for you that this seems to be a shortcut to our destination."

Dick narrowed his eyes. "You're just saying that."

Santana shook her head and moved closer to Dick. She took a paper map from her bag and pointed at the spot where they stood. "This here is where we are. Over there is the Nureguard Valley. We were heading on a long route around higher ground. That would have added at least another mile, but I know that path better than this one. At least this way," she dragged her finger along the paper, showing a straight route toward the valley, "we can cut out some distance and also do a little bit of prospecting along the way."

"Prospecting is mining," Dick stated.

Santana nodded, pocketing the map. She cut the rope and freed her bullwhip. "Correct."

She dug the knife into the cracks between the stone with one hand, then cracked the whip toward the thick overhanging branches of the trees above her. She bashed the heels of her boots together, and small blades extended at the front, sticking out about an inch from the toes. *Dorothy's shoes have nothing on these.*

Working swiftly, Santana steadied herself and pulled upward with the whip while alternating her grip with her feet and her hand digging in the dirt. Her ascent was fast, and soon she was high enough to know that a fall could be deadly if she slipped. As she cracked her whip to gain higher traction, a flock of birds took to the sky. A few moments later, a second flock of birds took wing, these some distance back from where she had come.

Santana turned her head, hoping to get a view of the top of the canopy, but the trees were too large. Instead, the distraction caused her foot to slip. She quickly jabbed her knife into the wall to save her from the drop.

"You okay up there?" Dick called.

"All fine!" she confirmed.

At the top of the wall, Santana gripped the edge of the brick and levered herself over. She straddled the wall and looked out over the jungle.

"Whenever you're ready," Dick shouted.

Santana chuckled as she dug into her bag for more of the yellow rope. She secured one end into a knot around the nearest tree, then let the rest fall to Dick. A moment later, the rope went tight as he scaled upward, following in Santana's tracks.

As Dick followed her, Santana hopped down onto the other side of the wall, appearing in a small courtyard of sorts. A doorway stood not too far from her. She headed toward it, her heart thumping as excitement began to take over. Scribbles and scratchings stained the wall, detailing the messages of the German people who had once occupied the island.

Santana stepped to the door and reached into her bag. She withdrew a rag, doused it with part of a small bottle of alcohol, and wrapped it around a thick branch.

A *thump* came from behind. "That was a workout."

"You're losing your edge," Santana replied.

Dick laughed. "It's not often I have to climb a rope in my line of work. Mostly it's cardio."

"Should consider drinking and smoking less," Santana offered.

Dick scoffed. "I don't tell you what to do in your line of work. Leave me alone with mine."

He drew closer, his heavy breaths reaching her ears. "Whoa. What's this?"

Santana lit the end of her makeshift torch and couldn't hide the wonder on her face as the door came to light. She took another picture with her phone, allowing the app to translate the words. "Servants of Hitler…allow me your secrets."

The door was thick steel, lightly layered in dust blown from the winds and crawling with stubborn vines. Santana ripped them away, her hand tracing gently over the engraved swastika in the center of the door. It was easily as large as a New York pizza, and although the inhabitants had long ago abandoned this place, Santana couldn't help but feel the ghosts of those who had been before.

She turned back to Dick with a mischievous fire in her eye. "Can you feel it?"

"What?"

"History." Santana shoved the door open and let light burst inside.

CHAPTER EIGHT

Camila Sokolov's voice filled Santana's head. "There's history there, in the forgotten things. You can smell it, can't you? The remnants of the people who came before, in a time before anyone conceived the notion of ourselves. It's magical to think that history remains and that, even when we're gone, our memory can live forever in the very fibers of the places we once resided."

Dick shuffled in behind Santana. Santana turned, half-expecting her mum to have walked in with them. She was right, of course. The minute Santana stepped inside she could feel the past speaking to her. The building held its breath around her, but she could sense the things that once happened here. They called to her from beyond the grave.

She activated the flash on her cell phone and further illuminated the darkness. She was in a bare corridor, the walls and ceiling simply exposed brick. Another door lay at the end. She made her way forward, thinking nothing of the rotting skeleton slumped against the wall as she stepped over its long white legs. A round steel helmet sat crooked on the bare skull, blocking the pits of empty eyes beneath.

"You're not looking so bright, friend," Dick muttered.

"Didn't have you down as a Nazi sympathizer," Santana offered.

Dick scoffed. "That was a bit of a jump, wasn't it?"

Santana opened the second door. The darkness seemed thicker than ever. The smell of something rotten filled her nostrils and forced her to cover her nose with the crook of her elbow. Dick followed suit, bringing the folds of his jacket to his nose.

Inside the large room were three large stone tables. Large maps sat on the surface, yellowed and crisp from years of neglect. The corners turned up, edges bitten by rats and insects. Stacks of books lay piled nearby, glued together with an adhesive blanket of spiderwebs.

Dotted around the room were more skeletons, some slumped over chairs, others against the wall, a few strewn across the floor. Old maps and sheets covered the walls. There were several strange electrical devices on the table surfaces that Santana had never seen before.

"I wonder what happened to them," Dick asked.

"Something bad." Santana's gaze stayed fixed on the room.

"No shit." Dick ran a finger across the table, leaving a clean trail. "It takes something big for a group of people to die where they were working." He stopped by a skeleton sitting at a nearby table. He grabbed the back of the skeleton's head and peeled it off the surface. He examined the remains of the fabric that had once been the person's uniform and spied the dark stains of blood. "Must have been some kind of raid."

Clinking drew Santana's attention to her feet. A couple of tarnished shell casings rolled on the floor. "I guess so."

Santana pulled a mini DSLR camera from her pack and took pictures from every angle, documenting everything she came across. She used to take photos with her cell phone but learned that it was a best practice not to mix business and personal on one device. Besides, most thieves aimed for the mobile, forgetting about a simple camera.

As she journeyed around the room, she stumbled across candles on the desks. She lit a few with her torch, and soon a soft flickering light bathed the room.

She ran a hand over the maps, examining the cartography printed on the page. Sketches showed the layout of the surrounding jungle, crude drawings of monuments, and landmarks that might once have helped guide the soldiers around the jungle.

She took more photos of the maps, then with a click of a button, she batched the photos she'd taken and sent them off along the 6G trails toward her home. It was a custom function she'd had rigged, a way to transfer evidence to a secure hard drive at her apartment. Once the files had transferred, they would erase themselves from the camera entirely.

Dick strode around the room, more interested in the skeletons than the artifacts. Somewhere in the distance, another report of gunfire came.

Santana took an empty seat beside a skeleton and reached into her bag. She drew a flask of water and took a long sip, her nose finally beginning to adjust to the stink. "Oh, sorry. Did you want some, pal? You look mighty thirsty."

She held the bottle to the skeleton. "No? Suit yourself. If you're not careful, you'll find yourself dehydrated, and there's no coming back. Life is short, you know. Take each moment as it comes and make the best of it."

Santana's eyes grew glossy. "Like my mom once did. You never know when your time is going to come."

A distant look fell over Santana.

Dick approached her from behind. "You okay?"

Santana drew a long breath, then shook her head. "Yeah. All fine. These guys make bad party guests."

"You're telling me," Dick replied. "I've seen more life in a care home."

Santana laughed. She turned her attention away from the skeleton, then rifled through the papers on the desk. The books were useless at this point, and the loose leaves even more so. They were yellowed parchment with the ghosts of messages that had long faded into nothingness.

"You looking for something in particular?" Dick glanced over his shoulder at the door where they could hear more gunfire, increasing in frequency.

Santana strode around the room, grabbing all she could take. "Anything that could be sold or used to propel further knowledge of the past." Among a host of items retrieved were some more Nazi currency, a rusting pocket knife, a faded photograph of a harsh-looking woman with dark lipstick, and a signed letter of instruction by the battalion's commanding officer, which the soldier's pocket had protected.

The gunfire reached a fever pitch. Dick exchanged a glance with Santana.

"Come on," Santana stated. Satisfied there was nothing left to discover, Santana made her way to a door by the far wall.

The gunfire stopped.

"Give me a hand with this, won't you?" Santana instructed.

Dick appeared by her side, pressing his shoulder against the door. It opened slowly, cracks *popping* from the rusted hinges.

"Well..." Dick muttered. "There you go."

The open door revealed a long corridor with a dirt-packed floor that led into darkness. Strings of wet moss hung from the ceiling. The ground sloped down, strewn with broken bricks and a large umbrella of mushrooms. The sound of running water hissed toward them.

Santana took a step inside, her boot squelching in a small wet puddle.

Dick remained where he stood. "You're going down that way?"

"Of course." Santana wondered why he asked.

"What's down there?"

"We find out." Santana took another few steps then turned back. "Don't tell me Dick Chambers is afraid of the dark."

Dick chuckled. "It's not the dark that gets me." He brushed some dust from his sleeve.

Santana raised an eyebrow. "Oh, I get it. Worried about your jacket getting messy? Should've thought about that before you entered the jungle with me."

Dick laughed. "Fine. Lead the way, Lara. Show us the treasure."

"A *Tomb Raider* joke? How original." Santana rolled her eyes.

Dick stepped inside, "Just make sure no booby traps spike or poison me, and I'll be okay."

"Really? For someone who drinks as much as you do, I find it laughable you're worried about poisoning your body." Santana put her hands on her hips.

Dick smacked his lips. "Great. Now I could do with a drink."

Something *thudded* behind them. Voices followed the disturbance.

"In here!" The voice was female and commanding. Footsteps echoed loudly.

Santana and Dick ducked behind the door. She cut the light from her cell phone and left them in the gloom.

Peeking around the corner, she saw three figures appear in the doorway. An athletic woman led the way, an assault rifle in her hands as she swept her aim around the room and took in her surroundings. Behind her, a large man limped in, supporting another man who appeared to be unconscious.

"Put him in one of the chairs," the woman commanded.

The large man eased the unconscious man into a chair, then stretched. The unconscious man lay beside the skeleton, mimicking his position in the chair. Even from here, Santana could see the gaping wound at the back of his head and the spill of blood running down his ear.

"Fuck," the woman exclaimed. "Did they see us come in here?"

The large man shrugged. "How am I supposed to know? If I'd turned around, we'd never have gotten him out of there in one piece."

"Is he okay?" she asked.

He craned over the unconscious man, examining the wound in his head. "He needs patching up. I don't have any equipment on me, though. Do you?"

The woman glared at him. "You think I had a chance to grab medical supplies? That was a fucking shit show. Jesus."

Santana exchanged a glance with Dick.

The woman sat on one of the tables, her gaze moving to the nearest candle. "Hold on. Did you light these?"

"And *I'm* the idiot," the man replied.

The woman stood, alert. She arced her rifle around the room, looking for signs of movement. As she found Santana's door, she paused. "Someone's here."

"Or maybe they were, and now they're gone?" the man replied.

She advanced on the door slowly, gaze fixed into the darkness. Santana took a step back, readying herself. She loosened her bullwhip and clutched it in her hand.

Something sounded down the tunnel. The woman's eyes widened. She pulled the trigger, sending a bullet into the dark. Santana spun, saw Dick toss another rock. "Now," he commanded.

Santana reached an arm out and cracked the whip. The end coiled around the barrel of the rifle. Santana tugged, the rifle pulled free from the woman's grip, and skittered across the floor. She stepped out into the open. Dick stepped behind her, pistol aimed at the woman's face.

The large man reached for his gun.

"Make another move, and I'm turning her head into pulverized meat," Dick stated.

The man froze, a sour expression on his face.

They stared each other down, the air pregnant with tension. After a moment, the woman spoke. "You're with them?"

Santana cocked her head. "With who?"

"Whom," Dick corrected.

Santana ignored him.

The woman's lip curled. "The assholes who wiped out our whole division." She looked Santana up and down, then turned her attention to Dick. "You're not dressed like them."

"I don't know who 'they' are," Santana replied.

"Bullshit," the man growled.

"No bullshit," Dick replied. "What's going on out there?"

The woman turned to the man, and the pair had a silent conversation. The woman stepped back, resting her rump against the table's edge.

The bleeding man grunted, a haunting sound emanating from his throat.

Santana nodded his way. "I can patch up your man. I have supplies."

"Why should we trust you?" the man asked.

"You shouldn't," Santana replied. "Not if you're smart."

Without waiting for approval, she strode toward the injured man. The large man's lip curled, his eyes darting to the woman. For a moment, it looked as though he was going to block Santana from helping until she took off her pack and drew out a small med-kit.

She rested the green box on the table then took out the various items she was looking for. Blood trickled lazily from the wound, matting in the man's hair. Santana poured ethanol onto a cloth and cleaned away the worst of it. When she could finally see the injury, she took out a needle and thread and began to stitch up the scalp.

The entire time she operated, silence filled the room. Dick held his aim on the woman, fixing her in place. No one moved. No one spoke.

Santana worked carefully, finally sealing the wound closed. He would need to see a professional since a chunk of his skull had been chipped away, but at least the gash was closed, and the bleeding could stop.

"There," she stated at last.

She supported the man's head, then flashed the light of her cell phone in his eyes, checking for their dilation. The man blinked, then closed his eyes.

"He needs the hospital," Santana announced.

"No shit," the man replied.

The woman looked their way. "He's still with us?"

"Just," Santana replied.

"Thank you," the woman offered.

Santana put her equipment away. "Don't mention it." When she finished, she placed her hands in the air. "Look, we're not here to get anyone into trouble. We're independent explorers hunting in the jungle. Whatever is happening out there, it's nothing to do with us."

The woman looked at the man.

The man waved a hand. "I believe them."

The woman's shoulders slumped. "Me, too." She turned to Dick. "Mind lowering that thing, now?"

Dick moved to the rifle on the ground and kicked it behind him. "Fine. Just keep your hands where I can see them."

"John…" Santana warned.

It took a second for Dick to realize that she was speaking to him. "Fine." He holstered the gun.

Santana turned her attention to the pair. "Talk to us. Tell us what you know. First, start with your names."

The woman indelicately shoved the skeleton off a nearby seat. She dusted the chair with her fingers then sat. "We're with the Atlantican Historical Preservation Society. My name is Rowena. This is Declan. The man you patched up is Alex."

Santana glanced at Dick. He caught her gaze.

"I'm Santana," Santana offered.

"Dick," Dick added.

Rowena gave Dick a strange look.

"For God's sake," Santana whispered.

Undeterred, Rowena continued. "We'd recently been assigned a job exploring a newly discovered entryway to a hidden temple. The Society sent its best and brightest to explore and look for hidden relics to display at the Atlantican History Museum."

She sighed, a sadness falling over her. "It was beautiful. A hidden doorway among the ivy. Stairways that led deep underground. The architecture, the inscriptions, the temple appears to have been a relic of Incan proportions."

"So, thirteenth century?" Santana asked.

"I'd say so," the woman replied.

"But that's impossible," Santana offered. "The Incans were a Columbian American Empire. There's no evidence that they would have made it across the ocean to land somewhere like here."

"Tell that to the inscriptions on the walls," Declan commented.

"It's beautiful," Rowena marveled. "Paintings of Viracocha, Pachacamac, Mama Coca and more. Some of them faded but in great condition."

"And Inti?" Santana asked.

Dick looked perplexed, the others speaking in a foreign language to him.

Rowena smiled. "You've heard of the temple before?"

"The Temple of the Summer Crown." Santana tried to hide her excitement. "Inti, the Sun God, hid chambers around the world to channel sunlight. Places in which heat and energy could be stored on Earth in the event of extended nightfalls and mischievous activities from the other gods. The first was rediscovered in Peru in the 1600s, with more found in the nineteenth and twentieth centuries in South America."

"It's true." Rowena smiled. "The temple exists. We've been in it."

"So, what was the problem?" Dick asked.

Declan sighed. "The chambers—if there are others besides the ones we found—are hidden. Legend tells of La Daga de los Días Sin Fin—"The Dagger of Endless Days"—hidden somewhere in the chamber, but we found nothing to evidence this."

"We looked for two whole days," Rowena continued. "The team brought in equipment to scan and seek the hidden chambers. We found something in the detectors but couldn't find the entrance."

"Why couldn't you blast the walls?" Dick asked.

They all turned simultaneously.

Dick held up his hands. "Right. History geeks. Got it."

Rowena turned to Santana. "We thought we'd come close when… When *they* came."

"Who?" Santana asked.

Rowena sighed, her gaze straying to Alex. "We don't know. Mercenaries in black. They swarmed us, picking off our team one by one, stealing our research, taking our machines and technology. We abandoned ship, running at the first sign of gunfire. They got Alex as we sprinted for the trees. Someone shot our attacker. We ran… We ran…"

A single tear tracked down her cheek. "So much opportunity… Gone."

Dick took a step forward. "Was there another team down there? More people searching the temple?"

Rowena gave him a strange look. "There was." She gave a derisive snort. "Bunch of amateurs. All pickaxes and hammers.

They were going to destroy the whole damn site to find what they were after." She cocked her head. "You know them?"

Dick glanced at Santana, silently communicating. She was thinking the same thing as he was. Dick's client's team had been down there.

"What happened to the other team?" Santana asked.

Declan shrugged. "The hell if we know. We got out of there the moment shit hit the fan. They're all dead, for all we know."

Santana glanced at Dick, each one thinking the same thing. Whatever was going on down there was bad news, and it was where they needed to go.

"Which direction is the temple?" Santana asked.

Rowena thought a moment, then pointed.

They all turned toward the open doorway and the dark slope leading downhill.

CHAPTER NINE

"It can't be," Dick stated.

Santana half-shrugged. "Maybe not. Maybe so."

Rowena looked at Declan.

Declan mimicked Santana's shrug. "Who knows where that leads to in this Godforsaken jungle."

Santana stepped toward the tunnel and shone her flashlight inside. The light only stretched a few meters before the shadows claimed it. "It may be nothing. But it leads in that direction, so we'll check it out."

Dick rolled his eyes. "I knew you'd say that."

"Problem?" Santana asked. "Isn't your client and their wealth of the utmost importance to you?"

Dick didn't reply.

Santana took another step.

"I'm not sure if this needs to be said," Rowena started, "but we're not coming with you."

Santana waved her off. "Never expected you would. What are you going to do? Drag around an unconscious friend through a series of unknown and potentially dangerous tunnels?"

Rowena raised a placating hand. "Just saying." She looked uncertainly back at the entryway behind them.

"What is it?" Dick asked.

"They don't know how to get back," Santana finished for them.

Santana stepped back into the room, then placed her backpack on the table. She rooted around inside until she pulled out a scrap of yellowed paper. With a stubby pencil, she drew a series of lines and zigzags, detailing landmarks that would be handy to help them out of the wilds. "This should help you."

She handed the paper to Rowena, who examined the contents and gave a weak smile.

"Thank you." Rowena turned to Declan. "You think you can carry him a little further?"

"What choice do I have?" Declan scooped Alex up and hauled him over his shoulder. "If we get attacked by jaguars, it's on you to defend me."

Rowena held out a hand to Dick. Dick hesitated, then tossed the rifle to her.

For a heart-stopping moment, Santana believed Rowena would turn the firearm on them both and mow them down. Instead, she shouldered the rifle, then turned to the door. "Thank you," she muttered over her shoulder to Dick and Santana.

"You're welcome," Santana replied.

Dick gave a quiet, "Sure."

Then they were gone. Santana waited until they'd shuffled from the safety of the ruin before returning her attention to the tunnel. She strode confidently toward the door.

"I hope you know what you're doing," Dick called after her.

Santana smirked. "I hardly ever do. Isn't that the beauty of it?"

Dick took a candle from the room before closing the door behind them and closing off the outside world. Santana shone her flashlight, the cone of illumination only reaching so far into the dense void.

The ground was wet and slick. The stone walls had cracked, each lightning bolt break filled with moss and lichen. They trod carefully, taking their time as the floor gradually sloped down.

After a short while of walking in silence, Dick asked, "You sure this is the best idea? They told us that mercenaries raided the temple. Their teams were shot and wounded. For all we know, they've already found what they're looking for."

As if to further his point, the ground rumbled slightly. The sound of a large blast came from the world above them.

"Isn't *that* the point?" Santana replied. "If it's so important that people are out there looking for the item, it's worth fighting to find. So many times dangerous objects have fallen into the hands of the wrong people, and the world has had to live with the repercussions. Not on my watch."

She noticed Dick looking at her but refused to clarify further. Camila Sokolov's face appeared to her in the gloom. Somewhere in the distance of her memory, she could hear the rumble of rock as a cave closed in.

She blinked away the ghost, the walls widening out on either side as they entered an underground chamber.

Dick stumbled. His foot slipped into a small stream of water running in a broken channel between the rough-hewn path that appeared before them. Santana arced her light around them, revealing the handcrafted work of a civilization come long before.

Pillars were broken and toppled. A modest stream cut through the center, chattering as it ran off into the distance. At the far end of the chamber was a door standing crooked, and in either direction, the room stretched into the shadows.

"What is this place?" Dick asked.

Santana held her flashlight high, sending its beam as far as she could. There were markings on the walls, frames for torches, and weaponry scattered around the place, as though a troop had once lived here and all that remained were their effects. "Some kind of entrance," she offered.

She hopped across the stream, then jogged toward the doorway. The ceiling stood around twenty feet high, with jagged stalactites looming above them.

The door was a thick slab of wood that had warped and swollen with time and now fit snugly in the frame. Santana pressed against it but felt no give. She pushed her shoulder against it, and the door creaked.

Still, it didn't give.

She stepped back, examining the surrounding wall.

"Need a hand?" Dick asked.

"Nope," Santana replied. "I'd rather you just stood there watching the pretty lady at work." She turned over her shoulder and cocked an eyebrow.

Dick chuckled. "Here." He stepped beside her. They both pressed against the door. For a moment, nothing happened. Then, the door creaked.

It buckled, the center of the wood wetly splitting. They lurched a couple of inches forward. The frame grumbled, small rocks spilling down. Beside them, a stone the size of a volleyball tumbled.

Santana hopped back, pulling Dick with her. Another few rocks fell. The wood bent further, then stopped.

Santana waited a moment for everything to settle.

Dick glanced her way. "We good?"

Santana remained silent. After a minute, she confirmed, "Yeah. We're good. Although I'm not sure that doorframe is going to hold its shape once we move the door."

Dick nodded. "Agreed. So what do we do?"

Santana turned her light to the left of the door. A small distance away was a hole.

"Really?" Dick asked.

"You wanted to intern as an explorer. We do what we must."

She closed on the hole, shining the light inside. Rocks and debris surrounded the opening. The crawl space was tight, but it might be enough to get them both inside.

"Up for a challenge?" Santana asked.

Dick scratched the back of his neck. "I'm getting too old for this shit."

"I'll take that as a yes." Santana lay on her front and approached the hole. She took the move slowly, using her arms to propel her forward. She could feel the heat of Dick's gaze on her. "This isn't an excuse to stare at my ass."

"Like I ever need one," Dick replied.

The air was dusty, and each movement disturbed the particles around her. The space stretched for ten feet before opening up, and soon Santana was on the other side. A couple of small rocks rolled around her, but she had no concerns as she dusted herself off and called for Dick to follow.

Soon came the sounds of scuffling. She turned to check the room as Dick worked his way inside. A hallway stretched before her, the angles of the walls and ceiling neat and sharp. Along the walls were doors made of bronze bars that had tarnished over years of neglect.

Dick grunted. Something *clacked*. "Uh...a little help?"

Santana turned to find Dick's head poking out of the hole. She smirked. "I didn't have you down for a claustrophobe."

"I'm not." Pain shot through Dick's face. "I accidentally kicked my leg, and something fell on it."

Santana crouched, aiming her flash into the hole. "Keep crawling."

"What do you think I'm trying to do—"

Dick's leg kicked again as he struggled forward. The impact disturbed another rock, and the wall began to shake.

"Shit. Move," Santana ordered. She dropped her cell, then grabbed Dick's wrists. Bracing back, she tugged Dick toward her.

Dick slipped along the stone, groaning as the rough surfaces scratched his stomach.

The wall wobbled. Rocks fell. His legs freed from the space as the wall began to slip and move, the stones that had been undisturbed for years now crashing down around each other.

Santana continued dragging Dick until they were both clear of the fall. She looked up at the ceiling, checking for any signs of further breakage, but the roof held firm.

"Ouch," Dick offered, pulling his wrists from Santana and working his way to his feet. White dust covered his black tee and jacket. He brushed himself off before looking back at the place the crawl space had been. "Thanks."

"Don't mention it. This is fascinating."

"Where are we?" Dick cast a furtive glance back. "More importantly, can we get out again?"

"There's always a way out." A sharp pang hit Santana's stomach as she remembered that wasn't always the case. "It looks like an Incan passageway. Could be another outpost of some kind. Could be part of a larger network. See those doors? The Incans were one of the first large cultures to utilize bronze in ornamental figures and architecture." She grinned. "Fascinating…"

"Yeah." Dick was unimpressed. "I'm more interested in the 'way out' path. Think we can get there?"

"We can only try."

They crossed the room, Santana moving slowly past the bronze doors and shining her light inside. Numerous skeletons lay behind the doors, as well as several shields and rudimentary swords. Occasionally a squeak emitted as a rat scurried by somewhere in the darkness.

"What happened to them?" Dick asked.

Santana shrugged. "Could be anything. Could be the same thing that affected the Nazi soldiers above."

"You think they ever came down here?" Dick commented.

Santana considered this. "If they did, they didn't bother to come this far down. Maybe they took the easy way along the running stream. It could've been them who warped the door. It's all guesswork at this point."

"Isn't all of history guesswork?" Dick asked.

Santana chuckled. "A lot of it. Not all. We're often smart enough to deduce what happened in the forgotten realms below the world." She tapped her chin. "If only we could solve Atlantica."

Goosebumps rose on her flesh.

At the end of the passageway, a broad set of stairs led them farther beneath the ground. They walked in relative silence, accompanied only by the echo of their feet. On one occasion, glittering black beads appeared in the flashlight beams, and a dozen bats screeched as they flew over their heads and out the tunnel behind them.

The stairs led ever deeper, stopping at a large archway that led to an even bigger chamber.

Here the ceiling arced forty feet above their heads. A cool chill ran around the room. Santana couldn't make out how big the chamber was until she found several torches fixed to the walls. They were dry wood that would spark like tinder. She splashed a few drops of alcohol on each, then touched Dick's candle to them. Methodically working their way around the room, they soon had the place lit.

"Jesus..." Santana breathed.

Dick echoed the sentiment.

The room was spacious, with a central raised dais in the center. Evenly spaced around the dais were eight smaller platforms with what appeared to be stone bird bowls filled with water. The central dais displayed an ornate carving of a stubby, fat man with a large, arcing headdress. The carvings were ornate, with decorations trailing around the entire statue. Eight arms protruded in the direction of each of the stone bowls, with golden bracelets circling the wrists.

As Santana circled the statue, she noticed four additional faces, each in a particular state or emotion. One had its eyes closed, another its tongue sticking out, the third clenched its teeth, while the final one winked.

"Hey, look over here," Dick called. His voice carried easily across the chamber.

Santana crossed to Dick, who stood before the fading remains of a large, painted mural. Red and black and brown and white and yellow inks painted a portrait of a sun rising over the horizon. The upper half of the portrait was bright and sunny. Where the horizon crossed, everything below bled. Men and women lay dead, spears and arrows in their chests. Rivers of red ran around them, dripping off the edges.

"It's a story of Inti," Santana mused. "Inti was the Sun God, an ancestor of Incas. Incans worshipped Inti, believing that it was under his hands that the sun shone and crops thrived. But here… Here something is terribly wrong."

She traced a hand along the painting, the rough stone texture scratching her fingertips. They came to rest on the only man standing among the sea of the dead. "There's the dagger."

The man held the blade in the air, its point shining in the rays of the sun. Even now it glinted, as though the sun was still shining through it.

"The dagger was believed to have been one of the token idols which Inti had handed to humankind. It was revered and a gift to each reigning king in turn. When the Incan race faded, they immortalized the dagger in the Temple of the Summer Crown where it would always point at the sky and fend off the darkened nights."

Dick nodded, impressed by Santana's knowledge. "So why all the blood?"

Santana turned back to the room. "Now, that I don't know."

She crossed to one of the stone daises and looked into the water. Despite the fact that there was no natural way to fill the bowl, it was full to the brim. The water was spring clear, with no sign of moss or fungus. "Interesting…"

She examined the other bowls and found all but one full. When she circled the place once more, Dick pressed a hand against the stone wall between two torches.

"Trying to push your way out?" Santana asked.

Dick took a step back. A cigarette hung from his lips, a ribbon of smoke trailing above him. "Not quite." He narrowed his eyes. "There's some kind of outline here among the stone. It's thin, but…"

Santana stood behind him, seeing now what he was seeing. Tiny spiderweb fragments created an image they couldn't quite see.

"It's all connected." She looked at the central dais. "This has to be an activation chamber."

"An activation chamber?" Dick asked.

"Find the hidden treasure, unlock the door," Santana clarified. "Simple, really."

Dick scoffed. "Like a video game?"

Santana nodded.

"Are you kidding? I thought that stuff was all fabricated?" Dick replied.

"Every story has a morsel of truth. The human imagination can only take you so far."

She worked her way around the room a few more times, taking in additional details where she could. She examined the artistry, investigated the layout of the room, attempted to read the fragmented remains of scripture on some of the walls.

Dick's cigarette had burned down to a stub. He plucked it from his lips and tossed it onto the ground. "Any luck?"

Santana chewed her lip. "The central statue has a tiny receptacle that looks like it fits an item of some kind. An orb, perhaps? Maybe even just a gold, round locket."

"Like your pendant?" Dick smirked.

Santana nodded. "Perhaps."

"You're not serious?" Dick replied.

"Not on this occasion," Santana returned. "The receptacle is far too large for the pendant. It needs…" She grumbled. "I don't know. See if you can find something spherical that might fit into the hole—if you've finished setting your lungs on fire, that is."

"You disapprove of smoking, too?" Dick asked.

"Not really," Santana replied. "People can do what they want."

Dick chuckled. "You hate it."

Santana shot him a look.

They split up, each working their way around the room, Santana now studying each nook and cranny with excruciating detail. Dick kept his hands in his pockets, eyes narrowed. Though he looked like he was only giving half effort, Santana knew that Dick's work was meticulous.

Still, they found nothing.

They united at the central statue. Santana showed Dick where the receptacle was. He stuck his finger inside and examined the space. "Definitely looks like something belongs in there."

"Yep," Santana confirmed. "But what?"

They glanced around the room. Santana's attention was drawn to the empty bowl.

"Why would they all be full, except that one?" she mused aloud. She moved closer, running a finger across the base of the bowl. "Dry as the desert."

"Is there a way to fill it?" Dick asked.

Santana reached into her bag and drew out her canteen. It was half-full. She emptied its contents into the bowl.

Something made a noise, stone grinding on stone.

"Something happened." Santana extended a hand to Dick. "Quick, give me yours."

"And if we get stuck down here and need water?" Dick asked.

Santana marched over and snatched the flask from his hands. She unscrewed the top and was about to pour it in when—

"Stop!" Dick exclaimed. "That's not the water."

Santana brought the flask to her nose, then instantly pushed it away. "Really? What did you think you'd need booze for in the jungle?"

Dick shrugged. "That's my business. Here." He chucked his other flask. Santana threw the whiskey back.

She emptied the contents into the bowl, filling the basin around a third full. The basin lowered into the ground an inch. The central statue turned one degree.

Excitement passed between the pair. "We need more water," Santana offered.

Dick looked around. "There's nowhere here. The stream is on the other side of the collapsed tunnel and the warped door."

Santana's brow creased in thought. "Maybe it's not about the water…"

She removed her backpack and set it on the bowl. The base absorbed some of the water, darkening its color. The bowl sank another few inches, the central pillar rotating a few more degrees.

"Is that as far as it goes?" Dick asked.

Santana pressed her weight on the lip of the basin. A part of the edge crumbled away and smashed on the ground. Water spilled from the edge.

"Shit," Santana replied as the basin raised and the central statue turned back. She spun and sat in the center of the bowl, her ass going cold from the water.

The bowl sank. The statue turned until one of the faces was looking at the mural. "There's a hole in the center," Santana called.

Dick moved closer, finding that Santana was right. He could now clearly see through one of the face's eyes and straight through the center of the statue. "The dagger…" Dick noted. "It's sparkling."

Santana hopped off the bowl. The statue returned to its original state. She approached the mural, taking a closer look at the dagger the man was holding. Something was behind the picture, sparkling and glowing.

"Help me with this," Santana instructed, looking around for a way to get behind the stone.

Dick appeared beside her. "It was brighter a minute ago."

"What do you mean?" She glanced back at the bowl, then touched her ass. "I have to sit in it again?"

"I never asked you to the first time," Dick replied.

Santana crossed to the bowl and sat. From there, she saw that the mural shifted slightly, allowing the strange glow to burn brighter. Dick pincered his fingers into the hole but couldn't reach the item. "My fingers are too big."

"Time to swap places." Santana hopped off.

Dick burst into pained groans. "It's closed on my finger!"

"Shit." Santana hopped back on, the water soaking up into her ass again. "I feel like I've wet myself."

Dick freed his finger. "I'd rather that than almost losing my finger." He sucked on the reddening skin. "Your turn."

Dick took Santana's place, the stone sinking an extra half an inch.

Santana smirked as a hole wide enough for her hand opened behind the mural.

Dick patted his stomach. "It's only a little holiday weight."

Santana raised her eyebrows.

Dick scoffed. "Just grab it, will you? My ass hasn't been this soaked since I was in nappies."

"Keep your kinks to yourself. Whatever you choose to do on your weekends is your business." She reached inside the hole and clasped the round, glowing object. It was warm to the touch, little tickles of electricity trailing over her palm. When she drew it out, she was unsurprised to find the glowing ball of Atlanticore in her hand. "Always the way on Atlantica…"

"Good to hop off?" Dick asked.

"Yep." Santana held up the nugget.

"Atlanticore?" Dick hopped down. The hole closed and the statue shifted back. "Did the Incans use Atlanticore?"

"Seems so," Santana offered. "Unless these aren't Incan ruins at all."

"What are you saying?" Dick asked.

"I'm not sure yet." She grabbed her DSLR from her bag and took a picture of the core. "Hard to say. Until now, I wasn't *certain* of Incan activity on the island." She glanced at the statue. "Let's see if this works."

They approached the receptacle. Santana placed the orb inside. It fit snugly, Santana having to give a gentle nudge to drop it into the chamber.

The Atlanticore orb glowed brighter. Something inside the statue *clicked*. A humming of power sounded around the chamber.

"Whoa…" Santana stepped back as the circular dais slowly began to rotate. Dick jumped off with her.

The statue spun, the eight arms moving up and down as if on pistons. From where the Atlanticore sat, light bled out, trailing along the carvings of the statue until the whole thing was practically alight.

When the statue had lit, the light trailed along thin channels on the ground, working toward the eight smaller daises. They too began to rotate slowly, the water inside splashing and sloshing out of the bowls. Light emitted from the center of the bowls, magnified through the remaining water until they illuminated the chamber in an alien blue.

"Look." Santana pointed at the nearest dais to the wall with markings. The light continued along its course on the ground until it reached the wall. It crept up, coloring in the lines until an ornate doorway appeared. Another *crack* sounded, and the entrance opened.

Santana beamed, her breath caught.

"This is unreal," Dick muttered.

"This is history," Santana replied.

Dick made his way toward the door. "There's light down here. Come see."

Santana took one step forward, then glanced back at the Atlanticore. The statue had stopped spinning, and now it stood motionless, the blue glow teasing her.

"Leave it," Dick called, Santana's intentions clear in her eyes.

Santana's fingers twitched.

"Santana, come on," Dick insisted.

Santana held up a finger. She reached for the Atlanticore and tried to retrieve it. The orb wouldn't budge. There was no way to get a decent grasp on it.

"Santana…" Dick warned.

Something rumbled nearby.

Santana drew out a wide pair of tweezers from her bag. She gripped either side of the orb and pulled. It budged a fraction.

Something *crunched*.

Santana tugged harder this time. The orb popped out of the hole. She caught it before it hit the floor.

The lights around the door began to recede. The door started closing. Dick's eyes widened. He called to Santana. She shoved the Atlanticore in her bag.

"Come on!" Dick urged.

Santana ran for the door. The statue and the daises spun. The light bled back to the statue, crawling to its source. As Santana ran, she was sure she heard voices calling somewhere nearby.

The door was almost closed. She sprinted, running to the place where Dick was standing, clear of the path of the closing entry. She dove, managing to squeeze through the final crack before the door closed.

The door *clicked* shut. Santana coughed dust. She picked herself from the floor and found Dick staring at her, a cold judgment in his eyes.

"Was that necessary?" Dick asked.

Santana smirked. She drew the Atlanticore from her bag. "You tell me."

In the chamber behind them came a series of angry cries and calls, followed by a sudden barrage of gunfire.

CHAPTER TEN

Santana and Dick took a step back from the wall.

Bullets spattered across the thick stone. Fragments chipped and *tapped* onto the floor. No shots made it through.

"Son of a bitch!" someone called from the other side. "Find a way in. Now!"

A muffled response replied.

"I don't give a shit. I want in, and I want in now!" the first voice continued.

Santana exchanged a look with Dick. "Friends of yours?"

Dick took a cigarette from his pocket and placed it between his lips. He shook his head.

"Get the C4," the voice called. "If we can't get in, we'll blow our way in."

"We should get going," Santana muttered.

"No arguments here," Dick replied.

They turned, leaving the chaos behind them. Although neither acknowledged it, they walked at a pace faster than before.

The walls were smoother here, with stone tiles cut into squares. The passage wound on along a slow curve that headed west. Now and then, great knots of tree roots had invaded the tiles and claimed the corridor as their home.

Several passages opened around them. Across the walls, Santana could make out the trails of thin lines and wondered if this was also part of the network. If the Atlanticore would've lit the way and showed them the right direction.

Too late for that, now.

"That was stupid back there," Dick commented at last.

Santana didn't answer.

"You could've gotten us killed," Dick pressed. "Or trapped, at least. Do you need to grab every shiny object that comes your way?"

"Yes," Santana replied simply. "It's my job."

"To die underground?" Dick asked.

Santana's lips thinned.

Dick quieted. He knew he'd gone too far.

The passage rumbled behind them as an explosion sounded. Santana wondered how many charges they'd need to break through stone that thick. "This way," she muttered, steering Dick along an offshoot of the main passage and into what appeared to be an underground cave system.

Thickly packed earth formed the entrance, the tangles and wires of tree roots holding open the space. A little farther in, stalactites protruded from the ceiling. Santana held up her flashlight, illuminating a large underground lake on their right. The water was deadly still.

They only took a few steps ahead before Dick stopped.

"Problem?" Santana asked.

Dick thumbed over his shoulder. "We were in a ruin. Why are we heading out to the caves?"

Santana sighed. "Two reasons. Number one, the first place they're going to look is in the safer, inhabited spaces. They're not going to want to go out into the wilder natural systems."

"And two?" Dick asked, unconvinced.

"The temple is this way," Santana clarified.

Dick frowned. "What?"

Santana pointed at the darkness. "The temple is northwest of our original location. That way is northwest. Those passages are taking us southeast."

Dick studied her a long moment. "Your inner compass must be impeccable." He caught the object Santana threw at him, examining the compass. The hands pointed in the directions Santana had outlined. "That's amazing."

"It's what I do," Santana replied. "Now get a move on before we lose time and whoever those fuckers are find us."

The cave magnified every sound. The still lake water glittered with the light from Santana's cell. Halfway through the cave, she reached into her backpack and connected the cell to a remote charger.

Dick chuckled.

"Something funny?" she asked as they veered around a large rock jutting out from the ground.

"Jungle girl loves her some tech." Dick flicked his cigarette away. It landed in the water and floated for a few moments before sinking from sight. "Shouldn't that be broken? You put your bag in the water in that bowl."

Santana took the charger out and held it in the air. "Waterproof charger." She turned to show her bag. "Waterproof bag."

"Makes sense," Dick agreed.

Santana put the charger back. "You think I wouldn't have thought of that? It would be a stupid thing to dunk all my electronic devices in the bowl just for the sake of progress."

"I've never seen you in your native environment," Dick stated. "I'm impressed."

Voices whispered along the cave. Santana placed a finger on her lips.

In the distance, a small bubble of light appeared. They looked back at the cave entrance, able to make out several small, indistinct figures. Santana put her cell phone in her pocket, shutting out the light.

They lingered at the cave entrance, shining lights inside. Santana prayed that her instincts would be correct, and as they shuffled further on their passageway and left the cave behind, she let out a sigh of relief.

"Come on," she whispered, taking Dick's wrist in hers.

"Are you crazy?" Dick replied. "Turn on your light."

"It's fine," Santana replied.

"No." Dick pulled away. "I may have seen a bunch of crazy shit in my time in this city, but I will not believe you can see in the dark."

Santana chuckled. "I can't."

"Then how can we trust that we won't fall into some endless chasm?" Dick asked.

Santana took his wrist again. "Because some of us are observant enough to examine the way ahead." She pointed, although she knew Dick couldn't see. She left it a few moments before he spotted the line of bioluminescent mushrooms scattering the path before them. "We'll be fine for a short distance at least. We follow the shrooms."

"I once had a dream like that," Dick commented.

Santana guided the way. After a few minutes, she was confident enough to light their way again.

The cave stretched for a long while before them. Occasionally they noted large dark holes on either side of them, but Santana knew better than to investigate. She had once lost a friend to curiosity—Jerry Fingel, a great man—who crept as close as he dared to the edge of a dark pit, only for his footing to slip and for Jerry to tumble down into the darkness.

It wasn't endless. Santana heard his final cries as his body smacked the ground.

More lakes opened around them, and as they moved deeper into the cave, an ambient chorus of *drips* accompanied them.

Santana shone her light to the ceiling, finding small holes where water freely trickled, and the stalactites were stained green.

"We're at the bottom of the valley." She pointed for Dick's benefit. "The river must be above us."

"Which means we're…" Dick started.

"Approaching the temple," Santana replied. "Providing we can resurface again."

She left her comment trailing in the air. As they continued, the sound of rushing water came from above, muted by the thick rock. A little farther in, a waterfall flowed freely into the only lake with white foam on its surface. There the water pooled in a crater before flowing down into another endless hole. Occasionally Santana spotted the glittery silver of a fish, presumably taken a wrong path and falling to its doom.

"Up ahead," Dick called.

Santana didn't need Dick to point it out. An illuminated thick stone doorway showed. A hole in the surface allowed fragments of natural light to shine as though some deity was guiding them forward.

There was only one issue.

"I don't swim that well," Dick stated, staring across the large body of water that barred their way.

Santana secured her bag shut, shutting a load of clasps and zips and ensuring there was no leakage inside. She strode into the water, fully clothed, disturbing the mirror-still pool.

"You're going without me?" Dick asked.

Santana closed her eyes, enjoying the clean chill of the water. The walk through the cave had made her skin sticky. "Who said I'm going anywhere without you?"

"You're swimming."

"You're not." Santana spun and flashed a smile. She ducked under the water, then re-emerged, her body responding to the cool. "Get your ass in, Chambers."

Dick cocked his head.

"If you want to go back, then go," Santana offered. "The only way out is ahead. Your choice." She grinned. "Didn't have you down for a wimp."

Dick scoffed. "It's not the water."

"What is it then?" Santana moved her arms to keep afloat.

Dick glanced farther out into the lake. "What's beneath it?"

Santana turned, then shrugged. "You've seen *Lord of the Rings*, right?"

"Funny," Dick commented.

"I thought so." Santana smirked. "Come on. Get over yourself. We'll be on the shore in no time."

She ducked her head beneath the water and swam. Arm over arm, she cut through the water at speed. The water was clean and smooth, likely undisturbed for years. Only once did she open her eyes, but with little to light the way, she couldn't see the bottom.

As she neared the shore, fragments of light filtered down, allowing Santana her first glimpses into the strange void. A fine layer of sediment covered the sloping rock toward the surface. A few tiny schools of fish skittered nearby. Bleach-white crabs crawled along the bottom of the water.

Something slid past her leg.

She continued, undeterred. Her feet touched the sand. She walked out of the water, running her hands through her hair to push the water away from her face as she'd seen in several James Bond movies.

She spun and sat on the shore. Bubbles and disturbance in the water indicated Dick's location, though she couldn't see a part of his body. Perhaps he'd decided to swim underwater.

Bubbles rose. The movement came closer. Santana cocked her head, gathering her breath. An arm came out of the water.

Not an arm—a fish.

The fish was barrel black and as long as a cutlass. Santana caught the flash of scales, a strange crimson stripe running along its body. Small dagger-like teeth jutted from its jaws.

It splashed into the water and was gone.

"Argh," Dick complained, surfacing with a grimace. "Son of a—"

Something dragged him under again. Santana rose to her feet. She couldn't see beneath the surface from this angle.

She ran to the water and dove in.

She streamed toward Dick, propelling herself through the water with her arms. Something slid by her again. She opened her eyes, barely able to make out the dark shape of a man and several small objects orbiting him. When she neared, she recognized more of the fish.

She reached for the dagger strapped to her waist and pulled it free. One of the fish barreled toward her. With a swift move, she caught the fish in the side of its mouth. Its propulsion pulled it along the blade, the serrated edge slicing along its body.

Thick red misted her vision as the fish stopped moving and sank to the bottom.

She continued forward. Something bit her shoe and pulled her back. She grunted, spinning to track the creature, but it was already gone.

Dick... She thought the name she preferred not to say. She closed in on Dick, who had fought his way to the surface again. Three of the creatures were dragging him back down.

Santana slashed the knife, catching one of the three in the flank. The fish thrashed, flashing angry eyes. Before it could react, Santana plunged the blade through one of its eye sockets.

The water was murky with blood. Santana looked for another attacker and saw the wound on Dick's leg, a tear through his trousers. A flash of movement drew her to the right, and she twisted in time to avoid the jaws of another of the creatures.

Santana needed air.

She kicked to the surface, taking a deep lungful of air. Dick was beside her.

"Motherfuckers," he grunted, gasping.

"Hold still," Santana replied. She dove back down, hacking at one of them until all that remained was one.

It came at her. She slashed with the knife but missed. It swam off into the darkness and out of sight.

She waited a few moments, knife at the ready until she had to come up for air. Finally, she surfaced. "Come on," she instructed. "It's not that far."

"Farther when your leg has been hacked open," Dick retorted. Still, he followed.

Santana kept her wits about her, guarding Dick as he closed in on the shore. She looked around, watching out for any flashes of silver, but all she could see were smaller fish drawn to the cloud of blood out of curiosity. A few plunged into the depths to digest the fallen creatures.

As Dick took his first step onto the shore, something splashed behind them. Santana's toes touched the sand. She spun as the fish arced in the air and came for her throat. She jabbed the knife in an uppercut and caught the fish on the blade. Its weight bore toward her, and she barely managed to stop its teeth a few millimeters from her lips.

The fish's jaws snapped wildly for a moment. A few seconds later, it fell limp.

"Get out of the water," Dick urged.

Santana obeyed, bringing the skewered fish with her.

"What's that for?" Dick asked.

Santana propped the fish on the shore. "Dinner."

Dick chuckled, then groaned as a fresh wave of pain rocked through him.

Santana gave Dick a pitying look. "Straight after we fix you up, of course."

CHAPTER ELEVEN

The wound wasn't as bad as it had looked in the water.

Teeth marks peppered his legs. There was a small section where the tissue showed, though Santana was able to cover up the worst with a couple of stitches and a series of bandages.

"I'm glad that water was cold," Dick offered as Santana secured the bandages in place.

"Why's that?" Santana asked. "Most men don't like what the cold water does to them."

Dick chuckled. "It numbed the worst of it." He winced as a shot of pain ran through him. "That's wearing off a little now."

"Are you okay to walk?" Santana asked, abandoning her probe of the small fire she had got crackling on the shore. The fish lay in the sand beside the flames.

Dick accepted Santana's help to his feet. He put his weight gingerly onto the leg, face screwing tight. "I think so. It won't be nice, but I don't want you carrying me around this place." He glanced over his shoulder. "Not when there are more of them around."

"If we only knew who 'they' were," Santana replied.

Dick took a few cautious steps, limping slightly.

"Are you sure you're going to be okay?" Santana asked.

"I'll let you know," Dick replied. She could tell he was acting brave, but she didn't want to question him. He was right. This job needed them both mobile. "What were those things?"

"Not sure. They looked like barracudas, but they behaved like piranhas."

"I thought piranhas swarming and attacking innocents was a myth? I'd heard they only attack non-moving, dead targets."

Santana smirked as she returned her attention to the fire. She held the strange creature over the flames, filling the air with the scent of cooked fish. "Someone's been doing their homework. That's correct, but who knows what these things are? I've never seen anything like them. Could be a new island discovery."

Dick shook his head, then flopped down beside her. "You could call them Santanas."

"Or the Chambers fish." She smiled.

Dick laughed and looked down between his legs.

"Did I say something wrong?" Santana asked.

Dick lifted his head and looked out over the lake. "You struggle to call me by my proper name, don't you?"

"Your proper name is John."

"Dick."

Santana chuckled. "John."

"Dick."

"John."

Dick shook his head, a smile on his face. "Why's it a problem for you?"

Santana drew a long breath, rotating the blade to cook the fish evenly. Some of the larger scales had curled and blackened, but she knew it was the meat inside that counted.

"Because it's all bravado and ego with you men. Every man and his dog want admiration for their sexual prowess. Every warm-blooded male wants to play up to his buds and prove his macho stature. You're one of a long line of men who can't accept the fact that a woman won't bow to your wishes and embrace a name that they find personally offensive."

Dick frowned. "Really?"

Santana laughed. "Nah. I just refuse to embrace a name that's synonymous with a penis. Plus, I can tell it grinds your gears."

Dick rolled his eyes. "What if I changed your name?"

"Try," Santana insisted.

"Penelope," Dick replied with a smirk.

Santana scoffed. "You can't make names up. At least I'm calling you by your name—your *given* first name." She removed the fish from the flames and laid it across a clean slate of stone she'd found nearby. "Besides, it's not like Dick is short for something. If your name was Richard, I might accept it. But how does 'John' become 'Dick?'"

"You've asked me that before," Dick replied.

Santana smiled. "I never got an answer." She started cutting the fish into small, bite-sized cubes.

"You still won't," Dick replied. He eyed the fish. "Are you sure that's safe to eat?"

Santana picked up a cube of pink fishy flesh and sniffed it. "Smells like salmon."

"Poisons like blowfish," Dick shot back.

Santana touched her tongue to the meat. It was salty, despite the freshwater she knew filled these lakes. Satisfied, she popped the chunk in her mouth.

The meat exploded in wet flavor. She chewed until all was mush, then swallowed it. For a few moments, she allowed herself to sit and feel the food working through her body.

"Well?" Dick asked.

"Seems fine," Santana replied. "Guess we'll find out in an hour or so."

Dick chuckled uncertainly. "You're kidding, right?"

Santana nodded. "It's a barb-toothed pike," she clarified. "One of Atlantica's native species. They're found everywhere in these cave systems, and they're quite delicious."

Dick's mirth vanished. "You knew the whole time?"

Santana popped another cube in her mouth. "Sure did."

Dick looked as though he had something to say but bit back the retort. "Pass me some," he settled on.

They ate in relative silence until their stomachs were full. When they were satisfied, they gathered their things and extinguished the fire.

"Ready to rock?" Santana asked.

Dick looked down at his leg. "That a joke?"

"You have been in the wars, haven't you?" Santana replied.

Dick stayed quiet.

The light had faded some when they stood by the door. Craning their necks skyward, they could make out the small breaks in a rocky chasm above, which gave some light to the outside world. It was no wonder no one had stumbled across this door. Overgrown greenery grew thick above.

She turned her attention to the door, its frame carved in ancient lettering.

"More Incan?" Dick asked.

"More Incan," Santana replied.

Somewhere nearby an explosion sounded.

"They're going to tear the place apart," she stated.

Dick nodded. "We better get moving, then."

They entered the doorway, met by a walkway with angled walls carved in a yellow stone. Their feet echoed loudly around as they followed where the path led, stopping by a thick stone door. They pushed the door open, stone grinding on stone until they found themselves in a large room lined with thick pillars.

Doors led off each of the three walls. The first led to an ancient bathroom, complete with holes in the floor that dropped at least fifteen feet into a gently running river.

"No better time," Dick announced, causing Santana to turn and shield her eyes as he unleashed a yellow stream into the hole.

They approached the next door and found a room lined with rotting tables and chairs. Gold and bronze plates lay on the table, thick with spiderwebs and food that had become dust. Along the walls were various golden ornaments embedded in the rock itself.

"I've never seen anything so preserved as this," Santana stated. "Most Incan ruins are simply stone and dirt, with little remaining until you dig. Something must've happened here to make them leave all their possessions behind."

Dick stopped by a bench. He reached down to an object then held it up for Santana to see. He waved the skeleton's arm. The rest of its body lay flat on the bench, so grey and rotten that it blended in with its surroundings. "They didn't go anywhere."

"More of this?" Santana shook her head disbelievingly. "There's something strange with this island. How many more examples of past cultures must we find where entire civilizations die without a known cause? The Incans, the Germans, the US soldiers..."

Mom.

"Does that mean you're saying what I think you're saying?" Dick asked.

"Probably not," Santana replied.

Dick chuckled. "You think an apocalyptic event wiped out these cultures. Something that swept through and took them out?"

"Maybe," Santana muttered.

Dick drew a long breath. "If that's the case, what's to stop it happening again and wiping out Atlantica as we know it?"

Santana shrugged, not answering his musing. "Perhaps."

Dick chewed his lip. "Who knows...We can't rule it out. The question is, what's happening to them?"

Santana examined a nearby skull that had fallen off its owner and rolled to the floor. From an educated guess, she identified the skull as belonging to a female Incan. She turned it to face Dick, who raised an eyebrow. "That question has been on the tongues of historians for almost a century," Santana replied. "But nice to see you're paying attention."

She snapped some pictures, then they returned to the previous room, turning their attention to the final door. This one showcased an image of Inti on the front, carved into rotten wood. They opened the door together, both keeping an eye on the stone frame above lest they repeat their past mistake, and stepped inside.

Santana gasped.

The space was huge, the walls sloping up toward a central point to complete the pyramid. Dotted around the place were tiny holes that allowed a thousand thin shafts of light to illuminate the space and highlight the swirling dust motes in the air. In the center of the room was a towering statue, at least thirty feet tall, with a face Santana had repeatedly seen on this journey.

"Inti..." she breathed.

Inti was in pristine condition, a monolith of gold and stone. He held his hands out on either side, palms up. On his head was a towering headdress of gold. Large, carved-out hollows showed where the eyes should have been, and in the center...

"There," Santana announced, pointing at Inti's face.

Inside the eyes, something was giving off light. This time it wasn't blue but golden and pulsing.

Dick rested against the wall, leaning for balance. "Okay," he muttered, eyes larger than they had been since they set off into the jungle. "But what about that?"

Surrounding the statue was a large ring of water that had turned green from moss and algae. Bubbles floated lazily to the surface, and Santana wondered what delights awaited inside the pool. The only way across was several platforms which steadily rose in a spiral around the statue, eventually reaching the height of Inti's head.

"We climb," Santana commented. She glanced uncertainly at Dick. "Or, rather, I climb."

"I can come," Dick offered.

"Is *that* why you called yourself Dick?" Santana winked, already working toward the first stone.

It was an easy enough leap, Santana's jump taking her six feet over the water. Her feet landed securely in the center of the stone.

She looked at Dick. "Easy enough."

Something rumbled. The edges of the stone grew wet as it began sinking into the water.

Dick shook his head. "Got a habit of speaking too soon, don'tcha?"

Santana uncoiled her bullwhip and snapped it toward the second stone pillar. It coiled around an outcrop of rock, but as she tugged to check its security, the rock crumbled away.

"Shit."

She snapped the bullwhip again, finding another small crop of rock. This time she leaped, one hand reaching fingers toward the lip, her feet finding purchase in small grooves on the side of the pillar.

She looked back, the first stone already sunk in the water.

The pillar shook.

It started sinking.

She climbed, using her elbows and swinging her leg over to get to her feet. "It's like a shit game of Mario," she called.

Dick retorted, "A good workman never blames his tools."

Santana scoffed, lining up her jump to the next pillar. "What does that even mean?"

She jumped.

"Doesn't matter," Dick replied.

Santana climbed onto the top, briefly brushing herself down

as the pillar followed suit with the others and started to sink. The platform was around four feet in diameter, giving her one solid step to gain momentum for the next jump.

"No, you said it," Santana insisted. "So stand behind your words."

"I simply meant maybe you were a shit Mario player."

"I never played Mario." Santana took a step back. Her heel slipped and sent a smattering of stone into the water.

"That's my point," Dick called.

Santana shook her head, focusing on the pillar ahead. This one had a jagged crack running along its length, which she didn't like the look of one bit.

She leaped. This time, her stomach slammed on the top. She clung to the edges and crawled onto the platform. As she stood, she felt the pillar swaying beneath her.

"Santana, watch out!" Dick shouted through cupped hands.

Santana readied to jump, knowing that time was short. She was about to leap when the stone lurched downward. A segment of the center fell out, and the pillar jolted. Without a second thought, she leaped toward the next column with her arms spread wide. She was short of the top but managed to cling to the stone. Her muscles coiled. She craned her neck to the top as the pillar slowly started sinking.

She reached for the lip but was an inch away. She dug in the toes of her boots, attempting to get the extra distance, but the smooth stone yielded no friction.

"Fuck..." she grunted.

"Santana, grab the top!" Dick called.

"What do you think I'm trying to do?" Santana groaned, gripping tightly with her fingers. She tried again, using both feet in one froggish leap. For a moment, she was weightless, floating twenty feet above the ground.

Her fingers snatched the edge.

She roared, raising herself.

There was no time to settle on top. She'd already lost valuable time, and there were three pillars left.

She jumped for the next, fingers barely catching the lip. She chanced a glance down, seeing now how high she was. Although the water was beneath her, she didn't want to drop. Bubbles frothed and foamed beneath the murky surface, and after her encounter with the pike, she didn't want to know what awaited below.

Another leap.

Another climb.

Finally, she saw the end of the road in sight.

"Almost there!" Dick announced.

You think I can't see that? She rolled her eyes. *This is why I work alone.*

She stopped at the final hurdle, measuring the leap. It was larger than the others, with a little bit of a drop this time. Still, she could feel the pillar sinking beneath her.

"How are you going to get down?" Dick called.

Santana shot him a look. "Can't I focus on getting there first? I'll explore the options for a safe descent after."

She took a step back, coiled her legs. Assessing the gap, she leaped. The world fell away beneath her. The second and third pillars had sunk into the water. She focused on the landing, a smooth stretch of gold filtered with a fine layer of dust and grit.

She landed firmly on her feet.

Her feet skidded.

She fell onto her rear.

She slid toward the sloping descent of Inti's headdress.

"Fuck…" she grunted, spinning onto her stomach and attempting to grab anything she could find to stop her fall.

Metal disappeared beneath her feet, then her legs. The sharp drop of the flat of Inti's headdress fell below her. Her fingers were grazed, grown hot by her attempt to slow the fall.

She clutched the lip.

Her body crashed into the gold front of the headdress. Air expelled from her lungs. She hung there for a moment, catching her breath.

"You okay?" Dick called.

Santana ignored him. She looked around, working out her next step. The front of the headdress had deep grooves etched for detail. These she found she could dig her toes into as she scaled down the adornment, finally coming to a stand on the brow of Inti, one hand clutching the gold as an anchor.

She looked for Dick. He had moved to the edge of the water—as close as he could get without crossing it. He was so small beneath her. She gave a weak thumbs-up.

"It looks like there's a way to climb down by his right ear," Dick offered. "See where the trail of hair spirals?"

Santana looked where Dick was pointing. She nodded, then shinnied along Inti's brow, finally making it to the strange spiral ladder.

She lowered herself, finding that she was only a few feet away from the hollow of Inti's eye socket.

"Almost there," Dick stated.

Santana's nostrils flared. She looked for an easy way but could find none. All around her was the smooth gold front of Inti's giant face. "Here goes nothing," she breathed.

Before Dick could protest or warn, she leaped. The eye socket was as tall as she was, and she managed to jump smoothly into the hole. She dropped to her hands and knees, breathing a huge sigh of relief.

For a moment, she allowed herself to catch her breath. Her fingers stung. A sheen of sweat made her forehead sticky. When she looked up, she had to shield her eyes.

She wasn't sure how it was possible, but dozens of razor-thin fragments of light shone inside Inti's head. Coming through unknown holes, concentrated by...she couldn't figure it out. The lights all angled toward a single object in the center of Inti's head…

A dagger.

"La Daga de los Días Sin Fin," Santana breathed, mouth agape.

The blade was gleaming as if exploding in white light. She barely made out the definition of its edges, the dagger resting in a groove that allowed it to stand upright, pointing at the sky.

She crawled closer, one hand blocking the worst of the light. The nearer she got, the more she felt the hum of energy exploding from it. Her hair obediently stood on end as if electricity were coursing through her.

She touched the hilt, her aching fingertips growing warm. She tugged the dagger…

But it wouldn't move.

Her eyes stung. She tried both hands, but the damn thing wouldn't budge. She tried once more, then sat back, trying to see something that she must be missing through the barrage of light.

It rested on the ceiling above the dagger, a small hollow the size of a small ball. Taking the Atlanticore orb from her backpack, she rose and placed the ball inside the groove. It fit snugly inside, locking in place, and Santana had a moment to feel smug about being determined to bring it with her.

The moment didn't last long.

Energy pulsed from a space between the dagger and the Atlanticore. It threw Santana backward. She grunted, sitting up to see a strange line of electric energy passing between the Atlanticore and the tip of the dagger. The shafts of light grew wider, beginning to move in all directions, blinding her.

The dagger rose from its cradle, suspended in the air by this strange new rush of energy.

Without thinking, Santana reached for the dagger and took it. She brought it toward her, breaking the bond between Atlanticore and dagger. Another pulse pushed her back, sending her skidding to the open edge of the eye socket.

"Santana!" Dick called, urgency in his voice.

She turned to find the water glowing a vibrant blue. The bubbles frothed and foamed as if the water was heating from below by an unknown source.

"I've got it!" Santana called, holding up the dagger.

"Great!" Dick replied dryly. "Can we get the hell out of here now?"

Energy hummed behind her. Light traveled in great streaks across Inti's body, lighting the statue the same way the smaller replica had a short time ago. Something lurched inside the figure, and before Santana knew what was going on, the arms shifted, rotating in their sockets.

"Santana!" Dick called.

"Okay!" she called back.

She desperately looked around for a way down. The statue began to lower, falling into the water in the same way the pillars had. Santana looked at the slowly rotating arms, wondering what mechanisms were inside to make such a heavy, grandiose display of wealth move so smoothly.

She lashed out her whip, the coils snaking around one of Inti's fingers. With a bold jump, she swung through the air, holding back the urge to jungle-call like Tarzan.

She reached the end of her swing, then started back in the opposite direction. This time, as her swing brought her close to the ground, she flicked her wrist, loosening the coil and allowing her to fly the last few feet onto solid rock.

She yelled, lowering herself into a clumsy roll as she attempted to dissipate her momentum.

When she stood, she turned to find Dick on the other side of the room. He was pointing behind her.

She looked at the wall, pleased to find a glowing door had appeared. "Come on, then!" she called. "Get your ass in gear."

Dick hobbled toward her. The statue continued its strange dance, causing the chamber to rumble around her. Stones rained down. Dust spiraled around them. More shafts of light appeared as the ceiling began to cave in.

"Come on!" Santana yelled.

Dick narrowly avoided a boulder falling on him. He stumbled toward her, limping with each step. Another rumble came from the far wall.

Dick reached Santana. "That one wasn't the statue…"

Santana and Dick turned to the source of the rumble as another came. A moment later, the smell of explosives and the cry of enraged voices followed a blast of light.

A small group filtered into the chamber through the hole they'd made. Santana caught a flash of sunlight glinting off their weapons before she turned and ran for the door, dragging Dick in her wake.

CHAPTER TWELVE

"I'm getting déjà vu," Dick called.

Santana pumped her arms, allowing Dick to lean on her as they ran through the passage. "Shut up and run!"

Shouts rang from behind them. Rocks fell. Bullets fired, *pinging* off the walls. Santana glanced over her shoulder and saw the ceiling caving in, the lit doorway falling from sight as a tumble of rocks came down and blocked them in.

The rocks worked their way toward them. Dust kicked up, pushing them forward as they sprinted through the crafted passageway. The walls cracked. Detritus drifted down around them. At the end of the hallway was a framed stone door.

"Fuck. Run!" Santana instructed. Dick weighed heavy on her, but she pulled him along anyway, the pair of them closing on the door. Stones fell on Santana's head and shoulders, pain blossoming where they landed.

"What do you think I'm trying to—"

"Now's not the time for sarcasm—" Santana stopped, yelling as a boulder grazed her heel. She could hear nothing other than tumbling rock.

They were within reach of the door. Santana used the last of her strength to swing Dick forward, chucking him through the oblong as she swiftly dove after.

The doorframe was solid, holding back the tide of rockfall. They spun, watching with trepidation until stone barred the way back. Somewhere far away, gunfire continued.

"Holy shit…" Santana panted, regaining her breath.

Dick lay beside her, one hand covering his face. There were red slices across his jacket and arms, as well as his cheeks. "Remind me never to go exploring with you again."

Santana let out an incredulous laugh. "Honey, this is just a Monday for me."

"My point exactly." Dick pushed himself into a sitting position and looked around. Soft golden light filtered in from a shaft high above them. The sky had turned pink, looking as though the sun was setting and nearing dusk. "Where the hell are we?"

Before Santana could answer, they heard voices above. She helped Dick move out of sight of the shaft toward the darkened edges of the chamber.

"It came from over this way," one of the voices called. Three heads appeared at the edge of the hole, silhouetted by the burning sky. "Shit, that's a long way down."

"It's too dark," one of the voices stated. "Got your light?"

Santana tugged Dick sharply, dragging him behind a nearby boulder. A powerful beam of white light trailed down and scanned the place. "Looks like just another crevice." The light honed in on the door. "Oh, hello. Wait a minute."

"What's that?" one of the voices said.

"A way in?" another suggested.

The light scanned around the room, finding a passageway leading off the chamber. "There's another one down there. Go, tell the captain. It could be the way inside."

"Didn't you hear Dresden?" one of the voices retorted. "The captain is busy. Reckon they found a way in themselves."

"Oh, right," one of them laughed. "Like blasting holes through the rock is going to get them anywhere."

"Go, fetch your abseil gear," the first voice commanded.

They disappeared. Santana looked at where the light had shone toward the second passage. With a nod, she motioned for Dick to follow.

The door was more of a crevice that they both had to squeeze through. The walls were tight, pressing against their curves and edges. Dick followed Santana, grunting as his larger frame struggled to break through.

After a short distance, the crevice opened into a rough stone cave. They walked in silence, listening for the sounds of those they'd seen before. Although they couldn't see anyone around them, they couldn't fight the feeling that they were in a dangerous position and one wrong move would unleash a hive of activity.

The cave curved to the left. They trod over lumps and rocks, climbing on a couple of occasions where the gradient of the floor increased. It was slow going, and by the time they reached the level surface again, they were both panting.

Dick's stomach rumbled loudly.

"Shhh," Santana shot back.

Dick raised an eyebrow. "I'm hungry, so sue me."

"No. Shush." Santana pointed ahead of them.

There was nothing in sight, but they heard the faint murmur of voices.

"Wait here," she commanded.

She stalked ahead, listening intently. She couldn't make out what they were saying, but they were somewhere nearby. She crept close to the walls, careful where she trod. She reached a point by a large flat expanse of the wall where she heard the words more clearly.

"...give us one." The voice was male, rough.

A feminine voice replied, "Catch," and threw something.

Santana picked up the rustle of a food wrapper.

She looked around, trying to find a way to see what was going on. Beside her was a rock that she trod on to gain a higher vantage point. A series of small holes lined the rock face, a few of them the size of a dime and allowing her to see through the wall.

A man and a woman sat around a small fire. They wore black uniforms with a symbol on their left breast that she couldn't read. The man was tucking into a chocolate bar while the woman worked at some food stuck in her teeth. Hovering over the fire was the desecrated corpse of an unidentifiable mammal.

The woman prodded the animal with a stick. "This is boring."

"It's supposed to be," the man replied.

"Why are they having all the fun?" she asked. "They're off playing with TNT, and we're stuck here keeping guard over the equipment. What do they think is going to happen? Some jaguar is going to come and take our packs?"

"It's necessary," the man replied. Beside him, resting on the floor, was a sleek black pistol.

"It's bullshit," the woman continued solemnly.

Santana looked past the two, toward where a corridor led away from the room. Several objects lay scattered in the passage. When Santana's eyes adjusted, she recognized them for what they were.

Bodies.

Santana glowered at the pair. If her guess was right, they'd stumbled across a parallel walkway to the temple's main body.

That meant one thing: the way out.

Fuck.

Santana worked her way back to Dick, leaving the pair behind. When she reached him, he was lying with his eyes closed, his breath coming in long drags. "Wake up."

"I wasn't asleep," Dick's eyes opened as he peeled himself off the ground. "What did you find?"

"A way out," Santana replied. "I think."

"Great to have a bit of certainty in these trying times," Dick quipped.

"Keep it down," Santana reprimanded. "There are people there."

Dick shut his mouth and followed Santana to the wall. She stood on the rock, looking through a hole. The pair had stopped talking, the man now fast asleep as the woman dealt with the fire and removing the shredded, cindered carcass.

"Hey…" Dick whispered, waving a hand.

Santana moved beside Dick.

"There's something here," Dick stated softly, pointing at a large groove in the rock. "Think you can fit through?"

Santana threw an uncertain glance in the direction of the two through the wall. "I can try."

She stepped a leg inside, then squeezed into the space. As she pressed against the rock in front of her, it budged away from her, allowing her a chance to breathe. She exchanged a glance with Dick, then pushed harder, finding that the rock started to roll away from her, widening the gap.

"Huh?" The woman's voice.

Santana paused, waiting a moment until all was quiet. Holding the rock from her, she found there was now space to fit Dick inside, too.

When he was beside her, he took the weight of the boulder. The farther she crawled in, the more she saw of the large rock, noting that it must have been balancing precariously as it was for years, and their final effort determined its direction of falling. As Santana wormed her way through, she came across a small crawlspace blocked by tangles of roots and plants.

She cautiously lowered to her stomach and looked through the roots. From here, she could crawl into the space with the two in black uniforms. Working slowly, quietly, she reached back and brought her backpack beside her head. She rooted inside for the tranquilizer darts Emily had given her, then loaded them in her dart gun.

The dart *clicked* into place.

The woman's ears pricked up. She glanced toward Santana.

Santana pulled the trigger.

The dart flew toward the woman, finding a home in her neck. She brought her hands to the projectile, about to call out when her eyes drooped, and her body went weak.

The woman *thumped* to the ground, unconscious.

Holy shit, that was fast.

She turned her attention to the man who was still fast asleep on the floor. She had a limited number of darts and wanted to save them where she could. Instead, she holstered her gun, then reached for her knife.

She worked on the roots, creating a space big enough to crawl out. When she was free, she steadily rose to her feet, eyes fixed on the man.

She tiptoed toward him. Dick scuffled after, emerging from the hole like a baby slipping free from the birth canal. Santana drew her pistol and held it at the man's face. He looked peaceful, serene. She wondered what he was dreaming about.

Dick drew up beside her. "Going to shoot him at point-blank range?"

Santana shook her head and nodded at a length of rope coiled nearby.

Dick took the signal, returning a moment later with the rope. He stood beside Santana and held up a black roll of duct tape that had been near the rope. He ripped off a length and slapped it on the man's mouth.

The man woke sharply, grunting behind the tape. He sat up, then froze under the withering glare of Santana's pistol.

"No fuss. No sound," she warned.

The man glared at her as Dick bound his ankles and wrists.

He glanced toward his comrade, eyes widening at the sight of the dart in her neck.

Santana knelt beside him with the gun pressed to his temple. She spotted the embroidered logo of a scythe on his breast. "I'm going to remove the tape, now. You're going to answer some questions for me. Got it?"

The man nodded and frowned.

Santana pinched the corner of the tape. She peeled slowly, the man's skin rising and falling as she removed the adhesive until half of his mouth was exposed. "What's your name?"

The man didn't answer, his breathing rapid.

Santana tore the strip of tape off in one go. The man grunted. "What's your name?"

"Gyles," he replied. "Gyles Forde."

"Nice to meet you, Gyles," Santana crooned. "What are you doing in a place like this?"

Gyles met her gaze. A glob of spit left his mouth, landing on Santana's shoulder. She nonchalantly wiped it away, then pressed the gun harder into his temple. "I'm not here to fuck around, Gyles. I want answers. Got it?" She thumbed off the safety.

"Yes. Yes," Gyles mumbled. "Sorry…"

"Who are you with, Gyles?" Santana's voice was soft but firm.

"The Order," he replied. "I'm with the Order."

"Which order?" Dick asked.

"The Order of the Scythe," he answered.

Santana glanced again at the logo.

"Who is The Order of the Scythe?" Santana replied.

Gyles looked at his friend, then back at Santana. "Historians. Documenters of history. We're treasure hunters, same as you." He nodded at the tunnel filled with dead bodies. "Same as them."

"That's how you treat fellow treasure hunters?" Santana asked.

Gyles narrowed his eyes. "I was only following orders."

"You mowed down an entire faction," Dick commented, lip

curling. "Barged in with firearms to tear up this place and take out those who were one step ahead of you." He shook his head, reaching into his pocket for a cigarette. "I thought treasure hunting was about delicacy? Fragility? The tender touch?"

Santana smirked. "You've been paying attention."

"It's what she wants," Gyles grunted. "She only wants the main prize. She doesn't give a shit about the rest of it, for decorated walls and inane trinkets. She has her eyes on the big goal and will get there by any means necessary."

"Who?" Santana asked. "Who will?"

Gyles glanced around him as if someone would turn up and shoot him for talking. "The boss."

"Who's the boss?" Dick urged.

Gyles closed his eyes and drew a long breath. Santana adjusted her fingers on the pistol. Gyles swelled. "I'll tell you. But if I do, you have to let me go."

Dick scoffed.

Santana raised an eyebrow. "You hardly have bargaining power here, my friend. Give us a name, and we're gone. Don't give us a name, and we're gone."

"Going to be hard to find your way out of the labyrinth without running into more of us," Gyles remarked. He glanced toward Dick's leg. "Especially with a hobbling mess at your side." He turned his gaze to Santana, an earnest look in her eye. "You need me."

Santana turned from the man to the tunnel. In the distance, she could make out movement and more voices.

"Fine," Santana replied.

Dick gave her an incredulous look. "You're kidding?"

"My operation, my choice." Santana reached beneath the crook of Gyles' arm and helped him to his feet.

"Unbind his feet," Santana instructed.

Dick reluctantly obliged.

Gyles held out his hands.

"They stay tied," Santana informed. "As long as you're with us, you're directing. You don't need your hands."

"I want to point," Gyles replied.

Dick exhaled a cloud of smoke. "And I want cigars, bourbon, and a pretty lady on my lap. We're all in the same fucking boat here."

Santana nudged Gyles forward. "Over to you, Theseus. Take us through the labyrinth."

CHAPTER THIRTEEN

Santana tugged Gyles back. "Hold back."

The passageway split into two directions. Flame torches lined the walls. They had trodden over several bodies of men and women who all looked as though they didn't deserve to die. Peaceful expressions masked their faces, a contrast to the pools of blood littering their bodies from the bullets the Order had rained down on them.

Two people approached from the left walkway. Santana glanced at Dick, sending silent instructions to wait and be ready.

The footfall grew louder. Gyles hung back with his lips clamped closed. As the two emerged into sight, Santana and Dick sprang.

Their fists connected with faces. Santana hooked a leg behind her victim, sending him sprawling to the ground. His head hit the stone floor, and consciousness left him.

Dick's attack was almost as smooth. His target had some fight and threw a punch back. Dick pulled his head back, the man's fist scraping his chin. Dick returned with an uppercut straight into the man's jaw. His eyes rolled back as he fell.

They quickly dragged the pair into the walkway with the

bodies. Gyles led them down the right corridor. Doors opened on either side, Incan in design, but cleaner and more modern than the chambers Santana and Dick had left behind.

As Gyles led them through the many corridors and rooms of the temple, Santana couldn't help but wonder if the reason no one had been able to find the main heart of the temple was that someone had built this new one on top. No wonder they needed to blast through the muck to find the dagger at its heart.

They encountered more groups, the activity getting steadily busier as they ascended the levels toward the surface. The farther they got, the greener the surroundings, with trails of roots, leaves, ivy, and tangles invading the stonework.

They reached a room where a group of the Order was working away. They'd set up several makeshift tables, and some of them were brushing and dusting off artifacts they'd claimed from the temple. Others patrolled with large rifles in their hands, occasionally shoving the workers who sat at the tables.

Santana shot a look at Gyles. He'd been good so far, leading them ever upward. She was beginning to think she might be able to trust the man.

"They're hostages," Gyles whispered. "Members of the Albatross' team, working to help the Order. The Order of the Scythe mostly focuses on retrieval and upheaval, not survival and revival."

"Catchy slogan for your TV adverts," Dick retorted.

Santana's eyes lingered on the group.

"Santana, no," Dick stated, reading Santana's intent.

"We can't leave them," Santana replied.

"Yes, we can," Dick retorted.

Santana crept closer. "No. Not on my watch. They're good people." She looked at Dick. "They're members of your client's team."

Dick's lip curled. "This is happening, isn't it?"

Santana replied by creeping closer to the doorway. Nearby

was a man with his back to her. He monitored the room, sweeping his gaze across the tables.

Santana slowly reached for her bullwhip. She fixed her gaze on his rifle, then lined up her aim.

"Santana…" Dick warned.

Santana checked the locations of the others around the room. With a quick snap of the wrist, she latched the coil around the end of the rifle, then pulled it back.

The rifle slipped from the man's grasp and flew toward her. The man shouted, alerting the rest of the room. Santana secured the gun in her grip and pulled the trigger.

All hell unleashed. She carved a path with the bullets, mowing down the assholes in black who had their hostages withering under their glance. She swept it back on an arc, keeping her aim at head height to not accidentally kill the hostages.

After a few seconds, she released the trigger. The room went quiet. Bodies lay scattered on the ground, weapons fallen from their hands. The first guard Santana had stolen the rifle from stared at her in disbelief. She aimed at his thigh, then shot once.

The man knelt, clutching his injured leg. Santana met his gaze. "Tell the others what you saw."

She tossed the rifle away from the man, then addressed the rest of the room. "There's no way no one else heard all of that. I advise you to run for your lives before the cavalry comes. You've seen what they're capable of."

Without another word, she turned from the room, shoving Gyles ahead of her to lead the way.

She walked confidently ahead. Dick jogged to catch up. "Want to tell me what the hell happened back there?"

"You got a problem with justice?" Santana asked.

Dick smirked. "Who hurt you?"

Santana stopped, turning to face Dick. "In Atlantica, there are good guys, and there are bad guys. In this line of work, I've seen my fair share of assholes. I've done things I'm not proud of, and I've done necessary things."

She pointed back the way they'd come. "They were going to kill all of those workers the minute they had no more use for them." She looked at Gyles. "Am I wrong?"

Gyles shook his head.

"The jungle has its own laws," Santana continued. "When they finished with them, they were going to destroy any evidence they'd existed. It's the only way to ensure that the artifacts you recover remain yours, and you get recognized for their discovery. The victors write history."

She marched ahead, dragging Gyles with her to find her direction. A commotion rang out behind them. Footsteps and shouts came from before them.

Santana kept her cool, pulling Gyles into a recess in the walls. Dick joined them. They remained quiet as a group of men and women in black raced past them, eyes fixed ahead to the gunfire's source.

Once they were gone, Santana drew out again, marching with Gyles. He took them through twists and turns until they reached a set of sandstone steps.

The way up was clear and wide. At the end, they saw the purpling sky. They ran up the stairs, Dick struggling behind them as they neared the surface, the cool night air licking their faces. Scattered around the stairwell were more bodies of the fallen, all in various uncomfortable positions, trails of blood already dried on the steps.

They reached the top. Around them was a thick curtain of forestry. Ahead of them were several guards who turned at the sight of the three at the top of the stairs.

A moment's hesitation followed as they recognized Gyles' uniform. When they finally understood the situation, they fired the first shots.

Santana shoved Gyles forward. Without his hands to protect

him, he fell flat on his face in the soft mud. She dove to the side, uncoiling her whip and lashing it at the nearest attacker. She caught his fingers, leaving a bright red trail across his knuckles. He dropped his weapon.

Dick followed up his first shot with another that went straight into the chest of the second man in black. The man groaned as he fell to the ground, dead.

Santana made a break toward the nearest trees, using the thick boughs for cover. Bullets followed her, splinters raining into the air. She leaned around the trunk, swapping her whip for her pistol as she sent two shots at the other guards.

The first hit. The second missed, disappearing into the trees across the way. She ducked away again, listening for Dick. More shots fired, filling the air with chaos. Birds took to the sky.

Santana glanced back at Gyles, who remained on the ground, slowly using his knees to worm his way toward a metal container that appeared to hold several cartridges and magazines.

A bullet whistled past Santana's ear. She turned, staring into the dark canopy to find a shadow moving nearby. Light glinted off the woman's pistol.

Santana shot, the woman disappearing into the undergrowth.

"John!" she called, running to the next bough. She peeked around, looking for Dick across the other side of a dirt track. "John?"

Reports called in answer. She narrowed her eyes, trying to identify the moving shapes in the distance. A man cried out as he flew backward. Another's gun sparked with life as they shot. A moment later, she heard a fist *smack* against a face.

Santana broke toward the chaos, gun leading the way. When she made it through the growth, she found Dick leaning heavily against a tree.

"You okay?" Santana asked.

Dick shook his head, indicating his leg. "Bastards opened the wound."

"You need help," Santana commented.

"No shit," Dick replied.

Santana looked around for some kind of prop or cane Dick could use to support his weight. She settled on the crawling man, now kneeling over the metallic container, drawing a pistol from its depths.

Santana's heart dropped. *Bastard. After all we've been through...*

She walked slowly toward Gyles, appearing through the large, fan-like leaves. She pointed her gun at him. He aimed his at her. "Gyles... Think about what you're doing. We can help you." She motioned behind her. "John's in trouble. Help us out of here, and you'll be greatly rewarded. More than any of those guys can offer."

She saw the glint in his eye and knew she was in trouble.

"Please..." she offered, finger tensing on the trigger. "Don't make me shoot."

The report silenced all other sounds. Santana ducked as Gyles fired. Fire burned in her eyes, anger in her stomach. It was only when the weight of something heavy crashed on her that she realized what had happened.

The woman in black lay unconscious atop her, weapon fallen from her hand. Santana shoved the woman away, rolling onto her back. As she looked up, Gyles stood over her, his bound hands outstretched toward her. "Need a hand?" he offered.

Santana accepted the help, rising to her feet. Gyles pointed toward the trees. "He that way?"

She told him Dick was. They moved into the cover of the trees, Gyles offering a shoulder for Dick to lean on. They started their walk away into the wilds, Santana leading them far into the dense trees until the sounds of gunfire and shouting faded into the pregnant silence of the waiting jungle.

Sasha Chechik's heart raced.

She already knew what the outcome would be. Even as she watched her team assemble their ropes and belays and scale the monolithic statue of Inti, she knew that it would already be gone.

Inti rested on his side, mechanisms whirring but arms not moving. The chamber was a mess, with rocks scattered everywhere and dust coating the entire place. They'd had to wait until the worst of the fall subsided before they could enter the chamber. Her team had reported two figures running away through a door they could no longer access, and she knew they had it.

The dagger was gone.

It was confirmed a few moments later when a solemn-faced woman with a short crop of hair stood on Inti's cheek and shook her head. She hopped down, over the remains of a filthy lake where a dozen or so mutant-looking fish had hopped free of the water and died on the land, then made her way toward Sasha.

"No sign of it," Parna stated.

Sasha gritted her teeth.

"There's something else, though," Parna informed her. "They found a nugget of Atlanticore. Must've been part of the activation sequence to enable the mechanisms to work." She gave an appreciative half-smile. "Masterful crafting."

Sasha looked past Parna to the statue's eye socket where two men emerged, one holding the bright blue orb. The whirring mechanisms died, and the last of the light in the chamber faded. "The Incans were a masterful race," she muttered. "But the Atlanticans are greater."

She curled her fist into a ball, announcing to the chamber, "Move out. There's nothing more to do here. We search for the fuckers who took the dagger. We get them before they have any chance to escape this Godforsaken forest and make it back to the city."

She marched toward the blasted entrance into the chamber.

Parna walked alongside her. "Who do you think it is, Great One? Who could have thwarted us like this?"

Sasha didn't reply. She had an idea, but she didn't have enough information to base her idea on anything solid. As she stalked through the halls back to the main surface temple, her ears picked up the raging roll of gunfire.

With any luck, by the time she reached the top, they would have the interloper dead and the dagger in their possession.

CHAPTER FOURTEEN

Santana led them through the darkness.

Their progress was slow, with Gyles only able to aid Dick for short periods without rest. They trailed down the steep slope of the Nureguard Valley toward the wide river ravine that rushed through its basin. When they reached the water's edge, they paused and gathered their breath.

Clouds of midges followed them, feasting on the two men. Santana took out a handful of power bars and handed them to Dick and Gyles. "Eat. Get your strength back."

Dick plopped onto his ass, feasting hungrily on the snack. When he finished, he edged toward the water, then scooped handfuls into his mouth.

"Be careful," Santana warned.

Dick looked at her. "What for?"

She nodded at the water.

When he turned back, he spotted the dark glint of the crocodile's eyes, ten feet from the shore.

Dick scooted back, using his one good leg to put distance between himself and the beast.

The crocodile edged closer, snout appearing above the water. Two stubby legs touched the mud shore.

Gyles reached for his gun.

"No need," Santana stated, holding out a hand.

Gyles looked at her uncertainly. It was now only a few feet from Dick's legs as he scooted back.

The crocodile snapped its jaws. At the same time, Santana snapped the whip at its snout. The croc growled. She snapped again. Then once more.

The croc froze, head shifting to Santana. She held the whip ready, prepared to strike again. "Try me," she warned.

The crocodile decided against the attack, turned, and made its way back into the water.

They allowed their food to digest. Santana took a moment to stare at the sky and get her breath back. Her muscles ached. Her body yearned for rest, but they weren't done yet.

"We've got to get across the river," Santana announced, looking down into the foamy depths and wondering where their passage had taken them beneath when they'd walked through the caves.

"How?" Dick asked. "I can't see a bridge or a boat around."

"There's a crossing a mile up that way," Santana informed him.

Gyles raised an eyebrow. "How do you know that?"

"You've seen *George of the Jungle*, right?" Dick asked.

Gyles nodded.

"She's Georgina." They both laughed.

Santana smirked.

Gyles looked at Santana. "Hey, Georgina?"

"What?" Santana asked.

"I haven't said thank you yet," Gyles offered, glancing down at his feet. "I know how hard it is to take someone at their word. You spared my life, and I thank you for that."

Santana tilted her head. "I'll be honest. It doesn't always go down that way. Most of the time I end up having to kill my guide. Thank you for keeping to *your* word."

"Well, kinda," Dick offered.

Santana nodded. "Right."

Gyles looked momentarily confused. He remembered his promise, looking between them both. "Her name is Sasha Chechik. She's the head of The Order of the Scythe—some refer to her as the Great One."

"Oh, great," Dick stated. "We've upset a cult."

"You're not far off," Gyles replied.

"Who is The Order of the Scythe?" Santana asked.

Gyles narrowed his eyes. "We...I mean...'they' are an order dedicated to historical artifacts of magical properties. The Order takes its identity after the Grim Reaper, utilizing the scythe as their logo, and Sasha's weapon of choice." He pointed at the logo on his breast. "It's pretty fucked up."

Dick frowned. "You speak pretty negatively about a cult we found you working for."

Gyles offered a weak shrug. "Honestly, I didn't know what it was all about when I joined. A few friends of mine were involved and told me there was great money to be had. The Order looked after anyone who worked for them. They spoke of items that could change the world, gave pretty persuasive speeches about being on the cutting edge of the rest of the world, making history by finding history. Honestly, for a while, it was a good time."

Santana eyed him curiously. "You've had a sudden change of heart?"

Gyles nodded. "To be honest, this was my first true search with them. I've only been a member for a few months, and up until now it was all parties, booze, and..."

"Sex?" Dick asked.

Santana shot him a look.

Dick held his gaze.

Gyles gave a resigned nod. "Yeah." He raised his head. "I

honestly didn't realize how far they'd go to get whatever it was they were looking for. There was a lot of talk about some kind of dagger that would unlock something or other, but I was in it for the fun." His eyes went glassy. "So many people are dead… because of us."

"Because of *them*," Santana corrected. "That's how groups like that get you, by convincing you there's no other option than to assume group responsibility. That wasn't you."

"But I did it." Gyles' eyes welled with tears. "I played my part. Men, women who will never get to see their families again."

He hunched over, racked with sobs. Santana turned to Dick, exchanging a pitying glance. She shuffled up closer to Gyles until their hips were touching and stared into the fire. "We all make mistakes. That doesn't mean we can't rectify them and make amends."

Gyles sat up straight, wiping his eyes with his forearm. "No?"

Santana shook her head. "No. You can do penance."

Gyles chuckled. "You sound like Her."

Dick took his hip flask from his pocket and took a long gulp. He swatted at a cloud of midges floating by his ear, then gave a satisfied gasp. He raised the flask to Santana. "Thanks for not wasting this."

Santana rolled her eyes. "Gyles, we could use you."

Gyles met Santana's eyes.

"You know the Order," Santana continued. "I have a strange feeling that we're going to end up encountering them again at some point down the line. Tell us what you know. How do they work? What do their levels look like? Where do they operate?"

Gyles sighed. "It's over. The minute I go back to the city, they'll find me and execute me as a traitor. Christine will wake up and realize I'm gone. She'll assume. They know where I live. They'll hunt me until I'm gone. I've seen it happen. There's no escape."

"There will be," Santana offered. "There are places to hide."

Gyles smirked. "No. No, there's not. Besides, don't wrap yourself up in this shit. Run far away and leave them to it. They didn't see you. You can get on with your lives. You'll never encounter them again, I'm sure."

Santana tilted her head. "I wouldn't be so sure." She drew the gleaming dagger from her backpack. The faint silver from the moon glinted along its keen edge, highlighting the engravings on the side of the hilt. The blade hooked slightly, and a single notch rested two-thirds of the way up it.

Gyles' eyes grew wide. "That's not…"

"It is," Santana replied.

Dick's gaze hardened. "Santana."

"Yes, John?" Santana replied innocently enough.

"Should you be flashing that around?" Dick asked. "My client is *very* keen to acquire the blade."

"He'll have it," Santana replied.

Gyles held out his hands. Santana handed him the dagger. His eyes grew wider, a hungry look in them. "It's beautiful."

Dick's gaze burned more intensely. "Santana…" he warned.

"What?" Santana replied casually. "It's not like he's going to run off with the damn thing. He tries, we kill him. Easy pickings."

Dick seemed unconvinced but remained quiet. Santana held out her hands, and Gyles handed the dagger back. She put it in her backpack.

"They're going to come for you," Gyles stated.

"They can try," Santana replied. "That's why we need you to tell us all that you know about the Order."

A shot fired in the distance, closer than Santana would like. Their heads turned toward the noise's source, tracking the flock of birds sweeping through the sky.

"Not now, though," Santana commented. "First, let's get out of this jungle." She motioned to Dick's leg. "You okay to continue?"

Dick held up a finger before downing the remaining volume of his drink in one. When the flask was empty, he put it back in his pocket and climbed awkwardly to his feet. "Sure. Let's do this."

Gyles moved to his side, offering Dick an arm. Dick tried a couple of steps, then after stumbling, accepted the help.

They followed the riverbank, Santana occasionally snapping her whip at curious creatures drawn to them by their heavy footsteps. They were more exposed than Santana would like, but at least from here, they could see the way ahead. Soon enough, the river crossing came into sight, a dark shape on the horizon, stretching between two cliff faces.

They climbed up, Gyles following Dick and letting him use his shoulders as a support platform. Santana was first up and offered a hand for Dick to take. She pulled him up, and Gyles swiftly followed.

The bridge was rickety, but it held fast. They made the crossing one at a time, Dick using the rope supports to keep his balance. The whole time the bridge gently swayed under him, she watched the far bank, keeping a keen eye out for members of the Order. More shots fired, closer than she'd like, and as Gyles sped across the bridge, they saw the first sign of headlights scanning through the trees on the other side.

"Hurry," Santana called.

Gyles was nearly across. The bridge wobbled precariously beneath him. Dick continued to the lining of trees, taking a moment to rest against a trunk, his face pained. Gyles panted, pumping his arms as he closed the final distance.

The lights grew brighter. A car stopped somewhere in the trees, two bright headlights pointing in their direction.

"Over there!" someone shouted.

Santana readied her pistol.

Three figures appeared in the dark, tiny red dots moving near Santana, zeroing in on Gyles.

"Run!" Santana called, although what other option did Gyles have?

He let out a strange yelp as he dove to the safety of the grass. A shot fired. Another followed, then a third.

Santana fired back. Alarmed calls rang across the valley.

Santana sprinted for Gyles, grabbing his arm and dragging him toward the trees. A bullet hit the ground beside her, kicking up dirt and creating a small divot.

Santana fired back, distracting them with a volley of bullets. She reached the cover of the trees. The figures approached the bridge, one of them already a good distance across it.

Fuck.

Santana crawled, minimizing her size. She tucked behind a wooden anchor rod that held the bridge in place. Drawing her knife, she feverishly sawed on the rope, slicing until one of the tethers snapped.

The bridge lurched.

Voices cried out in alarm.

Another shot fired, this time grazing Santana's thigh.

She worked on the next rope. Behind them, the headlights shrank as the car sped away, presumably looking for another way to cross to intercept the trio.

The rope snapped. One of the men was halfway across, eyes close to the sight of his pistol, about to fire. He slipped, his body hurtling toward the ravine. A *splash* announced his arrival in the water.

The other two held back, blindly firing into the dark. Santana crawled to the other side and severed the two ropes. The bridge fell flaccidly against the far cliff face.

She retreated, tucking into the undergrowth. She allowed herself a moment to recover before Gyles thanked her and encouraged them forward. Santana agreed with him, guiding the three into the shadows, in the direction she knew the city to be.

Hoping that she wouldn't have to encounter those mother-fuckers again.

CHAPTER FIFTEEN

It was midday when Santana, Dick, and Gyles finally broke out of the jungle.

The lack of greenery and trees was a welcome sight. Even Santana had grown tired of the all-encompassing forestry as she walked with the two men at a glacial pace. The further they got, the slower they became, Dick clearly in need of a rest, and Gyles struggling to bear his weight.

"Wait here," Santana instructed. "I'll call a cab."

Thirty minutes later, the driverless cab rolled into sight, leaving a rooster tail of dust clouds in its wake. They climbed inside and were all silent as the car brought them back into the city. Nervousness clung to Gyles, his eyes darting around as the cab played a soft melody from some jazz station Santana didn't care for.

They pulled into the city proper a little past two. The cab pulled to the curb beside a diner with condensation-beaded windows and several hand-drawn signs. She helped Dick out of the cab, Gyles taking the other side, and together they approached her apartment building. They were an odd group, gleaning a few stares from nearby civilians, but soon they were inside and riding up the elevator.

Santana unlocked her door, then closed it behind her, leaving the pair outside. She attended to the many traps and tripwires around her apartment until the majority of them were disabled. Her fingers worked the switches and levers without conscious thought, a dance of a ritual that had existed since she first installed the security measures.

Eventually, she opened the door. Gyles brought Dick inside, then dropped him on the couch. He was asleep before his head hit the cushions, lying on his front with his cheek squished against the soft fabric of the couch. In broad daylight, she saw the tatters of the injuries on his legs. She would have to tend to the wounds, but it wouldn't hurt to let him sleep for an hour or so.

"Thank you," Gyles offered, breaking the heavy silence.

Santana glanced up, momentarily forgetting he was in the room with her. "Don't mention it." She pointed at the floor to the folded bundle of sheets Terra had slept in. "You can sleep on the floor. They should keep you comfy. Kettle's there. Fridge is there. Help yourself. I'll be in there sleeping. Don't wake me. You'll regret it if you do."

She walked to her bedroom door. "Oh, and if you think of switching sides again and want to try to kill me, I warn you, this place is booby-trapped to the nines. The apartment will kill you before you can get to me." To reinforce her point, she raised her leg as if treading over an invisible wire.

There was nothing there, but Gyles didn't know that.

Santana awoke to brutish grunts and the overwhelming scent of bacon.

"Hold still," a voice crooned.

Santana looked at her bedside clock. She'd only been asleep

four hours, and boy did she feel it. She stretched, her sore muscles complaining as she rose from her bed, still fully clothed, and opened her bedroom door.

The first thing to greet her was a thick ream of smoke. She looked at the stove where a wide pan filled with strips of bacon released a plume of black smoke. Across the room, Gyles knelt beside Dick, holding a wet rag spotted with Dick's blood in the air. Dick growled at Gyles, looking more disheveled after a few hours of sleep.

"Get the fuck off me," Dick commanded.

"Stop being a baby," Gyles commented. "I can staunch the bleeding."

"What the hell is going on?" Santana cast a wary eye toward the edge of the sofa where she'd set one of her triggers for her traps.

Gyles threw his arms in the air. "He picked some dried blood off the wound, and it started pissing blood. I tried to keep him quiet and stop him bleeding on your couch, but macho boy got all weird about it."

Dick stared daggers at Gyles. "I can handle myself."

"The hell you can." Santana laughed. She sauntered over to the couch, taking the rag from Gyles. "I've got it."

Gyles stepped back.

Santana nodded over her shoulder. "Can you deal with the food now?"

Gyles jumped up, only now remembering. He groaned, throwing away the black bacon while Santana tended to Dick's wound.

The cut was fresh but was somewhat clean. Blood leaked steadily out of the wound. She dabbed and cleaned until the blood began to clot. "You're going to need to go to the hospital to get that checked out."

"I know," Dick replied.

Santana spoke without looking at him. "You could've let him help you."

Dick grunted.

Santana chuckled, shaking her head disapprovingly. "It's because he doesn't have the 'feminine' touch, isn't it?"

Dick tilted his head.

"Oh, don't play innocent with me," Santana continued. "You wanted a woman to play nurse."

"Bullshit," Dick replied, saying no more.

When the wound stopped bleeding, Santana fetched her medical box, placing a couple of stitches in the injury to keep it closed. Gyles finished his second attempt at breakfast and brought them both plates. They greedily ate, remaining silent until their dishes were empty.

"Thank you," Santana offered when she finished.

"Please," Gyles replied. "It's the least I can do." He took the plates and started cleaning them up at the sink. He cast a furtive glance over his shoulder.

"What?" Santana asked.

Gyles shrugged. "I don't know where to go from here. Until the Order is dealt with, I have a target on my back."

"Stay here," Santana offered.

Dick shot her a look.

Gyles shook his head. "I couldn't possibly…"

"I insist," Santana stated. "I'm rarely ever in this place. I hardly get visitors."

"Your security begs to differ," Dick grumbled.

"It's yours as long as you need," she finished.

Gyles turned, resting against the counter. "Okay. If you're sure?"

"I am," Santana replied. "Besides, John and I have some errands to finish, don't we?"

Dick nodded.

"We'll be out for a while, most likely, so use the space and make yourself at home." Santana crossed to her bedroom, pausing at the door.

"Thank you," Gyles directed at her.

Santana laughed. "You can stop saying that now."

Gyles laughed. Dick winced as he levered his legs off the couch and tested putting weight on his leg. Santana found a carved wooden cane in her room—a relic from a previous expedition—and tossed it to Dick. "Here, Grandpa. Yours until you're better."

Dick smirked.

Gyles chuckled.

Santana cleaned herself up, ready for the next part of her plan.

A part that she knew wouldn't go well when Dick found out what had happened.

"Why do they call him the Albatross?" Santana asked as the driverless cab pulled up outside a large white marble manor, the walkway lined with stone pillars reminiscent of Grecian temples.

Dick had refused to go to the hospital, instead choosing bourbon as his medicine of choice. Santana chided him the entire cab ride and managed to get Dick to go for medical advice once he'd completed his mission.

"You want to get paid, don't you?" Dick asked.

Santana shrugged. "At some point, it stopped being about the money, y'know?"

Dick nodded. "I know."

They exited the cab. Santana waited by the main gates as Dick thumbed the intercom and announced his arrival. When the gates automatically slid open, he held out a hand to Santana. "Time to pay up."

Santana hesitated, holding the bag in her hand. It was made of black leather and did a great job hiding the shape of the valuable contents within. "If only I could have also got the Atlanticore orb," she muttered as she reluctantly handed the bag to Dick. "At least I got to see the dagger. I'm part of history."

Dick smiled. "Thank you." He raised an eyebrow.

"What?" Santana asked.

"I thought it would be harder than that to get you to part with the dagger," Dick replied. "Given how valuable it is."

Santana shrugged. "There'll be more where that came from. Plus, a deal is a deal. I promised you I'd claim the dagger for you to give to your client. There's the dagger." She nodded at the building. "Go deliver to your client."

She waited beyond the closing gates as Dick made his way down the long walkway. He was a strange sight, a man limping in a long black trench jacket, clutching a bag in one hand. She glanced at the cameras by the gates and gave a coy wave, then headed off down the street.

When she reached the corner, she made a left, walking along the side fences of the property. The sun was setting in the distance, casting the city in a fuzzy spray of oranges and purples. She spotted the cafe in the distance and headed toward it.

She had some time to bide.

CHAPTER SIXTEEN

The people of the city fascinated Santana.

For the next three hours, she sat in Woodston's Cafe and watched the world spin by.

The cafe was mostly home to the elderly members of the local community. Blue-rinsed women and wrinkled men trying to hold onto the last strands of their receding hairline sipped from china cups and conversed through dentures and false teeth. One thing united all of the clientele of this place, and it was the decadence with which they clothed themselves.

Pearl necklaces, bracelets, watches of pristine gold, and rings ornamented with diamonds the size of playing dice. The chatter was constant and feverish, a mirthful atmosphere in the air. Only on the odd occasion did someone below the age of fifty enter the building, and they instantly drew the eyes of the current patrons.

Santana kept to herself in the corner, keeping a clean line of view into the outside world as the light failed and night took over. When the clock chimed ten, she paid her fee then headed back out into the street.

She felt the heat of eyes tracking her as she left. She made her way back toward the manor, tucking closely to the neighboring fences. She stopped by the fence, hidden by the veil of foliage, and glanced around for any sign of security cameras.

There was nothing.

The fence was almost twenty feet high, vertically barred to discourage those tempted to climb inside. Santana uncoiled her whip, used it to lever herself up, and soon straddled the fence, greenery shrouding her.

She swung her leg onto the other side, then scaled down the closest tree. Soon, her feet padded on soft soil. She sneaked through the foliage, working along the perimeter until she could get a closer glance at the building.

The main building's exterior was at least thirty feet away across a perfectly kept lawn. To her right, she spotted a large greenhouse that could easily have been a mansion itself. Surrounding the greenhouse was another cluster of fruit trees.

Santana made it to the greenhouse, wondering what security detail this place had. She fancied she heard the soft barking of dogs but couldn't be sure that it came from this residence.

She advanced, slaloming through the orchard. She froze in her tracks when she heard the muttering of nearby voices.

She peered around a tree, spotting two guards in navy blue uniforms. Strapped to their hips were pistols on one side and nightsticks on the other.

What are they, English cops?

She hid, waiting for the pair to pass. When they were gone, she tiptoed closer to the building, stopping when she reached the edge of the orchard.

A graveled path led to a large oak back door a short distance away, but that wasn't why Santana stopped.

Two Doberman dogs growled, their hackles raised. Santana met their gaze, bending her knees and holding out her hands before her. "Easy, now..."

They crept toward her, noses working overtime. She slowly

reached into her pocket, letting out a soft rustle. One of the dogs barked.

"Shh…" Santana urged. She held out a treat before them, shaped like a bone. They were a recipe of her creation, something she had crafted after years spent around canines in her formative stages. Not only that but she'd laced them with bergamot, a citrus scent known for calming dogs and helping forge friendships in modern training academies.

The first Doberman sniffed the treat, then gobbled it up. The second stared at Santana, accepting the snack from her hand.

A voice called from nearby. "Rex. Carnaby. What have you found?"

Santana met the dog's gaze. She smiled, then gently snapped her fingers and pointed away from where she stood.

For a moment, the dogs stared back. Santana could hear the footsteps of the approaching guards. As they neared her location, the dogs ran away, jumping up at the guards with excitement.

Santana waited where she was, praying the dogs wouldn't draw the men to her.

"What did you find, boys?" one of the guards asked. "What is it?"

The dogs circled their feet, tails wagging excitedly. Santana froze, awaiting the inevitable moment of them drawing attention to her…

…but it never came.

"Probably a bird or squirrel," the second guard offered. "Little bastards are getting more and more skittish. Need to get them back to the training camp."

"No," the first returned. "Nothing wrong with being excited, is there, champs?" He crouched, rubbing one of the dog's chins. "Who's a good boy?"

The men led the dogs away, returning to their circuit around the compound. Santana waited until they were out of sight before breaking across the grass. She rested her back against the building's cool brick with her eyes fixed on the cameras pointing away from her in either direction.

No matter how hard they try, there's always a blind spot. She glanced at the sky, the bright moon fuzzy overhead. *Unless satellite imagery is currently working over the city.*

She turned, looking up at the building. A window was open above her, the golden arm of the latch holding it open. A short, sturdy pole angled out next to the window.

With a flick of her wrist, the bullwhip latched onto the pole. She planted her feet on the side of the building and scaled it, moving quickly toward the shadowy darkness of the room.

When she reached the ledge, she craned her neck to peer inside. Someone was asleep in a king-sized bed, the lump in the sheets rising and falling slowly. Santana eased in, sitting on the sill. She slid off her combat boots and placed them delicately by the window. *I'll be back for you.*

Her socked feet padded silently across the room. When she reached the door, she flipped the lock, then eased the door open to slip through. Buttery light spilled into the bedroom, then faded when the door closed.

The carpeted hallway boasted a patterned rug that wouldn't look out of place in a British pub from the eighties. She stalked through the corridor, keeping her ears alert for signs of approaching guards. If she could be silent, so could they.

As she snuck along the corridor, she peered inside each room in turn, hunting for the object she sought. She came across a set of stairs and made her way up, pausing near the top as a camera came into sight.

Shit.

Santana's fingers twitched. She half-crouched on the stairs, using the railing to block her from sight. She would have to move fast if this was to work.

She eased her bullwhip from its coil, then prepared her flick. With a sudden rush up the stairs, she lashed out the whip as it snapped against the camera lens. The blinking light shut off, the glass lens cracked.

She moved swiftly, passing through doors into the upper story. To her right, she found what she was looking for, a double doorway with golden handles and a "Do Not Disturb" sign hanging down.

"Sorry. No can do," she whispered, sweeping to the doorway.

She tested the locks but found the doors wouldn't budge. Silently cursing, she noticed that the next door along was slightly ajar.

Santana slipped inside, finding herself in a study of sorts. A large desk lay against the left wall, an impressive TV hanging on the wall on the right. At the end of the room, a large window stood, curtains open, silvery light spilling inside.

She tiptoed across the room. When she was halfway across, light flooded her vision, and a voice called to her and caused her to spin.

The lights had activated above her. On the TV screen, a large face grinned her way. It filled the screen, white skin, golden teeth, and black hair combed back in uneven rows. "Hello, sunshine! Go get 'em. Today's your day to *conquer* your goals and achieve your dreams!"

Santana cocked her head and smirked. She examined the room, spotting the activation sensors near her hips against the wall. Had this guy created a self-motivational video to get him up and running in the mornings?

"Know that you can do this," the video continued. "Know that nothing can stop you. You can achieve whatever you want, as long as you try."

Santana's back stiffened as a shuffling came from the room next door. She hurried to the TV, finding the off-switch at the back. She moved to the window, opening it wide. Dark figures moved on the lawn outside, and she ducked as they turned her way.

She flicked her wrist, the whip finding the light switch. She was plunged once more into darkness.

She eased back to the window and watched the figures on the lawn. They remained stationary for a moment before slipping into the darkness. Craning her head to the left, she spotted what she was looking for—another open window with a short pole beside it. *What are those things for, anyway? Flags? Or something else?*

"It's a warm night in Atlantica…" she mused. "Lucky for me."

In mere moments she was swinging toward the open window, the whip tight in her hand, feet padding gently against the side of the building. She scaled to the window, paying no attention to the severe drop below her. She peeked inside the room and found a lavish space filled with ornate objects.

A four-poster bed sat against the wall, its occupant curtained and cut from sight. Objects of gold, silver, platinum, and bronze capped cabinets and various mahogany furniture, each one telling the story of eras long gone.

There, on the side by the bed, lay the dagger.

She recognized its shape through the plain white cloth that wrapped it.

The room was silent. Taking her time, she tiptoed toward the bedside, reaching out for the weapon. She peeled back one corner of the cloth and caught the gleam of metal. A grin appeared on her face.

Movement came from the bed.

Santana grabbed the dagger and broke toward the window. She leaped out into the night, twisting as she fell. She lashed the bullwhip toward a nearby pole and swung. She caught the next window, this time balancing herself before climbing to the second story.

She eased over the lip of the window, reaching out to grab her boots. She tucked them under her armpit, then used the whip to lower herself to the ground level.

She pulled on her boots as a voice called from somewhere

inside the building. Dogs barked on the other side of the manor. Santana broke across the grass, heading toward the orchard, then to the trees. With a hop, skip, and jump, she landed on the sidewalk outside.

She wasted no time in putting distance between herself and the Albatross' manor, soon slipping into a driverless cab and riding back into the city.

CHAPTER SEVENTEEN

"It's beautiful," Taylor Yungheim breathed.

The sun was high, golden rays streaming through the floor-to-ceiling window that filled the back wall of Taylor's office. From here Santana could see the hazy outline of the mountainous ranges beyond, hillsides cloaked in green. She had managed to rest, catching a few hours of sleep while Gyles fussed around her apartment, cleaning.

"You don't have to do that," she offered, rubbing her eyes as she emerged from her room.

"I know." Gyles' cheeks flushed.

Santana laughed. "You're bored, aren't you?"

Gyles nodded. "I'm going crazy already. I'm not used to stopping. I need to keep busy."

"As you were." Santana headed for the front door with the dagger in her backpack, Gyles naïve to its presence. She pointed beneath the stove. "You missed a spot."

She had traveled across town, her heart beating fast. The thrill of holding a highly sought-after object in her backpack got her adrenaline pumping and kept her with a buzz that woke her up as she navigated through the city. Taylor had been ready for her in his office, and as she handed over the wrapped dagger, his fingers twitched with excitement.

"Marvelous…" His voice was soft, filled with awe. She had to agree with him. The weapon was a thing of beauty in full daylight. Ornate carvings spoke tales of old, the blade impossibly keen and sharp after years of neglect. "You never fail to deliver."

"I told you I could do it," Santana replied. "One woman doing the work of five men." She held out her hand. "Now pay the piper."

Taylor chuckled. Reluctantly he placed the blade on the desk, picking up his phone to tap against Santana's. Her smile grew as the numbers in her account did.

"How was it?" Taylor asked. "Tell me everything."

Santana did, regaling everything from her conversations with Dick Chambers and his client's intent to take the dagger first. She told him of the hidden back corridor to the lost temple and the activation of the Atlanticore, sparing no detail when it came to the ancient mechanisms that somehow, years later, still responded to the magic of the core. She detailed her encounter with The Order of the Scythe, right down to their escape from the jungle.

"So you didn't work alone," Taylor offered, a sly twinkle in his eye.

Santana raised her eyebrow. "I might as well have. It would've been quieter."

Taylor picked the blade up again, holding it to the light. "There is magic in this world, Santana. Your mother believed that you know."

A heaviness fell on Santana, the mirth draining from the room. She cast her eyes down. "I know."

"She was a fine woman," Taylor continued, ignorant to Santana's shoulders softening, eyes fixed on the blade. "She'd be very proud of you. Years she spent finding me objects, yet never in a million years did she find an artifact with a legend of this magnitude."

"I'm not convinced that it's only legend," Santana offered.

Taylor turned to her, a dubious look in his eye. "Good. Then you're learning."

Taylor placed the blade down on the table, delicately, as if lowering a child to its crib. He crossed in his motorized chair to a bookshelf thick with texts, selecting one from the center. He brought it back to the desk, the large tome dusty and filled with cracked, yellowed leaves. He opened the pages, finding what he was looking for before presenting it to Santana.

Santana read, "La Leyenda de la Luz. The Legend of Light," she whispered.

Taylor nodded. He pointed at the imagery on the pages, ancient sketches of rays of light and angled gods. "The Legend of Light was first read in scripture in the early 2000s, discovered by Rowena Templeton on an expedition in the jungle's southwest quarter. While trekking through the trees, she stumbled across an ancient outpost with the story outlined on the wall."

"A story that corroborated with other tellings across the world," Santana interrupted. "Matching other wall paintings and carvings found across South America, and even as far as Central Asia."

"Correct." Taylor grinned. "No one has ever managed to find evidence of the legend that tells of a dagger—La Daga de los Días Sin Fin—which holds the key to unlocking an era of eternal sunshine. History tells of a historic drought, a period in which Inti, the Sun God, was angered by his people, punishing them with a decade of eternal sunshine. Crops withered, rivers dried, and an entire population was on the brink of extinction."

"Until the son of the chieftain, Ekkeko, stepped forward," Santana continued. "Ekkeko, the pure of heart, sought discourse with Inti. He scaled the tallest mountain, almost dying in the process, to end the drought and offer an apology for his people.

The legend says that Inti blessed Ekkeko for his efforts, providing him with the location of the lock and key that triggered the endless drought."

Taylor filled a crystal glass with an amber liquid. "Go on…"

Santana turned the pages, showing a man trekking across harsh elements toward a temple.

"Alone, Ekkeko followed Inti's directions, journeying through forest, field, desert, water, and sand, until he arrived at the location Inti described—El Templo del Sol. There, he found the lock and the key. He tried to draw out the key, but his pilgrimage had sapped his strength. Hours he tried in vain to remove the key from the lock as the world outside heated, and his people died. Sweat poured from his skin with no more liquid in his body left to cry."

Santana turned the page. "It was there, on the brink of failure, that Mama Quilla, Goddess of the Moon, appeared, blessing Ekkeko with the cold, silent power of the night. For the first time in years, a chill swept through Ekkeko. He cupped his hands, and miraculously they filled with water. He drank. He cupped again, his hands already filled with liquid.

"He drank until he'd had his fill, the strength returning to him," Santana outlined. "Soon, he stepped up to the key, this time successfully drawing the blade from its home. He held La Daga de los Días Sin Fin high in the air, hearing the tinkling cackle of Mama Quilla as, for the first time in over a decade, night shrouded the sun from the sky and fell over Ekkeko's people."

Taylor offered Santana a drink. She politely declined, finishing the story. "Ekkeko returned to his people triumphant. To prevent another drought of such magnitude, they separated the dagger from its home, burying it beneath the ground, locking it in the Temple of the Summer Crown, away from harm's reach."

"It's not a legend." Taylor's conviction shone in his eyes.

Santana nodded. "I know."

Taylor looked out the window, staring out toward the jungle.

"Santana, we have to keep this item protected. There's a great price on the dagger, and now that it has been discovered, people will be after it in droves."

"I know," Santana repeated.

"The Order of the Scythe…" Taylor mused. "The Albatross… They'll all want their hands on it. With the discovery of the dagger comes the roadmap to the Temple of the Sun."

This time, Santana reached for the blade. Taylor stiffened with a strange look in his eyes. Santana studied the blade's hilt, trying to make sense of the carvings and the inscriptions. "Any idea what this says?"

Taylor shook his head. "I'll have to inform Christina of our new item. She should be able to translate."

"Can we trust her?"

"No." Taylor grinned.

"Just as you taught me. Trust no one. Rely on some."

"Exactly."

Santana carefully set the blade down and laced her fingers behind her head. "This is huge."

Taylor nodded. "You need to keep yourself safe. Don't let your guard down. If anyone saw you out there, they'll be coming for you now. You'll be target number one."

"I've made my share of enemies," Santana commented. "I can handle myself."

Taylor nodded, falling into silent thought. He sipped his drink. "You couldn't have grabbed the Atlanticore orb?" He winked.

Santana chuckled. Lord, had she tried.

CHAPTER EIGHTEEN

Santana sat on the couch with a steaming cup of coffee in her hands. "This place is spotless."

Gyles grinned, glancing around her apartment. He gave a satisfied nod. "It took a while, but I got there."

"I didn't even know I had the cleaning supplies," Santana stated.

"You don't," Gyles admitted. "I had to improvise."

She glanced down at his leg, where he'd thickly wrapped a white bandage. A small bit of red spotted the gauze. "Are you okay?"

"You could've warned me about the trap to your room," Gyles stated.

Santana half-shrugged. "I didn't want people entering. I warned you."

"Who are you protecting yourself from, anyway?"

"Enemies." Santana didn't elaborate further.

They drank and spoke, the humid heat from the outside world shrouding them in sleepy comfort. Santana couldn't remember the last time she'd spent this much time in her apartment, nor when she'd last entertained for this long. Gyles was a nice guy. They spoke about his experience with the Order, Santana asking questions, trying to glean his ascension into the Order.

"It just happens," Gyles admitted. "You don't ask to become part of a cult. You walk into the water, and before you know it, the shore's gone. There's no way out."

"Sounds awful."

Gyles nodded. "I've had better experiences." He looked at her. "How do I free myself from the burden of their revenge?"

Santana chewed her lip. "You beat them at their own game and take out those in your path who stand in your way."

Gyles narrowed his eyes. "That's a brutal life."

"This is a brutal place." She stopped when a knock came on the door, furious fists that made Gyles flinch and retreat farther into the couch.

"Open up," a voice called.

Santana placed her coffee cup down calmly before rising to her feet.

"Who's that?" Gyles asked.

Santana held a placating hand. "Nothing to fear, don't you worry."

Banging fists came again. "Santana."

Santana unlocked the door. Dick Chambers walked in, leaning on the cane Santana had loaned him as he favored his leg. He spun to face her. "Explain yourself."

Santana turned up her lip. "I don't know what you mean."

"I think you do," Dick returned.

Santana returned to the couch, taking a seat beside Gyles. She picked up her cup and drank.

"Santana," Dick warned.

"Close the door, won't you?" Santana asked.

Dick closed the door.

Santana shuffled in her seat, staring at Dick. They remained in silence for a few uncomfortable moments.

Eventually, Gyles spoke. "What's going on?"

Dick held Santana's gaze, his voice a low rumble. "Ask her. See if Santana knows how the blade I handed over to my client yesterday afternoon is now missing from his possession."

Santana avoided Dick's gaze.

"Santana?" Gyles asked.

Santana shrugged. "I don't know what you're talking about."

"Oh, I think you do," Dick replied. "You think it's a coincidence that the blade goes missing hours after I deliver it to my client and he pays his fee?"

"So, what's the problem?" Santana asked.

That took Dick aback. "Excuse me?"

"You got paid, didn't you?" Santana asked. "The money is sitting in your account?"

"Well…yes…" Dick stammered.

Santana straightened. "So, hypothetically, even if it was me who stole the dagger, why does it concern you? You upheld your end of the bargain. You delivered the goods. You got paid. If your client can't hold onto the item you've delivered, how's that your fault?"

Dick's gaze softened. His straight lips broke into a grin. "You clever son of a bitch."

Santana offered another shrug. "I don't know what you're talking about."

Realization dawned on Gyles' face. "You're a genius."

Santana sipped her coffee.

"Whether it was or wasn't you," Dick continued, eyeing her suspiciously, "the heat has come back to me. The Albatross thinks I've betrayed him. He's threatening to set his dogs on me."

Santana gestured around the apartment. "There's plenty of room to hide out."

Dick chuckled. "You're impossible."

"You love it," Santana returned.

Dick moved over to the kitchenette and poured himself a

coffee without asking. He leaned against the counter. "So, where's the dagger now?"

Santana bit her lip. "You'll have to ask the thief."

"It's like that, is it?"

Santana smiled. "Haven't you got other cases to work on? Other mysteries to solve?"

Dick considered this. "I do. But I always find that once I've bitten into something juicy, I refuse to let it go. This isn't over, is it? There's more to this story that you're not telling us."

"The dagger?" Santana asked innocently.

"Those people wanted the dagger, and they were willing to murder for the privilege of holding the blade in their hands." Drops of coffee slipped from the mug as Dick gestured. "A larger game is afoot, and I want in. You have my services. Pro bono."

"You still haven't paid me for my services yet," Santana stated.

Dick rolled his eyes, removed his cell phone from his pocket, and tapped an amount in the Satiata Cash App. Santana's phone *chimed*. "There. Happy?"

"I'm not unhappy," she replied.

Gyles moved toward Dick, using a cloth to clean the brown drops from the floor. Dick spied his leg. "What happened to him?"

"Booby trap," Santana explained.

"I don't want to know about your sex life," Dick returned. He gave Gyles a pitying look. "Thought he might be jealous of my wounds and wanted to copy me."

"Don't flatter yourself," Gyles replied.

Dick waited until Gyles was away from his feet before turning his attention back to Santana. "Spill it."

Santana opened her mouth, but before she could say a word, Gyles spoke first. "La Leyenda de la Luz."

Santana and Dick turned to face him.

"It was all she could speak of," Gyles explained. "Sasha…she was obsessed with it. Wants to find the temple and see if the legend is true."

"Legend?" Dick asked. "What legend? Did I skip this class in school?"

Santana explained to Dick the tale of the Legend of Light. As she spoke, the pictures from Taylor's book sprang into her mind. When she reached the end, Dick touched his chin and sighed. "People can't believe this bullshit, can they?"

Santana eyed him.

Dick raised his hands. "What? You're telling me that a magical sun god cast the world into a drought that someone ended by removing a dagger from some kind of lock? All sounds pretty Freudian to me. Oh, and unbelievable."

Santana and Gyles exchanged a look.

"You don't agree?" Dick asked Gyles.

Gyles shrugged. "I've seen things, man. Sasha is convinced. She built her force to find the damned thing. That says something for their conviction."

Dick turned to Santana. "You surely have more sense in your head."

Santana half-shrugged. "How else can you explain the temple we found? The power from the Atlanticore and the mechanisms involved? Sure, a lot of legend and myth turns out to be mistranslated hyperbole, but there's always a grain of truth to the tale."

Dick ran a hand down his face. "Well, if the legend is real, wouldn't the dagger tell you where to go next? Where is this fabled temple, and how would anyone find it?"

Santana replied, "We're working on it."

"Who's we?" Dick asked. Santana could tell that Dick was angling for her to slip up and confess to last night's incident.

"It doesn't matter," she answered.

They fell into an uneasy quiet. Outside, the city hummed and buzzed, birds flying past the apartment window.

A vibration broke the silence. Santana looked at her phone,

her blood running cold as she read the words on her screen. "Shit."

She ran for the door, grabbing her pack and jacket before swinging the door wide.

"Where are you going?" Dick called after her.

"Wait here," Santana called over her shoulder. "I'll be back."

Dick and Gyles exchanged a look. Santana flew down the stairs, hailing the first cab she could get her hands on.

CHAPTER NINETEEN

Santana sprinted up the museum steps.

She sped toward the glass elevator before rapidly pressing the button to call it. She waited all of thirty seconds before she gave up and made for the stairs.

The glass security barrier was in shattered pieces. One of the guards stood on the other side, nursing a red welt on the side of her head. Santana slowed on the approach, and she waved her past, recognizing her instantly.

Santana sprinted through the library, straight toward the large open doors leading to Taylor's office. She could make out his figure from here, sitting in his chair behind his desk, staring out the window.

"Are you okay?" she rasped. "What the hell happened?"

Taylor spun in his chair. Santana gasped as she took in the angry red groove gouged into the side of his cheek. The drywall was cracked behind him, the small glint of a bullet embedded in the center.

"They came," he replied simply.

"Who? Who came?" Santana's heart beat fast.

"The Order," Taylor replied. "They knew to look for you.

They broke in, a dozen of them at least, swept in and took it for their own." He tried to offer a weak grin but winced as pain flared in his cheek. "There was no way to stop them."

Santana skirted the desk, holding Taylor's face in her hands. She examined the wound, still trickling blood mixed with clear pus. "They shot at you?"

Taylor nodded. "Missed. Even at my advanced age, I'm too fast for them." He tried to grin again but took in a sharp breath.

"That looks bad." Santana's eyes stung. "Sons-of-bitches. How did you know it was the Order?"

Taylor pulled away from Santana, freeing his face from her hands before dabbing his cheek with a tissue. "They were surprisingly branded for a group that was breaking in." He shrugged. "I suppose they have nothing to fear from raiding private property."

Santana's cheeks burned. She looked around the room spotting a few of Taylor's employees straightening the place and putting things back where they belonged. A few priceless ornaments had smashed and were being swept up by robotic cleaners. "Shit." She shook her head. "They took it?"

Taylor failed to meet Santana's eyes. "They did."

"Double shit." She fell quiet, examining the office, trying to process this new information. "At least you're okay."

Taylor nodded. "At what cost?"

"What do you mean?" Santana asked.

"They're a rough lot, Santana," Taylor replied. "Even from just a brief encounter. They're organized. They're ruthless. They don't care about breaking and entering in broad daylight. They knew this place. Knew our people and their stations, as if they'd had months to plan a raid." He shook his head. "We're up against it."

"Did they leave anything behind?" Santana asked. "Something to follow them? Something to give chase and find those motherfuckers to bring them to justice?"

Taylor smirked.

"What?" Santana replied.

"I know you," Taylor explained. "You don't care for revenge. You care for the relic."

Santana saw no point in disagreeing. "Well…yeah."

"It's okay," Taylor stated. He nodded toward the large bookshelf that lined the wall. "Christine's through there. She'll have answers for you." He thumbed a button beneath the desk. Something *clicked*, and a doorway opened among the books. Santana walked through into a tiny research room.

There were no windows to allow natural light. A single bright bulb hung in the center of the room. Instruments, tools, and texts lined a square table, as well as several LED lights on flexi-cables that the researcher could angle to examine items from all angles.

Christine lay dead at the table. Her head rested on its surface, a pool of blood staining the surrounding papers.

Santana covered her nose. Already Christine's stink had started to fill the musty room. She eased around her, examining the table and looking at the papers and items. It was clear someone had been in here to raid and look for the dagger.

Santana spotted the long, clean slice along her neck and wondered if her attacker had used the dagger against her. Between that and the bullet wound in her back, there was no way she would've survived.

"Brutal," Santana whispered.

A small piece of paper clutched tightly in Christine's hand drew her eyes. She pried the stiffening fist open and pinched out the paper. Scrawled in rapid scribbles were the words, "Giant's Bowl."

She pocketed the paper and returned to Taylor, still staring solemnly out the window. "She's dead."

Taylor nodded. "She is."

"You could've warned me."

"Would it have made a difference?"

Santana saw a cold side of Taylor she hadn't encountered before. Would that be what it would be like if someone announced Santana's death to Taylor? Cold. Clinical.

"She translated the handle," Santana informed Taylor.

Taylor's interest sparked. He turned his chair to Santana. "Oh?"

"You haven't checked?" she asked.

Taylor held her gaze. "Cleanup takes time."

Santana drew a long breath. She showed him the paper.

"Giant's Bowl?" Taylor asked. "The crater?"

Santana saw it in her head, a large bowl-like structure in the middle of the forest. The tree-lined land scooped down dramatically into a large basin where the local tributaries combined to form the main body of the river that led out to the ocean. It was also one of the main sites of significance, with several explorers having trodden but never returned from it—a place rumored to be haunted.

"That's where the temple is?" Santana asked.

Taylor shrugged. "Seems so."

They were both quiet for a long time. Eventually, Santana helped herself to a drink from the crystal glass. She poured one for Taylor. She held up the glass, and he *clinked* it.

"You'll be careful?" Taylor asked.

Santana sipped her drink, wincing slightly as the brandy burned through her body. "I always am."

Taylor chuckled.

Footsteps announced someone's arrival. Taylor's gaze met the gentleman's, and the mirth slipped from his face.

Santana turned. She could've sworn she'd never seen this man before, but there was something familiar about him—a smell or an aura?

"Jakob," Taylor offered.

"Taylor." He turned his head. "Miss Sokolov."

Santana raised her eyebrows.

"Your reputation precedes you." The man offered a hand. "Jakob Masque. Pleased to meet you."

Santana's heart paused. Jakob Masque…the man she'd stolen the dagger from.

Santana remained tight-lipped. Jakob was an older man with a face covered in wrinkles. His green eyes were set deep into his face, with large bruise-like bags beneath them. His black hair was swept back in uneven rows, and though he wore a pristine silver suit, it hung awkwardly from his body, as though his hunched form once would have fit it but had now withered away beneath.

"What do you want, Masque?" Taylor asked, an edge to his voice.

Jakob raised an eyebrow, examining the scene. "I'd argue that you might have something that belongs to me, but it appears as though someone beat me to the punch." He shot a daggered look at Santana. "Don't you hate petty thievery?"

Taylor narrowed his eyes. "We don't know what you're talking about."

"Oh, I think you do," Jakob offered. "Don't take me for a fool. I'm sure you already think I am if you continue with this petty charade. You think my security cameras didn't pick up the form of a slender young woman vanishing into the night with my goods?"

Santana remained silent, a small grin on her lips.

"Whether we know what you're talking about or not, it's gone," Taylor stated. "There's nothing here for you."

Jakob chuckled. "Hurts, doesn't it? To be so close to the thing you desire, only to know that it's not truly in reach." He scanned Santana up and down, a strange look in his eye. "Still, perhaps this could be of some benefit to us. The enemy of our enemy is our friend, correct?"

Taylor held his gaze, silent.

"Fine…" Jakob nodded slowly. "I'll take that as a no. Still, it's a shame, given the Order is already two steps ahead. I figured it might have behooved us to work together to stop them before… you know…"

He turned to leave. When he reached the door, Santana stopped him, breaking her silence. "Wait." She turned to Taylor. "The Order wiped out most of his exploration team. Those who remained were kept prisoner with the Order. I managed to free some, but they might still be lost in the jungle. I don't know if they made it." She turned to Jakob for confirmation.

"Some did." He chose not to elaborate.

"He's right," Santana replied. "We're in the same situation. The Order has taken some from each side. Why not use each other and pair up to solve the problem at hand before the wrong side discovers the truth behind the legend and potentially fucks up the island?"

Taylor considered this for a long time, eyes boring into Jakob's. Eventually, he nodded. "Santana, leave us."

She stood, about to take her leave. Taylor held his hand out to her. She took it. "Prepare yourself," he stated, fingers discreetly passing a paper into her palm. "Be ready to move."

He winked at her.

Santana nodded, then left the room. When she was out of sight, she looked at the paper, rereading the same two words and picturing the site in her head.

Giant's Bowl.

CHAPTER TWENTY

Gyles lay sprawled across the couch, eyes fixed to his cell phone. His thumbs danced across the screen as Santana opened the door with gusto and paced across the apartment.

She disappeared into her bedroom, rummaging around for various items and pieces of equipment she knew she'd need. When she returned, Gyles was staring her way.

"Everything okay?" he asked.

"Where's John?"

Gyles raised his eyebrow.

"Don't make me say it," Santana warned.

Gyles chuckled. "He went out for coffee."

She turned to the coffee pot. "There's some there."

"Well, and takeout." Gyles sighed. "You have *no* food in this place. Plus, I was craving interaction from the outside world."

"You've only been here twenty-four hours."

"Don't I know it? I'm going stir crazy."

"What are you playing?"

"Soduko."

"Sudoku?" Santana clarified.

"Sure." He sat up straight and stretched. "You okay? You seem flustered."

"We're heading back out on the road," she replied.

"We?" Gyles shot up, excited. "Thank God. Thought I'd be stuck in this place forever."

"No, not you," Santana amended, flustered. "Me. I'm going."

"Where are we going?" Dick appeared in the doorway, a grease-stained paper bag in one hand and two takeout coffee cups in a holder balancing on the other hand.

"Not you, me." Santana sighed. "You two stay here."

Dick laughed. "I don't think so." He set down the various items of food and drink. He looked at Santana, concern in his eyes. "What happened?"

"Nothing," she insisted.

"Bullshit," Dick replied. "I'm a PI. I can read people. Something's wrong."

Santana wiped a hand down her face. "They took the dagger."

"I know." Dick air-quoted as he said, "they."

"No," Santana replied. "The Order. They stole the dagger. It's in their possession."

Dick's face fell. He turned to Gyles with an accusing look.

"What?" Gyles protested. "Don't look at me."

"It's not him," Santana replied. "Your employer, Jakob, showed up, too. Everyone is on the dagger, all vying to be the first to confirm or deny the legend. The Order killed our translator. They'll have the location of the lost temple before we know it."

"Fuck..." Dick sat. "How the hell are we supposed to go after them if we don't know where the temple is?" He turned to Gyles. "Any ideas?"

Gyles shrugged. He had several French fries already in his mouth.

"We don't need the dagger," Santana offered. She held up the small slip of paper, flashing the words on its surface.

"Is that blood around the edges?" Dick asked.

"Ignore that." Santana tapped the words. "Giant's Bowl."

"What's the Giant's Bowl?" Gyles asked.

"It's a crater in the center of the forest," Santana explained. "A place for which many have trekked, but few have returned."

"The temple is there?" Dick asked.

"Supposedly," Santana replied. "Of course, nothing is for certain. But that's where the Order will be heading. Even the Albatross will be sending his men there, likely my client's people, too. It's going to be a bloodbath unless we can get ahead of them all and claim what's ours."

Dick looked longingly at his food. "Can we eat first?"

Santana shouldered her bag. "No. Not if you want to come, too. I'm leaving, and if you're not ready in the next thirty seconds, you'll lose your chance."

"You want us with you?" Gyles asked hopefully.

Santana leveled her stare. "Truthfully, no. I realize you're going to follow me either way, so I'm going to make it easier on myself. Just know that if you fall behind, you stay behind. I'm not coming back for you, and I might be your only hope of surviving in the jungle."

Gyles rose to his feet, licking his fingers. "She's a badass, isn't she?"

Dick didn't answer, but she could read his answer on his face.

The driverless cab stank of greasy food as the city slipped into the night.

Gyles munched eagerly on his burger, his fingers slick with its juices. Dick nibbled on the fries he'd bought, occasionally sipping his takeout coffee.

Santana sat between them, a steady drift of today's pop chart floating around the cab. The artist was vastly abusing the autotune feature, to the point that it was almost impossible to decipher the words.

"Can you believe that this is music?" she asked.

Dick shrugged. "No different to some of the crap that came out when I was a kid."

They had stopped by Dick's place on the way out of the city. It had been brief, allowing Dick to arm himself with a set of pistols, tossing one spare to Gyles, who happily took the firearm. They didn't know what they were going to encounter in the jungle. All they could guarantee was that this wasn't going to be easy, and The Order of the Scythe was already ahead of them.

The city soon disappeared. Fields rushed by with crops as tall as houses. Before they knew it, they were at the entryway to the jungle, several headlights drawing their attention.

"Stop here," Santana commanded. The automated vehicle obediently drew to the side.

They were two hundred meters from the other vehicles that steadily drove between the trees. Santana grabbed Dick and Gyles and pulled them into the density of the nearby cornfield.

Raised voices called from afar. They stepped deeper into the field, losing sight of the road as footsteps approached the cab.

The cab didn't wait for them to approach. Already interested in its next trip, the cab turned in the road, then headed back for the city.

"Who's there?" a voice called.

Santana nodded for Dick and Gyles to follow, the trio slipping through the rows of corn, heading for the trees. They had some idea of who could be calling for them, but they didn't want to wait around to confirm it.

At the edge of the field, the trees took over. They slipped into the shadows, able to make out the headlights and torches a short distance to their right.

"Stay close," Santana instructed.

They obeyed, following keenly in step. The trees were

sparse enough that their roots didn't offer much of an obstacle at this point, but Santana knew that would soon change. They crept onward, Santana guided by her internal compass as she aimed for the river she knew would soon meet their path—a river where she had once taken a woman in vibrant red clothing.

The gentle hum of the car engines faded as the jungle took over. Insects buzzed, birds chirped, larger creatures shuffled and roamed in the undergrowth. A thin layer of sweat peppered their brows as the humidity and dense foliage closed in.

Something hissed.

"Fuck," Gyles complained, stepping to the side sharply as something flashed nearby.

Santana lashed the whip, the bright yellow snake coiling back and speeding away into the bushes.

"Watch your step," she warned. "Remain vigilant. The Order isn't the worst of the creatures we'll encounter in this place." She dipped into her bag and drew out a bottle of insect repellent. "Here."

She chucked the bottle to Dick. He fumbled, struggling to track its movement in the dark. When he picked it up, he clicked his tongue. "You had this the whole time, and you let me get devoured by midges?"

Santana offered a smile before taking out a small flashlight from her bag. "Take this, too."

Dick finished spraying himself, then offered the bottle to Gyles. A sour scent hung in the air as Dick turned on the small beam of light. "You sure it's safe?"

Santana nodded. "They're out of sight. If you listen closely, you can still hear them, but they'll be hard-pressed to detect us this far into the undergrowth."

The trees rattled above them as something large swept above their heads. It was quick, the dark shape disappearing as soon as it had arrived.

"Howlers," Santana informed them. "We're in howler territory."

"Howlers?" Gyles asked.

"Monkeys," Dick replied as another swung above them.

They arrived at the river, the water rushing past them in silky streams. Several rocks spiked out of the surface like teeth. It was at least forty feet across. A wooden bridge stood around half a click to their right.

There were no signs of the Order's vehicles.

"Who's up for a swim?" Gyles asked.

Santana stepped into the water.

"I was joking," Gyles remarked.

"Me, too." She grinned, stepping back. "We take the bridge. It's infinitely easier." She grinned again, remembering her crossing with the Red Countess.

"What are you smiling at?" Dick asked.

"Nothing." Santana shrugged him off. They skirted the river's edge, finally making it to the bridge. Deep tire tracks in the dirt told of the Order's passing. "They're ahead of us."

"How are we going to beat them to the bowl?" Gyles asked.

Santana straightened. "The road will only take them so far. Soon they're going to have to go on foot. Then, we take them."

The bridge was sturdy. Once across, the three followed the road for half a mile before Santana took them into the brush. An hour into their trek, they came across their first signs of local ruins and rubble. Gyles marveled at the architecture, but Dick showed no interest, his limp gradually growing with every step.

They reached a rocky outcrop beside them as the land began to rise. The mouth of a cave opened, and they stopped there to set up a fire and fill their stomachs. Flames flickered and crackled as the light danced along the uneven cave walls, the shadows stretching for a long way inside.

Santana disappeared from the group for a few minutes, soon returning with a tapir's heavy carcass dragging behind her. The creature was large, and the skin gave way to her sharp knife. She roasted the beast over the fire in chunks, passing the cooked pieces to her comrades.

Gyles eyed her impressively. "Where did you learn all of this?"

"You mean you didn't learn all this in your local schools?" Santana returned.

Dick chuckled.

"No." Gyles grinned. "Strangely enough, our teachers didn't deem hunting and surviving the wilds as a credible use of our time. They'd rather focus on Pythagoras' theorem and the periodic table of elements."

"Don't forget sedimentary erosion," Dick chimed in.

Gyles nodded, taking a large bite from his cooked meat.

Santana considered this. "My mother and father were keen to teach me survivable skills from as young as I can remember. He was Russian. She was Mexican. I guess you could say they came from equidistant, juxtaposing hostile environments."

"I guess you could." Gyles threw Dick a confused glance.

Santana paid no mind. "My mother had always been keen on archaeology and the exploration of ancient civilizations and cultures. My father less so, but he was swept away by her fervor. The pair of them traveled across the globe to the site of various digs for their first few years.

"I was practically raised on Atlantica when Mother discovered rumors of a long-forgotten secret that could change how we see the world. She was obsessed, tortured by the mysteries of the Atlanticore, certain that there was more here than meets the eye. My father entertained the notion, supporting her on her adventures, though often my mother would travel with her crews, gone for days at a time."

"What was she looking for?" Gyles asked.

Dick gave her a knowing glance.

Santana shuffled in her seat, eyes boring into the dancing flames. Inside the orange and yellow hues, she saw the smiling face of her mother, her eyes alight with youth and energy and inner fire. "She sought the lost city of Atlantis."

Gyles snorted.

Santana shot him a look.

He stiffened, his laugh cut short. "You're serious?"

Dick chimed in. "It's not uncommon. There are many on the island who seek the lost city. Atlantis has captured the hearts and minds of explorers the world over for hundreds of years. When people discovered Atlantica in the twentieth century, it raised excitement. Hundreds of explorers thought they'd find the lost city."

"But it's only a story," Gyles protested. "Everyone knows that. Hell, even Disney made their version in the early 2000s. Flying ships and intricate mechanisms of ancient origin. It's a lovely fairytale." He turned to Santana, seeing her gaze return. "You don't believe in all that, do you? A woman of the *real* world."

Santana drew a long breath. "I don't know. What I *do* know is that I've seen many wonders appear in this world through the years. I've dug up artifacts and items from cultures believed to have been a legend. I've seen colleagues discover relics that have changed the course of our understanding of history.

"Hell, even this island, Atlantica, was made of legend a little under a century ago." She looked back at the fire toward her mother's smiling face. "When a woman with such a strong conviction that something exists raises you, I suppose you'll always sit and wonder."

They fell quiet for a moment, each one losing themselves to their thoughts.

"What happened to them?" Gyles asked.

Santana looked up.

"Your parents," he clarified. "You talk about them like they're gone."

Dick cast his eyes down. He'd heard this story before, had asked the same questions not all that long ago. "Father is back in

Russia. He took us there not long after Mom's passing. He couldn't take the pain of living on this island after she was gone."

Gyles narrowed his eyes, looking as though he wanted to ask more questions but wasn't sure he could.

"A cave-in," Santana answered for him. "Down in the Atlantica wilds, exploring a sub-sect of caverns. Only one member of their crew escaped to tell the tale. They've been traumatized ever since, living in a premium care facility out in a rural area. There was no explanation given, just a single misstep, and the rocks fell on them." Her eyes glittered as she looked up at the sky.

"I'm sorry to hear that," Gyles offered.

Santana rubbed her eyes, catching the look from Dick. She knew what he was thinking, that there was still some mystery afoot. It had only been a short time ago that Santana had hired Dick's services to help her recover her mother's pendant, and the questions of the codes and the pictures inside had been left unanswered. The buzz of mystery filled the area around them.

A rumble sounded. Santana looked at Dick's stomach. "Here." She handed him another skewer of tapir meat.

Dick raised a hand, his back stiffening. "That wasn't my stomach."

Gyles laughed. "There's no shame in it. We've had a long walk. Eat up."

Santana rose to her feet, turning toward the cave. Her hand moved to her whip. The rumble grew again, elongating into a rolling growl.

"That's not hunger," she commented as a dark shape strolled toward them from the cave mouth. "We have company."

CHAPTER TWENTY-ONE

The shape loomed out of the cave, a hulking beast as wide as the three of them and equally tall despite the fact it walked on all fours.

The bear growled, the light from the fire dancing across its face and casting harsh shadows around its eyes and snout. Black eyes glinted at them over bared teeth and peeled-back lips.

"Holy…" Gyles muttered.

Santana planted her feet, bracing herself. The bear stopped ten feet from the campfire, assessing the scene. Dick slowly moved his hand to his hip, reaching for his pistol.

"Easy…" Santana offered, one hand outstretched, palm up. "There's a good girl…"

The bear cocked her head, great nostrils flaring as she detected the nearby tapir carcass. She took a cautious step forward. Santana held her ground. Dick remained still, the pistol now aiming at the bear's chest. Gyles flinched.

The bear's head turned to Gyles. Santana spoke softly out the side of her mouth. "No sudden movements."

She could sense Gyles' anxiety. She offered a glance and saw the sheen of sweat on his brow, his body quivering under the stare of the hulking beast. The bear took another step. Then another. She closed on Gyles, eyes locked on him.

Santana clapped her hands once, the sound a sudden sharp cut through the quiet. The bear grunted, craning her massive head toward Santana. The woman narrowed her eyes, holding its attention. "Come on, miss. Let's all stay calm, shall we?"

The bear turned back to Gyles. He swallowed hard. The bear took another step, her massive teeth shining toward him. One more step and she lowered her face, sniffing the meat.

A large tongue rolled out of her mouth as she tucked into the carcass, teeth shredding the remaining meat off the bone. Bone crunched with each powerful bite. Gyles was pale, looking ready to sprint off at a moment's notice.

Santana met Dick's eyes. He nodded toward his gun. Santana shook her head.

The bear ate greedily, no display of delicacy shown as she demonstrated the power of her jaws. Soon, she raised her head, licking meat and blood from her lips, her attention back on Gyles.

"Santana…" Gyles breathed.

The bear took a curious step toward Gyles.

His eyes were pleading.

The bear sniffed Gyles, its powerful head nudging him back. He placed one foot behind him, holding firm and waiting for a command.

The bear sniffed. Suddenly, she stepped back, rising onto her hind legs, a mammoth figure towering over Gyles. Her roar was mighty, filling the air around them, and it was enough for Gyles to turn and stumble over his feet as he broke into a run.

"Fuck…" Santana muttered, exploding into action.

She tore toward the bear who lumbered at Gyles. Dick was on his feet, gun aimed at the bear's head.

Santana sprinted past him. "No!" she cried as she smacked the gun out of his hands, sending it spinning into the detritus on the ground. Gyles scrambled back to his feet, breaking toward the trees. The bear slammed back down onto all fours and broke toward Gyles.

Santana closed on the pair and snapped her whip at the bear's feet. The bear stopped, turning its monstrous head at her. She unleashed a roar at Santana, who kept her cool and whipped again. The bear turned its body toward her, uncertain at what she was dealing with. Santana cracked the whip a third time.

"You asked for it, miss," Santana commented. Out of the corner of her eye, she saw Gyles hiding behind a tree.

The bear rose onto its hind legs. Dick called to Santana. She ignored him, dropping the whip to the ground. She straightened to her full height, stretching both arms into the air, mimicking the bear with her lips and teeth as she roared back at the beast. The sound that came from her throat was strained and raw, but the pair filled the surrounding area with their calls.

Santana stomped the ground, taking a bold step toward the bear.

The bear took a step back, uncertain.

Santana advanced.

The bear retreated, whining as Santana picked up the whip and flicked at her toes.

The bear peeled its foot back, then twisted away from Santana. Without a glance back, it sped off into the forest, lumbering away. They heard it crashing for a fair distance before the world fell quiet once more.

Santana held her position, whip trailing from her hand. After a few moments, Gyles re-emerged, cautiously looking around for the bear. Santana stepped back toward the fire, resuming her seat. She picked up her abandoned food and started gnawing.

Dick grinned, resuming his dining experience. Gyles returned, his body still shaking slightly. A white pallor covered his face. "Seriously, where did you learn this shit?"

Santana shrugged. "Common knowledge in my business. The

law of nature is simple, to win, you must be dominant. If a bear tries to intimidate you, you intimidate the bear. The moment you run, they know that you're accepting your role as prey. If you strike back, they don't know what to do."

Gyles gave an incredulous laugh. "Thank you."

"Don't mention it." Santana laid down her stripped bone. "If you two want to grab some sleep, I'll take the first watch. We should rest as much as we can. Who knows what we'll find when we get to the Giant's Bowl."

"Whatever it is, I'm sure you can handle it," Gyles offered with a smile.

Dick's gaze grew intense. "Something tells me it's not going to be a hoard of bears we encounter down there."

They enclosed themselves in their thin sleeping bags, Santana taking her watch around the fire. Occasionally she'd watch the flames, looking for her mother's face, but it seemed she had taken a short hiatus from her visits. In the distance, she caught the rumbling growl of the bear and wondered where she'd gone. At some point soon she'd crave the safety of her cave and would make her way back. For now, Santana simply needed to remain alert.

The jungle sang around her, creatures of all sizes and shapes committing to their evening chorus. Santana busied herself whittling a lump of breakaway rock, creating a keen edge on a rough-looking blade that she might be able to use at a later date. A few hours later, Dick awoke and joined her. They spoke for a short while, speculating on the Order and what mischief they might be up to before Santana slipped into her bag and settled down.

She only caught a few hours' sleep before Gyles' shuffling and stretching awoke her. He had slept through his watch, not that Dick had minded, and soon the three of them packed their things and readied to set off into the forest. They erased all signs of their fire as dawn broke, leaving the remaining tapir husk in the cave's open mouth as an apology and offering for their mammalian friend.

The wilds grew closer around them. Santana maintained her internal compass, looking for signs of familiarity as they closed on their target. Soon the brush was so dense that it was almost impossible to break through. Thorns and barbs barred their way, branches and trunks tangled around each other to form a wall of nearly impenetrable brush.

Gyles grunted, his skin brushed by more thorns, angry red scratches lining his arms. "We'll never get there at this rate. This is taking ages."

Santana removed the stony blade she had sharpened overnight and set to work, hacking at the green and brown wall. The ground was soft beneath their feet, the sun unable to reach the forest floor and dry the moisture. Each step was sticky and laborious, but Santana hacked at the wall all the same.

With trained eyes, she hunted for the primary anchoring branches and swung, unleashing the thorns and carving a path for the three of them to follow. Sweat gleamed on her skin. Dick trailed at the back, quiet and solemn.

They made half a mile in a few hours, and Santana knew that time was against them. The Giant's Bowl was still a distance away, and she could only hope that the others hadn't found an easier path. With so much of the jungle still unexplored, it was always a case of trial and error. Not that she told the others this. They needed to have confidence in their leader, and Santana needed to remain confident in herself.

The ground sloped downward. Nearby came the sound of trickling water. A short distance down the slope, Santana hacked at a branch, her muscles aching, when her feet slipped.

She crashed onto her back, slipping down the wet mud beneath her. She slid beneath the wall of tangles, unable to stop herself as the ground dragged her left, then right, until she eventually rolled out, face down, into a small bog.

"Santana?" Dick called.

Santana grunted, pushing her head up. Thick, dark mud covered her. She pushed herself to her knees, unable to brush any of the muck away since it also caked her hands. "I'm fine! Just…dirty."

Although she couldn't see him, she imagined Dick smirking.

She struggled to stand, the mud sucking at her feet. She was almost positive this wasn't some kind of quicksand, but that didn't make it easier to move. Something nearby grunted at her, and she spotted a group of wild hogs staring her way, tusks protruding from the sides of their mouths.

Santana stuck out her tongue at them. Deciding that she was no threat, they returned to snuffling through the mud for food.

A body crashed toward her, appearing through the thickets. Gyles splashed into the mud at her feet, sweeping her onto her back once more. A moment later, Dick followed, a little more gracefully than the other two. Still, when they stood, they were all caked in a thick layer of mud.

Gyles tried to flick the mud off his hands. "I don't suppose there's water nearby to clean us up?"

Santana looked past the hogs to where a thin layer of fog hung above the ground. "That way, I'd imagine."

"What about the pigs?" Gyles asked uncertainly.

Dick took a step toward them. "They'll make a great meal." He took his pistol and shot at the ground near the closest one's feet. They bristled, then took off into the trees, the mud offering no obstacle to their speed.

"Why'd you scare them off?" Gyles asked.

Dick shrugged. "Not hungry."

They staggered through the mud together, the cloying ground draining them of their energy. Each step was an effort, and by the time they made it to firmer ground, exhaustion forced them to rest.

They drank from their canteens as Santana offered them a power bar each. Dick declined his, choosing instead to quench his thirst by draining his entire bottle.

A little distance ahead, the mist hung over a body of dark water. Unlike the clear running rivers or the lakes in the cave that Dick and Santana had witnessed, it was impossible to see what lurked within. Vines hung in great loops from the treetops, and strange creatures hummed and vibrated in the shadows.

They stepped cautiously into the water's edge, scooping up handfuls to wash off the worst of the mud. While Dick and Gyles focused entirely on getting clean, Santana kept her eyes fixed around her, detecting a couple of strange ripples in the water a short distance away.

"Crocodiles…" she muttered, nodding their way.

Gyles stepped out of the water. Dick continued cleaning.

"It's fine," Santana offered. "They know we're here, but they're stationary, for now."

"I suppose that's comforting," Gyles stated.

Once the worst of the mud was off, they navigated through the strange bogland. Soft verges made walkways between pools of stinking water, and occasionally even these vanished so all they could do was wade across the pools. Midges followed in thick clouds creating an irritating hum in their ears until eventually, the land began to rise again, and the waters fell away behind them.

"Why would man settle here?" Dick asked as they approached a large crumbling statue tucked to the side of the trees. It was at least fifteen feet tall, its intricate carvings weathered and faded until all that remained was half a face and a few patterns on its stomach.

Santana gently rubbed a hand across the stone. Dust covered her fingertips. "There's hardly a place on this green Earth where humans *haven't* settled. We're a destructive species. Selfish. We must own and dominate all."

They left the statue behind, occasionally passing more examples of human interference. As the land rose, so too did the heat, until eventually, they found a crown at the top of the rise where trees refused to grow, and they could see the sky. In the center was a structure that looked like a stone giant's seat.

They climbed to the top, settling on a large stone slab that made the main seat of the structure. At least twenty feet wide and twenty feet long, there was more than enough room for them to gather and look out over the forest.

The city was nowhere in sight. All was green for miles around. They looked back the way they'd come and couldn't make out any of the bog or marshland. It seemed impossible that beneath the canopy could exist a world so unlike their own.

Santana pointed to the east. "There."

They all turned their heads.

"What are we looking at?" Gyles asked.

"See there where the green dips into that large round bowl?" Santana asked.

Gyles nodded, waiting for Santana to continue.

Dick raised an eyebrow. "Really? You're not getting this?"

Gyles looked at him blankly.

"That's the Giant's Bowl," Santana stated. "That giant bowl? Yeah. That's it."

Gyles laughed.

"What's the point of it all, though?" Gyles asked. "Like, this seat, for example. Why would anyone make something like this?"

Santana tilted her head, opening up her chest and face to the sky, praying for the sun to dry the sweat from her clothes. "It's a vantage point, that's all. Mix that with the hubris of the creator, and you have a throne dedicated to a giant. It's not enough for people to make a ladder or a set of steps or anything that is simply purposeful. It has to be 'pretty' too and have a greater meaning."

"Or a giant could have lived here," Dick offered sarcastically.

"Yes, John," Santana replied dryly. "A giant lived here. Just the one. They sat here and ate from that bowl."

Gyles laughed.

Santana turned her head toward the large bowl. There was a clearing in the center where she knew a large round lake resided. She had only stumbled across this location once and hadn't had much time to explore. Part of her was excited to see what the bowl had to offer for wildlife and brush. The other part of her was nervous about what they'd meet when they got there.

"How far do you think that is?" Gyles asked.

Santana considered this. "Maybe two or three hours provided the way ahead is clear."

Gyles nodded, then sniffed his armpits. "Don't suppose there's a chance for a shower down there?"

Santana smirked. "Here's hoping."

They all stared at the bowl, wondering if the small flock of birds that had taken off to the north of the crater was a sign of something else approaching.

CHAPTER TWENTY-TWO

It was four hours later when the trees began to thin.

The sun was dipping, leaving a wash of watercolor paint in the sky. As they broke through the trees, the air felt fresher, cleaner, and they were all excited to see the clear waters ahead of them.

A rush of water met their ears, drawing attention to a ring of waterfalls at the far side of the large lake. White foam trailed over crops of greenery, rocks jutted out like teeth, breaking the perfect drop to the water. A small shroud of mist clung to its base.

Dotted across the lake were small islands stocked with wonderfully bright flowers and plants. Were it not for the hazy veil of fog hanging over the top of the forest and blurring the reddening sun, they might have considered this the paradise that was so often caught on camera and put into films.

Gyles made for the water. Dick stopped him with one arm.

"What the hell?" Gyles asked.

Dick turned to Santana. "You might want clearance that the waters don't hold dangers before you dive straight in."

Santana examined the water but was unable to see far into its depths. "There's only one way to find out."

She took her top off, standing there in just her bra. The two men gawked at her like teens who had just seen boobs for the first time. She rolled her eyes. "Honestly, if either of you can brave my stench right now, you're welcome to try and sleep with me."

She turned to the water, then jumped in, opting to go feet-first so she didn't hit her head or break her neck on unseen obstacles. The water was cool and clean, and the dirt and grime from the day slipped off her. She swam a short distance, then came up for breath. She brushed her hair from her eyes and floated in the pool, glancing around her.

"So far, so good," she offered.

The two men waited.

"Fine." Santana added under her breath, "Babies.."

She submerged herself again, this time opening her eyes as she looked around the depths. The water was a cool blue, and schools of fish swam around her. Fallen logs and boulders lined the bottom of the lake as far as she could see before the slope edged down into unseeable depths. A few larger fish stalked the schools, and she spotted a strange variety of catfish eyeing her while keeping its distance.

She surfaced, nodding at her backpack at the shore. "Inside are a few small wooden daggers I whittled last night. If you're worried, bring them with you and arm yourself, just in case."

Dick rooted through her pack, pulling out the wooden stakes.

"Toss me one," Santana ordered. Dick threw one of the daggers. She grasped it, then dove down to explore the waters.

She observed the fish with a smile, enjoying the way their colors shimmered beneath the water. She spotted crayfish and freshwater crabs on the sandy bed, and only when she spotted the dark shape of a crocodile in the distance did she make her way back to the shore.

Dick sat in the water in only his boxers, letting the gentle waves lap his legs. Gyles busied himself with scrubbing his body, not too far from the shore. Santana joined them, making a beeline for her clothes. She brought them to the water and scrubbed the cloth together to remove any remaining stink she could.

"It's beautiful down there," she offered. "A whole other world."

Dick brought a cigarette to his lips. "I prefer my concrete world, thank you."

Santana threw him a judgmental glare.

Dick rolled his eyes. "I suppose this isn't too bad."

"Just watch for crocs," Santana added matter-of-factly. Gyles tensed. "I saw one down there, so there must be more. As long as you remain still and don't draw attention to yourself, you should be okay."

Gyles got out of the water, resting on the muddy shore.

They spent a little time getting themselves together and cleaning off. Santana explored the surrounding shores, examining every rocky crevice and occasionally looking into the shadows of the trees. The instructions told her to go to the Giant's Bowl, but that didn't mean anything without specifics of how to find the missing temple.

After her first lap, she returned to find Dick investigating his leg. There was a nasty scab over the place where he'd been bit, but it would soon heal. Gyles busied himself creating a makeshift structure to hang their damp clothes to dry.

"Anything?" Dick asked.

Santana shook her head. "It's no surprise. They were never going to make things obvious. It wouldn't have been hidden for years if everyone could easily find it."

A shotgun fired in the distance.

"They're getting closer," Gyles announced.

Santana nodded, turning toward the forest. "If that's even them."

"What do you mean?" Gyles asked.

"We're not the only ones in here," Santana replied. "This place is filled with explorers, each hoping to be the ones to find the next big discovery. A place this large and dense holds more secrets than we could ever imagine."

"Why doesn't anyone use satellites and tech to scan it?" Gyles pressed. "Tech is so advanced now. Can't people IR it, or heat map, or something?"

Santana exchanged a look with Dick.

"The island protects," Dick replied. "The domesticated parts where the city lies show up on satellite imagery, but the wilds remain protected for a reason—we don't know what's in here. Any attempt at recording imagery of the jungle returns static and disruption. The island is hiding something."

Gyles frowned. "Fascinating."

"Exactly." Santana checked through the items in her bag, ensuring that everything was still where she needed it. She felt Dick's eyes lingering on her body.

"It's the same reason that so few explorers return from the jungle's depths. Something is here. Multiple somethings, even. Outside of the dangerous fauna and the predatory animals, there's something at work in the deep of the trees that we can't put into words."

As if to demonstrate her point, a flash of orange and black came from the pool's far side. They turned to the tiger as the majestic cat crept to the water's edge, where it stuck out a large tongue and lapped greedily. They remained stock still, the tiger drinking its fill before returning to the jungle.

"Why do you come here so often?" Gyles asked. "Are you asking for death?"

Santana chuckled. "I'm at home in the wild. Not all are like me."

"I'll say," Gyles commented.

Santana sat, stacking dry tinder into a pyramid. She drew a long breath, then stared out over the water toward the waterfalls. "Humans aren't supposed to encase themselves in concrete and drywall," she stated at last. "To eat fast-food and exercise only by running to catch the bus or the train.

"This world…the world in which you live, it's all just…fake. An ecosystem designed around the manipulation of resources that will eventually kill the planet. We're greedy. We're hungry as a species, and we don't think of the long-term implications of what we do. To come out into nature…to see the way things *should* be…that's the only home I've ever wanted."

She hit some rocks together and sent a spark into the kindling. The twigs ignited. "When I first came to this island and discovered the protective laws around the jungle, I was elated. There are fewer and fewer places on this green Earth where animals and wildlife are left to thrive. You could walk for hours in this place and never see the same thing twice. This is it. This is how life was…how it should be. Natural, and built with everything that we need."

She blew on the ember, fanning it to get the flames growing. Reaching behind her, she grabbed a long stick which she laid across her lap. She took some twine from her bag and wound the wooden dagger around its tip to create a makeshift spear. "There. See?" she announced proudly.

Gyles grinned. "It's no good if you don't know how to use it."

Santana smirked, rising from her ass and moving to the water. She waded into the shallows, the water licking her knees, and coiled in position, arm raised. Gyles smirked at Dick. Dick stared at Santana. After a few minutes, she lashed her arm out, plunging the spear into the water.

Violent splashes accompanied the medium-sized fish spiked on the end of the spear. Rivulets of red dropped into the water, and as Santana looked along the shore, she spotted a couple of crocs slowly making their way toward her, drawn by the blood.

She walked toward the fire, a smug grin on her face. "You were saying?"

Gyles chuckled. "I just wanted to see what you could do."

"You ain't seen nothing yet."

She cooked the fish, the scales curling and peeling under the heat of the flames. She dished out small portions to the two men, then sat back and tucked into her own. She narrowed her eyes at her surroundings, trying to zero in on where to begin their search as she ate.

The sun was high in the sky, the heat rising in the clearing. They had heard another gunshot not too long ago, but things had fallen quiet. As they ate, several creatures approached the pool and came to quench their thirst.

A series of splashes drew their attention as they were finishing up, and they watched as several crocs on the far shore fought over an okapi who had accidentally strayed into their territory. The creature thrashed and struggled against their might but soon stilled as they dragged its body into the water.

Gyles gave Santana a sideways glance. She ignored him, rising to her feet. She took off to the right of the pool.

"You're going *toward* them?" Gyles asked.

Santana shrugged. "They have what they want, but we don't."

Her walk was slow. When she was a short distance away, she looked back, seeing that Dick had taken to examining the other direction of the shore. She kept her eyes peeled, looking for any sign of human interference or manufactured structures that might lead them in the right direction or show some kind of sign that they were on track.

When she made it to the waterfall, she stopped and looked back across the water. She could see their makeshift camp but could no longer see Gyles.

I hope that's not a bad sign...

She explored around the edges of the waterfall. The water streamed down from a rise in the land above. Around twenty meters from the water, a natural tunnel allowed a walkthrough to the other side. She passed through the tunnel and found Dick on the other side, his gaze thoughtful.

"There's nothing," he commented. "Nothing that I can see, anyway." He turned to her, hopefully.

"Same," she replied.

His shoulders slumped. She could tell he was unhappy lengthening his time in the jungle. If she was honest with herself, so was she. The sooner they could find this place, the better it would be for all involved.

"Maybe we wait it out for the others to come?" Dick suggested. "Hide out, set some traps, let them do the work for us."

Santana considered this. "Perhaps."

"We haven't addressed the obvious, anyway," Dick stated.

Santana nodded. "I know."

She was thinking it, too. Even if they found the place, the most they could do was guard it and wait it out until they could recover the dagger, and that was a dangerous game to play.

"What happens if the Order succeeds?" Dick asked.

Santana shrugged. "Remains to be seen."

He nodded.

Santana motioned toward the far shore. "Where did he go?"

Dick turned up his lip. "Wish I knew. Thought he might have gone with you."

"As long as he hasn't wandered too far off, we should be fine," she stated. "I don't rate his survival skills by himself."

"No?" Dick asked, a teasing note to his voice.

"No," Santana confirmed.

"Do you think it could be below the water?" Dick asked.

Santana narrowed her eyes. "It's a possibility we can't rule out. I didn't see anything on my brief visit down there, but that doesn't mean it isn't. Anything is possible at this point."

Dick scanned Santana up and down, lingering on the smooth skin around her navel. "Fancy another dip?"

Santana considered this. "Sure. I'm going solo, though." She glanced toward the gathering of eyes protruding from the water's surface, accompanied by several long snouts. "Maybe from the other side, though."

They skirted back around the pool, finally arriving at their camp. Santana tested her clothes and found them dry. Dick shrugged back into his as Santana stepped toward the trees. "Gyles?" she called through cupped hands.

Dick glanced over his shoulder, tugging his t-shirt back on. "Anything?"

Santana shook her head. "Gyles?"

A twig snapped. Someone emerged through the trees. Santana's face lit up, then quickly dimmed as a second someone arrived, then a third.

Gyles led the procession with a pistol pressed into his back to nudge him forward.

CHAPTER TWENTY-THREE

Gyles held up his hands, slowly walking toward Dick and Santana, mouthing, "I'm sorry."

A woman with long blonde hair gathered up into a ponytail held Santana's gaze. The gun she pressed into Gyles' back looked like an old war pistol. The woman arriving behind her was muscular with a slight swagger to her walk. In her hands was an AR-15, which she pointed at Dick.

"You did well," the first woman announced to Gyles. "No bluster. No bullshit. Straight to your camp." She cocked her head with her eyes still fixed on Santana. "What do we have here?"

Santana remained still, her hackles raised. "A small group of explorers. What do *we* have here?"

The woman smirked before shoving Gyles aggressively forward. He staggered, landing on his front in the mud. "Mind your manners, sister. We only want to know what's going on here." She turned the gun on Santana. "Judging by your words, you're already lying to us."

"Lying?" Dick asked, hands hanging by his side. "How do you figure?"

She turned over her shoulder to the other woman, a laugh on

her lips. "One of you is an explorer, that's for damn sure." She glanced at the drying clothes. "But a leather coat in the jungle? That's a little much, I'm afraid. Looks like you two gents are out on an expedition, and this skinny bitch is your guide."

Santana's lip curled.

The woman at the back cocked her head at Gyles. "I still say he looks familiar," she offered.

The first woman didn't take her eyes from Santana. "Who cares? All I want to know is what brings this strange band of misfits into the middle of the jungle? Seems odd to encounter them at random around this lake."

Santana cocked her head. *They don't know this is the Giant's Bowl.*

"Names," the woman ordered, looking at them each in turn.

"Gail," Santana replied. "Gail Carnegie."

Dick followed. "Charlton Hestworth."

Santana bit back a laugh.

Gyles pushed himself to his feet, brushing his front down. "Taylor Foster."

"Well," the woman replied, "Gail, Charlton, Taylor…My name is Janice, and this is my associate Toya. We're explorers of a sort, too. Perhaps you could help us."

Santana tensed, sensing that to decline was not an option.

"We're looking for someplace in the jungle," Janice continued. "Commonly known as the Giant's Bowl. Supposed to be a big crater around these parts somewhere. You heard of it?"

Santana exchanged a glance with Dick.

"Nope," Dick offered. "You're in Lake Chambers, currently. A little watering hole for the local wildlife."

"So where is the Bowl?" she asked.

Santana glanced over her shoulder, pointing toward a nearby peak shrouded in green. "If memory serves, there's a bowl of that kind of description out toward Cragwell Peak. About two miles that way."

Janice looked perturbed. She finally peeled her gaze from Santana and wandered over to the makeshift clothes rack. Toya adjusted her grip on her rifle as they watched Janice stick her hand into Santana's bag. Santana took a step toward her. Toya muttered, "I wouldn't."

Santana remained still. They were all unarmed. What could they do?

As Janice bent over, Santana spotted another gun holstered in her back pocket. She took out some of Santana's effects, eventually giving up on her search. She looked through Dick's pockets and only found cigarettes and alcohol. She gathered the firearms the three had brought with them and piled them a distance away from the group.

When she had finished her examination, she glanced toward the peak. "Two miles that way, you say?"

Santana nodded.

"Gotcha." Janice drew her pistol again, moving quickly to Santana. She pressed the mouth to her temple. "Bullshit."

Santana tensed.

Janice produced the piece of paper from her bag, the scribble stating, "Giant's Bowl."

"You're looking for it, too," she stated.

Santana remained still.

She grabbed Santana's ponytail and shoved her toward her comrade. Toya aimed her rifle at Santana's chest. "We know some people who will be very interested in what you're looking for at the Giant's Bowl. Come along with us—all three of you—peacefully, and we'll make sure you're left somewhat alive."

"Somewhat?" Gyles muttered.

"And if we refuse?" Dick asked.

Janice turned to address Dick. At that moment, Santana ducked quickly out of Janice's grasp. She spun, putting herself behind Janice, and hooked an arm around her throat. With her other hand, she wrestled for the pistol, the firearm sweeping dangerously around the group.

Gyles threw himself back to the ground. Dick took the moment of chaos to dive at Toya, who only had time to spray bullets at the ground before he tackled her. Dick pressed down on her, fighting to pin her arms back.

Santana tightened her grip around Janice's throat. The woman's cheeks grew red as her brain starved of oxygen. Soon she was forced to choose between the pistol and the luxury of breathing. She dropped the gun, and Gyles quickly swept it up.

Santana released her hold slightly, ensuring she didn't kill the woman in her grasp. Dick had successfully secured the muscular woman, her arm pinned behind her back, her face pressed into the dirt. Gyles picked up the rifle, then moved a safe distance from the pair.

"Where are your people?" Santana asked.

Janice remained quiet.

She tightened her grip.

"Fine! Fine…" Janice gave in. "They're in the brush, half a click away. We went ahead to scout out and find the Bowl, a few of us moving out in each direction. This place is a fucking labyrinth of shit."

Santana's lip curled. "How many of you are there?"

"An army's worth." Janice chuckled.

Santana caught the pistol that Gyles tossed her.

"Fine!" Janice called again. "A hundred, perhaps. We didn't do an accurate headcount."

"You guys must really want what's in that bowl," Santana stated.

Janice smirked. "You could say that."

"Why?" Santana asked.

Janice tried to escape. Santana held her fast. Janice sighed. "Like you don't know. You think you're pulling the wool over our eyes by pretending you're in this place for other reasons?" She spat on the ground. "Bullshit. You want what we want. That's all there is to it."

"Say we do," Santana replied. "Say we're going to get there first, and there's nothing you can do about it. How about that, huh?"

Janice laughed.

"Something funny?" Santana asked.

"Yeah…" Janice replied. "The fact you're about to get swarmed and destroyed by The Order of the Scythe."

Before Santana could react, Janice reached into her pocket and drew her reserve pistol. To Santana's surprise, Janice aimed the gun high above her head. Reflexively, Santana pulled the trigger.

Janice slumped in her arms, but not before a burst of light exploded from the end of the gun, a bright orange flare arcing into the sky.

Warm blood spilled over Santana's body. She released Janice, allowing her to fold onto the ground. She was momentarily in shock, the color draining from her face. She turned to Dick, who stared back at her from atop Toya.

"You had no choice," he offered. "You thought she was going to shoot you."

Santana glanced down at the body. "Fuck…"

Toya glared at her from the dirt. "You're in for some shit now, bitch. They know you're here. They're coming, and soon you'll be fodder for the crocs."

Santana ran her fingers through her hair. In the distance, she fancied she could hear calls and shouts of alarm.

She ran over to her backpack, taking out her tranquilizer gun. She stood over Toya, lined up the shot, then aimed a dart at her neck. Toya's eyes closed and she flopped still.

Santana addressed the others. "Gather up your things, now."

Dick and Gyles obeyed. They busied themselves with erasing

their presence as Santana splashed in the water and cleaned off the blood. She shook herself dry, then dressed.

"We need to get out of sight," she instructed, listening to the steadily rising voices.

"What about the body?" Dick asked.

Santana instructed Gyles to help her send Janice's body into the water. They kicked it to float toward the center, where the creatures within soon claimed it. Santana retrieved the dart from Toya's neck, and Gyles helped her hide the woman in some nearby ground brush.

"Higher ground," Santana ordered, motioning to a tree with a large trunk and several twisting branches. She was the first to climb high, with Gyles following and Dick at the rear. The limbs were wide and stable, and soon they'd tucked themselves into the leafy canopy with a slightly obstructed view of the place where Toya lay sleeping.

They waited in silence. Santana kept her eyes on the tree line, awaiting the arrival of their guests.

She didn't have to wait long.

CHAPTER TWENTY-FOUR

They swarmed from the trees like ants from cracks in the pavement.

There were several dozen of them. Janice's headcount had been exaggerated. Most of their team wore black fatigues and carried firearms. Many wore tank tops revealing muscular arms glistening with sweat. They rallied around Toya, one of their team opening a medical bag to address her condition while the rest roamed around the edges of the pool, scanning with their weapons to secure the area.

They passed quietly below Santana, Dick, and Gyles. The three of them remained motionless and silent. As the intruders worked to examine their surroundings, the sun began its descent in the sky.

Santana kept watch of the modest splashes in the center of the water. She wondered what creatures had gotten hold of Janice's body. A pang of regret nibbled her stomach at taking a life so suddenly, but Dick had been right. It was her or Janice at that moment, and Santana was a survivor.

A short while later, the search groups congregated back

around the main body of the pool where a woman in a dark cloak holding a scythe stood among the cluster.

"What do you think they're talking about?" Gyles muttered.

Santana shook her head. "Hard to say. I never taught myself to lip read."

Dick drew a small pair of binoculars from his jacket pocket.

"Where did you hide those?" Santana asked.

Dick raised an eyebrow. "That a trick question?" He pressed them to his face and searched the group. "They're mostly meatheads with firearms. Looks like that woman with the scythe is their leader."

"Would make sense," Santana offered. "The Order of the Scythe wouldn't be led by someone holding a chainsaw."

"I can't read them," Dick stated. "They're looking for something, though. See by the trees? They have six people in scuba gear set up to head into the water."

Santana shook her head. "I didn't prepare for a diving mission."

"It's fine," Dick offered. "Let them go ahead and unlock the door. We'll storm them when it's open."

"How?" Gyles asked. "There are so many of them."

Dick handed him the binoculars. "Recognize any?"

Gyles shook his head. "Only Sasha. She's the one with the scythe. The head of the Order. The others I don't believe I've seen before, luckily. That would've been a turn of events."

Santana studied Gyles closely.

Gyles removed the binoculars, taken aback by Santana's stare. "What?"

"Where did you go?" she asked. "How did they find you?"

Gyles' cheeks flushed. He handed the binoculars back to Dick. "I..." he struggled to find the words.

"You what?" Dick asked, looking through the binoculars.

Gyles sighed. "I needed to shit."

Santana scoffed, trying to hold back a laugh.

"What?" Gyles retorted. "It's a natural thing, okay? I wanted to be out of sight while I did it. I was finishing up when I heard noises. I got disorientated, walked straight into the pair. Thank God, too. I thought it was that tiger again."

They watched as the divers went into the water. They were armed, their waistbands kitted with a utility belt as they submerged in the pool. Santana thought back to her brief spell in the water, wondering what they could uncover that she hadn't seen.

"It's not like they show it on the TV," Gyles commented. He reclined against the crook of the trunk, adjusting his ass to get more comfortable. "You watch *Tomb Raider* and *Indiana Jones*, and you think it all happens super quickly. Adrenaline-fueled hunting for relics. The reality is quite different."

"Yeah," Santana confirmed. "It's a lot of waiting around and searching. Unfortunately, viewers would get bored watching Lara hunt for three months in a jungle before she found the thing she was after."

"Depends on what she was wearing," Dick offered.

Santana playfully hit his arm. Gyles chuckled.

The sky grew darker. Soon the sun was sinking behind the horizon, bursting into shades of vibrant crimson and pink. Santana's eyes watered as she watched the fuzzy haze of the sunset, remembering a time she had crested the hills of Beluhka Mountain in Russia and sat with her mother and father on either side. She had been young then, the world unfolding before her. Cold wind kissed her cheeks, and she was happy.

That had been the same sun then, but it felt different now.

While they waited, the divers emerged from the water, then re-submerged, always with empty hands. Santana wondered what they found down there—if anything. As the sky turned dark, they utilized their flashlights. The three watchers now saw the milky white lights beneath the surface. For the most part, the crocs stayed at bay, likely put out by their unexpected guests.

Santana whirled as something grunted behind her. She found Gyles adjusting himself, eyes wide.

"What are you doing?" she hissed. Dick was a few branches lower, nestled in the crook of the tree. His eyes were closed, but she didn't think he was sleeping.

"Sorry." Gyles rubbed his eyes. "I must've drifted off."

Santana glanced down. A group of the Order was surveying the area, flashing their lights around the ground. "It's a long way down. I wouldn't recommend it."

They remained tight-lipped until the small party had moved away. The Order members made their way back to the far side of the lake where a large bonfire was crackling and illuminated the shadowy shapes of others. A few were lined in neat rows, asleep in sleeping bags. Others had fashioned seats out of stumps of nearby trees and cooked their food in the flames.

Her stomach rumbling, Santana helped herself to a power bar. She offered one to Gyles, who was on the verge of sleeping again. She rolled her eyes and pointed lower. "Go down there and get some shut-eye," she ordered. "You should be able to remain still in that crevice. I don't need you giving away our position again."

Although there was truth to her words, Gyles appeared pained at hearing them. He took the bar and clamped it between his teeth as he made his way down the tree. Soon he was resting peacefully in its bough.

Santana continued to monitor the situation, tracking the divers working their way around the lake. After another hour or so, three divers emerged, some large item carried between them.

Santana placed the binoculars to her eyes.

They were holding a large piece of stone. She couldn't make out what was on it since their bodies were blocking the way, and the fire silhouetted the visible bits. The cloaked woman—Sasha—approached and examined the rock. Another diver emerged shortly after, carrying a couple of items that glittered in gold.

Santana's curiosity burned too brightly. She hated not being able to see from where she was. Soon she was shinnying down the tree, keeping to the shadows around the lake.

She tiptoed closer, deep enough into the shadows to not be seen, close enough to be able to hear. She curved around the lake, slowing as she neared the large group.

The heat from the fire wafted toward her. She didn't like how close it was to the trees, but she could do little there.

She moved as close as she dared, tucking behind the thick trunk of a nearby tree. She crouched, adding another layer of cover from the surrounding brush, and cocked her ears.

Amid all the general chatter from the Order, Santana picked up a thin, feminine voice. "...leaving until we've found more. This is good. This is a *sign*. We're in the right location, so feed me more of this."

"There's nothing else," a voice replied.

Santana could hear the venom in the woman's return. "I'm sorry, was I speaking to you or your captain?"

The man was silent.

Sasha advanced. "Answer me, worm."

"The captain," he replied sullenly.

"Good." A crack whipped through the night as her hand struck his cheek. "Learn your fucking place, unless you want us to leave your body out here, far from where your family will ever find you."

Another voice chimed in, trying to salvage the conversation. "He's right, ma'am. There's nothing. Apart from these items we've found, there are no visible treasures or entries. We've excavated a large area beneath the water. Each time we have to wait for the sediment to settle. There's nothing. Only more dirt and grit."

Sasha examined the blade of her scythe. "We're in no hurry. Back in the water you go."

They didn't bother to argue. Soon they slipped back into the water, the only sign of them the glowing lights beneath the surface.

Sasha stormed past the fire as people moved out of her path. The flames harshly licked her features, but even Santana could tell she was a good-looking woman beneath the cloak. She was now only a short distance away. Santana shrank further beneath the shrub. She held her breath, convinced that the woman would discover her hiding place.

Sasha stared out into the trees above where Santana was hiding. A man moved to her side. "We'll find it," he offered.

"Of course we will," Sasha stated. "Because you know what will happen if we don't?"

The man nodded, casting his eyes down.

Sasha finished anyway. "We'll burn this fucking place to the ground."

The man looked back up, following Sasha's line of sight. Santana could almost swear their eyes met for a moment. "What of the missing one?"

Sasha smirked. There was something devilish in her eyes. Had they found her body? Did she even care? It was impossible to tell.

"Whoever did this to her, they're nearby. We remain alert. We remain keen. I've instructed the guards to shoot on sight. Nothing gets in our way."

"Nothing," the man mirrored.

"Nothing at all..." Sasha mused.

CHAPTER TWENTY-FIVE

Santana awoke in the middle of the night to a sudden disturbance in the water.

She sat up in the tree, rubbing her eyes. A nearby bird took wing, its dark shape fading with the night sky. For a moment, she glanced around, unsure where she was until she spotted Dick beside her. He placed a reassuring hand on her arm, his eyes glittering in the dark as he motioned down to the water.

Gunfire cracked in the darkness. Men and women shouted as dark shapes exploded out of the water and attacked a group on the far side of the pool. Flashlights darted in all directions as their owners flailed their arms.

More gunshots fired. It appeared as though several crocs had stealthily swum through the water, sneaking up on a small group near the shore. The commotion was brief, and one of the Order's number needed urgent medical attention.

Santana whirled with the binoculars, watching for Sasha near the fire. She sat still, hood up, not sparing a glance in their direction.

Beneath them, the lights still circled the water...

Below Santana, Gyles awoke from his cradle and stretched. He wiped away a stray string of drool from his lips and climbed up the tree. His body took a moment to adjust to wakefulness, his legs weak as he pressed onward.

Santana and Dick sat side-by-side, staring at the water.

"Quiet," Dick reminded Gyles.

Santana pressed her lips together, her focus on the water. For the last hour, the lights had moved in circles, searching for treasures. Now they'd congregated around the east side of the pool. They were too deep for any of them to see clearly, but they each watched with interest.

Santana handed Gyles a power bar, which he took greedily. She only had a few left, so she knew that if things remained like this for much longer, she'd have to hunt and risk alerting them to their presence with fire. For now, she observed.

Something bubbled beneath the water. All of the divers were engaged in this latest revelation. After another short time, they moved as one, slowly rising to the surface. Not too far away, the waterfall continued its roar, water streaming down its rocky surface. Santana turned her head toward the falls, a glint of something catching her eye.

She looked again. The glint was gone.

Excitement buzzed on the shore. The Order made way as the divers emerged from the water. First, the front few strolled onto the shore with ease, but as they exited the water and lost the advantage of weightlessness, the item they carried dragged them down.

More bodies went into the water. Those fully clothed waded into the shallows, working together to remove a large round object, easily the width of a car. It was at least six inches thick, with a series of patterns and decorations on its surface.

"It looks like a medallion of some kind," Dick offered.

"Or a chocolate coin," Gyles added. "Used to get loads of those at Christmas."

Santana silently agreed, unable to peel her eyes away. As the flames glittered on its surface, a familiar face looked back at her, its large headdress arcing above its head.

Inti.

"Holy shit…" she muttered.

Gyles looked between them, but Dick and Santana knew what they were seeing. Sasha approached the medallion and, for the first time, removed her hood. Dark hair spilled down her back. She ran a hand over the stone, a manic glee in her eyes.

Another glint caught Santana's eyes.

She turned back to the waterfall, cocking her head. In the darkness behind the waters, she could swear that light shone, a pinprick of white like the stars in the night sky.

Then it was gone.

She turned her attention back to the medallion. The whole team's spirits lifted as they cheered and got to examining their find. Several of their team surrounded the relic as the others lowered it to the ground. Sasha laughed in triumph.

"Still doesn't give them a way in," Dick argued.

Santana shook her head. "No. But there may be something on its surface that might."

She looked up at the sky, noticing that the black had begun to turn purple. On the edge of the horizon, a reddish-pink light appeared.

Santana turned back to the waterfall. That glinting was back, brighter now, with a pinkish hue.

She leaned closer to Dick. "Can you see that?"

Dick lowered the binoculars he had taken back from Santana, following where she was pointing. "No? What?"

Santana shifted him back a little, so he was in her exact line of sight. "What am I looking at?"

Gyles craned his head to try and see.

"The light," Santana explained. "In there... See?"

Dick narrowed his eyes. "What is it?"

"I don't know," Santana replied. "It wasn't there before."

Dick shrugged, turning his attention back to the medallion. "It's definitely Inti. Wait, where are you going?"

Santana slid down the tree, hopping between branches. She landed with a soft *thump* on the verge and swiftly stalked through the shadows.

The sky grew brighter above her. Santana knew that she'd have to move fast to avoid detection. She closed on the waterfall, thankful that the medallion had drawn attention away from the far end of the pool. When she was at the tree line, she remained low, using the jutting rocks as cover as she dashed closer to the water. Something jumped out of the water and splashed. She glanced around for crocs or other dangers but could see none around her.

She waded into the water, moving toward the falls. The roar of the falling water magnified. The ground was mossy rock, and she slid as she progressed closer to the falls.

She looked back at the trees, hunting for Dick and Gyles, and was glad when she could see neither of them.

Water poured down on her. She pressed a hand to her left, tracing the rock face, looking for where she believed the light to have been. A short distance into the falls, her head and body buried in water, the wall to her left fell away.

Santana fell sideways, landing awkwardly on her hip. There was no more water falling on her head. She looked out at the pool, through the falls, from the crevice in the rock. Around her, the space was tight, but several scratches and carvings in the wall forced her lips to peel back into a giddy grin.

"Signs of Incan activity..." she murmured. She rose to her feet and had to cover her eyes from the piercing pink ray of the sun through the water. A tiny rock jutted out, breaking the water's flow and creating a hole through which light could leak. Behind her, the water had smoothed a small section of the wall over the years, and as she moved, the light bounced sharply out through the water.

Santana beamed as she turned and looked around. Behind her, uneven, hazardous, and deadly, were most certainly a crude set of stairs leading down into the darkness.

She craned her neck, looking as far into the darkness as she could, which wasn't too far. Trickles of water channeled down the side of the stairs, smoothing the rock into a thin gulley leading down. Her heart raced. She returned to the waterfall and peeked out past the water.

Slipping back out into the open, she hurried to Dick and Gyles. As she neared the trees, someone turned her way, forcing her to dive. She paused, waiting for the moment to pass. Satisfied they'd seen nothing, they turned away.

"What were you doing?" Dick hissed as Santana appeared in the tree. "You trying to get yourself killed?"

"Grab the stuff," Santana ordered, ignoring Dick's reprimand. "Let's go."

"Go where?" Dick asked.

Santana didn't answer. Instead, she slid down the tree and waited at the bottom.

A growl came from behind. She glanced over her shoulder, jumping and climbing just in time to escape from the diving clutches of the tiger.

"Fuck...." She grunted.

She climbed higher, the tiger yowling at the base of the tree. Santana worked quickly, navigating toward the others, stopping them mid-descent.

"My bag. Now," she called.

Dick tossed Santana's bag to her. She rooted inside, returning a moment later with a small foil packet. She unwrapped the object and dropped it to the tiger.

Its attention caught, the tiger sniffed at the item on the jungle floor. Voices called, drawn by the disruption of the creature. The tiger turned its eyes upward to the three in the tree and started its climb. It reached the lowest branch, and Santana produced another treat.

The tiger hissed, long teeth bared. She waved the treat back and forth, the tiger tracking it with its gaze. After a few more waves, she tossed the treat out into the open. The tiger pounced, appearing at the shore and stopping several surprised men and women in their tracks.

A gunshot sounded. The bullet streamed past the tiger. The tiger coiled back and sprang at the group.

"Now," Santana commanded.

She dropped, landing heavily on the ground. Dick and Gyles followed, and they made a break for it, sticking to the trees until they couldn't any longer.

They dashed into the open, making a line for the falls. They were behind the first set of boulders before calls alerted the others to their presence. Santana moved through the roaring foam until she found the crevice.

Gyles was behind her, feet slipping all over the place. She grabbed his shoulder to help support him and dragged him back to his feet. Dick gave him a rough shove, forcing the pair ahead of him into the crevice.

The din from the falls, the tiger, and the gunshots mixed as Santana tried to slow Dick's momentum. He crashed into her, wedging Gyles between them. Santana fell back against the rough steps, and together the three of them tumbled into the darkness.

CHAPTER TWENTY-SIX

A buttery yellow light flickered off the cave walls. Large rocky teeth jutted up from the ground and down from the ceiling, and it was easy for Santana to believe that she was walking into the jaws of a monster.

"Hold my hand, sweetie," Camila Sokolov soothed.

Santana's hand was swallowed by her mother's. She giggled as they stepped into the mouth of the cave, Camila holding a flaming torch in one hand.

The air cooled several degrees. Santana trod slowly, comforted by her mother's presence, yet terrified of the stories she had heard of caverns beneath the ground. Dracula was a vampire who could turn into a bat, and bats lived in these caves. Terra had told her so. Terra didn't approve of Santana's mother's job.

"Look over there," Camila instructed, drawing Santana's gaze to a large black hole in the floor. Artificial rocks bordered it, staged to look like the real thing. They edged close, Camila lifting Santana to her hip so they could stare down.

"How deep is that?" Santana asked.

Her mother crouched. "Take a rock. See for yourself."

Santana selected a smooth brown pebble.

Her mother straightened. "Go on."

Santana giggled as she tossed the rock. It went further than she planned, bouncing off the far rim before ricocheting down into the hole. The flames from the torch illuminated it only so far, and soon the darkness swallowed it.

"Where's it gone, Mommy?" Santana asked.

"Hold on." She held up a finger.

They listened. A few seconds later, they heard the rock clatter to the ground an unknown distance below.

"Wow." Santana's eyes lit up. "That was faaar."

Camila smiled. "It sure was."

"How far was that?" Santana's eyes were wide.

"At least ten houses," Camila replied.

Santana gasped. "That's high."

"Mmhmm." Camila placed Santana down. "You wouldn't want to drop down there."

"What's down there?" Santana asked.

This time, Camila tossed a rock, aiming a little distance from where Santana had thrown the rock. A moment later they hear a splash. "Water, darkness, and more caves, probably."

"And monsters?" Santana asked.

"No, dear." Camila chuckled. "The monsters live in the city, remember?"

Camila took Santana's hand once more. They journeyed deeper into the cave, passing several information boards drilled into the rock. Flyers and coupons for discounts on tours littered their surface, as well as information on the age of the caves and their history. Santana ignored all of these, wonderment in her eyes as they descended a set of hewn stairs toward an underground lake.

LEDs flickered, emulating fire. Camila took Santana toward a bench by the lake's edge and sat. The cavern was expansive, stretching in either direction, the ceiling a good distance above them. Boats had docked on the water's edge.

Something squeaked.

Santana flinched.

Camila pointed at the ceiling. "They're not going to harm you," she explained.

Santana shrank into her mother's bosom. Camila gently eased her daughter's face to the cave ceiling. "Bats are as scared of us as we are of them. They live in these caves to escape people. They're shy, like you."

"I hate bats," Santana muttered.

"It's easy to hate what you don't understand," her mother stated. "But it's not in hate that we make progress. Love, kindness, and knowledge are the best tools to arm your mind to the world. We don't explore because we're scared, or we hate. We love what we do, and we thrive when we learn. You get that, don't you?"

Santana pursed her lips, unable to take her eyes off the small bats flying around above. Occasionally one would flit into the air and circle the others before roosting again.

"Remember when you were scared of the neighbor's cat?" Camila asked.

"Mrs. Whiskers made horrible noises at night," Santana stated, remembering the snow-white cat playing in the garden in the middle of the night, screeching at the other neighborhood cats.

"But when you met her, she was lovely," Camila continued. "Think of the bats like that. They're not going to hurt you."

Santana tracked another flyer. When it settled, she muttered, "Which one is Dracula?"

Her mother stroked a lock of hair from her face. She looked down into Santana's innocent eyes and met her gaze. "None of them. Dracula is a story. Those kinds of stories aren't true."

Santana thought about this. It didn't make sense. "What stories are true?"

Camila wrapped an arm around her, drawing her in tighter. She smelled of lilac. "You'll learn as you grow older. Don't believe all your friends tell you without finding out for yourself. Bats are omnivores, which means, what?"

"They eat meat and plants," Santana dutifully replied.

"Correct," Camila assured her. "They eat mostly bugs, worms, and berries from outside the cave's entrance. They don't suck blood or trans-form into people whenever they want."

Santana wrinkled her brow.

"I'll prove it," Camila stated. She twisted her backpack to her front, drawing out a small wooden box that gently rattled as she set it on a slender, chest-high rock a short distance in front of them on the lake's edge. She removed the lid, revealing a handful of berries and dried worms.

They waited patiently. After a few minutes, one of the bats swooped away from the roost, arcing down near the box before swooping back up. Another one broke free.

Another few minutes passed before the first bat came down to settle on the box. It dipped its head into the box, then fell to get airborne and flapped to gain height. A second landed, then a third, and soon four of the creatures were standing at the container, dancing around each other, eating their fill of food.

"See?" Camila whispered into Santana's ears. "They're harmless. They couldn't hurt you if they tried."

Santana's gaze remained fixed on the creatures. They were tiny, much smaller than she thought they'd be. Their eyes pinched closed, their nostrils wide as they sniffed their surroundings and licked their lips. They were like skinny hamsters with wings. She giggled. "They're cute."

"They are," Camila confirmed. "See? The real thing we fear is the unknown. Now that you've identified your fear, you can face it head-on, and you know it's not half as bad as you originally thought."

Santana snuggled into her mother, watching the bats with joy. When the container finally emptied, the bats returned to the cave roof where they settled again. Camila reclaimed her box, then continued taking Santana around the cave.

Santana beamed the entire way, pointing out more colonies of bats, catching the gentle splashing of fish in the lake, and even spotting one or two cave crabs. She only wished her father could be there with them, Santana holding each of their hands as she walked.

They neared the far end of a cave where a rough-hewn door stood. Although flames lit around the entry, beyond the threshold, all was pitch black.

"What's down there?" Santana asked.

Camila smiled, staring into the darkness. "Want to find out?"

Santana cocked her head. She stared into the darkness and could see the shapes of things moving, eyes glittering and the scuffling of feet on the rock. "No. No, thank you."

Camila crouched beside Santana. "What did we learn today?"

Santana rubbed her nose nervously. She shrugged.

Camila chuckled. "Fear is caused by the unknown. Identify your enemy, and learn what you can about them. Nothing is as terrifying as you think."

"You'll always be around to guard me, won't you, Mommy?" Santana asked, clutching her mother's arm.

"Yes, darling." Though Santana tried to meet her gaze, Camila looked into the darkness. "And, if I'm not, I know you'll be okay."

"How do you—" Santana cut off, her words trailing into a sudden scream as her mother shoved her into the darkness. The shadows swallowed Santana, the floor sloping harshly down. She felt the bump of steps on her body as she was flung into the unknown, stars sparking in her vision with every bump and bruise...

The darkness was absolute. The only source of light was the pulsing colors flashing through Santana's head. She groaned, her body battered and bruised. The ground was rough and cold.

She eased herself into a sitting position, gingerly checking all of her joints and ranges of movement for fear of fracture. There was a nasty bump on her head, and her thumb was tender, but after a few stretches, she was satisfied that it hadn't broken. The hushed roar of the falls was far above her, though she could no longer see it nor any light.

Something shifted beside her. She heard Dick's signature groan as he shuffled in the darkness. A moment later, Gyles moved and grunted.

Above them, voices shouted and called. She didn't believe she'd been knocked unconscious, but her understanding of time had warped. She rooted in her pack, finding her cell phone. She activated the flashlight and illuminated the space around them.

She gasped.

Just a few feet away, the chasm opened before them. They were on a shelf, meters above the cavern floor, the drop severe and deadly. Rocks jutted from the ground below like spikes, and a fall would have meant instant death.

She eased back from the shelf and looked behind at the stairs leading down to where they were. The stairs curved upward, which would explain the absence of light.

"We need to move." Dick pointed out the obvious as the sound of footsteps coming down the stairs followed.

"Easy now!" a strange voice exclaimed. "It's slippery as shit."

"Watch it!" another chimed.

Santana cautiously rose to her feet, aware that the stream of water passed around them and down the shelf, creating a slippery surface. She shone her light to the left, finding a gentle slope leading down into the massive underground cavern.

"Come on," she instructed, taking Gyles beneath the crook of the arm and helping him to his feet. He limped for a few steps as he tested his legs. His face was pained as he cradled his elbow with the opposite hand. Santana could make out the lump in his shoulder where a bone had slipped out of place, but they didn't have time to address it now. "Let's go."

They eased their way to the slope and began their descent. They moved as quickly as the slope allowed, but all turned back to the shelf when a voice mutated into a shout, and someone slid down the same path they had. A body appeared a few seconds later as a man scratched against the floor, struggling to slow himself. He slid toward the edge of the ledge, his weight carrying him on until he disappeared over the lip.

His shouts stilled as a wet grunt escaped his mouth.

"Frankie!" a voice called down the stairs.

All went quiet.

A bat shrieked overhead. Santana shone her flashlight to the ceiling, finding a roost of black critters fluttering past above them.

She drew a long breath and proceeded down the slope with the others in tow.

CHAPTER TWENTY-SEVEN

"We need to hurry," Dick urged.

Sound traveled easily around the cave. There were a few more slips and falls from the Order, but no more deaths that they could hear. They'd learned from the mistake of their comrade. Soon the voices filled the cavern, and light illuminated the spaces behind them.

They hurried, the slope soon showing signs of human construction. A gentle wall grew at the side of the decline, protecting travelers from a fall. When they reached the bottom, a lake opened to their right. The cavern wall to their left stretched high into the air, and several carved entryways showed at its base.

"Which one?" Gyles asked, voice weak.

Santana picked one at random, tucking them out of sight as footsteps ran down the slope after them.

They hobbled along, following the tunnel as it banked to the left, then to the right. The way ahead looked as though nature had produced it, although Santana spotted small markings at regular intervals along its channel. In the cracks of the rocks were strange runes, which she memorized as they put distance between themselves and the Order.

Pathways opened on either side of them. They twisted and turned as Santana led the group on until all sounds of others faded into nothingness. They entered a small pocket cave with a natural pond in the center. Moss and mushrooms grew around its edge, the water as clear as the open sky. Beneath the water, a small group of fingernail-sized black fish clustered and swam.

Santana helped Gyles sit, his back against the cavern wall. Dick continued to the far side, eager to press on. "Why are we stopping?"

"He's hurt." Santana shone the flashlight at Gyles.

"Rather hurt than dead," Dick replied.

Gyles looked up at him, pain in his eyes. "He has a point."

"We can't run blindly into the unknown," Santana shot back. "We need tactics. Planning. They can't sneak up on us here."

"Want to bet?" Dick replied.

"We'd hear them," Santana returned. "Look, let's take a second to recalibrate, and then maybe we can keep running into the darkness, trailing through the labyrinth until we're lost."

Dick screwed his fists tight. "Santana…"

"No," she replied. "This isn't your terrain. This is mine. We keep running into the darkness, and we'll…"

"End up like your mother?" Dick snapped.

Santana's nostrils flared. She held his gaze for a moment, watching him regret his words instantly. He looked away. "Santana…I didn't…"

She held up a hand, crouching to address Gyles. Her heart beat fast, but she knew that Dick wouldn't have meant it. They were all tired, and adrenaline raced through them. Stressful situations brought out the worst in people.

Still…in the back of her mind, she heard her mother calling for help, the distant rumble of falling rock.

"Are you okay?" Santana asked Gyles, turning her attention away from her imagination.

"I'm fine," Gyles replied, clearly lying. "Let's continue."

"We don't need to," Santana replied.

"How do you know?" Dick asked, pointing the way they had come. "In case you hadn't noticed, there's an entire team of them out there, armed to the teeth. They're organized. They're *prepared.*"

"In case *you* hadn't noticed, we're heading in the right direction." Santana returned, gently touching Gyles' shoulder as he winced. "Definitely broken. Here." She handed him a white tablet from her bag.

"What is it?" he asked.

"Forget about it," she replied.

Dick came closer, eyes lingering on the fish in the pool. "What do you mean we're heading in the right direction? As far as I can see, we're in a coil of a maze, paths in all directions. Sooner or later, they'll find us."

A voice carried down the tunnel, as quiet as a whisper. They waited in tense silence, but nothing followed.

"The walls," Santana replied at last. "While your eyes stay fixed on the destination, I'm fixed on the path. There were runes along the walls, inscriptions carved at regular intervals along the way. Ancient symbols marking out instructions to lead travelers onward."

"Symbols?" Dick asked, perplexed.

"The pool is the first checkpoint," Santana replied. "Next will be a ladder. After that will be the doorway."

"And you picked all of this up from running through a tunnel?" Dick asked incredulously.

Santana nodded. She grabbed Gyles' arm, looking deep into his eyes. "Do you trust me?"

He hadn't finished nodding before Santana cranked his arm, bringing the hand of his broken shoulder to the opposite shoulder. Working quickly, she wrapped a length of cloth around his body, creating a makeshift sling.

"Fuck…" Gyles gasped.

"Sorry," Santana stated. "Better to ask for forgiveness than permission."

She rose to her feet, turning her attention back to Dick. They stared at each other for a long moment. "You don't have anything to say?"

Dick raised his chin. "I'm sorry."

"Good," Santana replied, crossing to him. She gently patted his cheek. "Now, if you don't mind, give Gyles a hand to his feet, and let's keep moving. We have a ladder to find."

At intervals along the way, they caught snatches of disturbances from behind. Voices echoed toward them from all directions, the occasional footsteps reaching their ears. Santana strolled confidently on, taking her time to study each of the runes that marked their path as they went. Dick shook his head in disbelief when she pointed out the first, and after another twenty, they came to a crossroads.

"Which way?" Dick asked.

Santana examined each direction, sniffing the air down each tunnel.

Gyles cocked his head. "What are you sniffing for?"

"Seeing where the air is fresher," Santana answered. "A trick I picked up from *The Lord of the Rings*."

Dick rolled his eyes. "If you could sniff out a ladder, that'd be fantastic."

Santana scratched her head. "It should be around here." She glanced at the floor, walking a small way down each walkway until turning back, just as confused as before.

"It's not going to look like a normal ladder, is it?" Gyles offered.

Santana continued looking. "Yeah. Exactly like your typical rusty stepladder. Those things survive thousands of years. Yep."

Gyles blushed.

Santana tapped her foot impatiently as a series of voices echoed down the tunnel. They looked at each other in turn.

"They coming this way?" Dick muttered.

"No idea," Santana replied. She closed her eyes, craned her neck back, and exhaled. When she opened her eyes, something caught her eye. She laughed.

"What's so funny?" Dick asked.

"All this time we were looking for a ladder going down…" She pointed skyward. "Look."

Above them, the ceiling puckered inward, another hole trailing up. At the lip of the hole was a series of rough grooves that looked almost like the rungs of a ladder. Santana stretched, her fingers at least two feet short of the first rung.

She glanced back at Gyles.

"Fuck…" Gyles offered.

Dick planted himself beneath the hole, lacing his fingers to create a small step for Santana. "You first. Then Gyles. Then me."

Santana nodded. At least when she was up, she'd be able to give Gyles a hand, then Dick.

Dick lifted her. She sailed through the air, fingers finding the first rung, then the next. She clamped her phone between her teeth as she braced herself against the opposite wall and offered a hand down. "Gyles. You're up."

Gyles reluctantly approached Dick. He trod in Dick's cradle, a worried expression on his face. He reached his good arm up, which Santana took. She pulled him until he was able to secure himself in the hole.

Santana shone the flashlight up. The ladder climbed at least twenty feet above them. "Are you good to try and climb?"

Gyles experimented by pressing his back against the rock and wedging his feet on the other side. With one hand, he could shinny up the chute a few feet before stopping to rest.

The voices grew louder below. Dick looked around uncertainly.

Santana slid to the lowest rung and offered her hand. Dick jumped, using Santana's pull to add an extra few inches to his jump. His fingertips clasped the first rung. He pulled himself up, Santana assisting. They managed to climb a few feet into the darkness before Dick hissed, "Turn out the light."

They waited, tensed and poised, as footsteps clattered toward them. Voices trailed, growing louder.

"…fucking maze. Never going to be able to find anyone in this shit hole," a male voice commented.

"It's better than being back there with the others," a female voice answered. "It's kind of exciting. A hidden maze beneath a giant lake. Can't you feel the magic?"

"All I can feel is dust up my sinuses and blisters on my toes," the first voice replied. The shapes appeared beneath them, pausing underneath the hole.

Santana, Dick, and Gyles stared down at them, each stranger carrying a powerful torch that shone at the floor.

"There's fuck all here," the man continued. "We've in a generic cave. Do you see any sign of ancient civilizations or any of that shit?" He shook his head. "I should be back with Diane right now. She does a killer roast on a Sunday."

"It's Tuesday," the woman replied.

"What are you two bitches chatting about?" a third voice offered, this one female.

"Tucker's scared we're lost," the first woman replied.

"Well, better pack it in," the third voice commented. "Turns out you numbskulls were heading in the right direction. One of the researchers is leading the others this way now. Something about symbols in the rock." She clapped, then rubbed her hands excitedly. "Can you feel the magic?"

The man snorted.

"Shall we wait here for them?" the first woman asked.

The second woman mused. "Nah, keep looking around. We might find something helpful to the case. If we can help lead the boss to the treasure, we might be able to increase our shares."

They moved away, muttering possibilities to each other excitedly. Santana waited until they were gone before activating the flashlight again. The three climbed as quickly as Gyles allowed them to until they eventually climbed out of the chute and onto solid ground.

Santana breathed a sigh of relief, taking a moment to gather her strength. Holding her position had been hard for her. Imagine how hard it would have been for Gyles.

"You okay?" she whispered.

Gyles stared at her, wonder in his eyes.

"Gyles?" she repeated.

Dick's hand landed on her shoulder. He spun her around to face the sight behind them.

A large golden door embedded in the rock, the emblem of Inti's face fixed to the top of the arch.

CHAPTER TWENTY-EIGHT

"Holy shit…" Santana couldn't blink, her body slowly dragging her toward the door. She couldn't pull away, as though she were the negative charge, and the door was the positive, magnetic forces dragging them together.

The door was double her height and six times as wide. Its golden surface had lost its shine. Moss, mold, and dust had dulled it. She ran a finger across its cool surface, leaving a clean trail behind. "The Temple of the Sun… It's real…"

Dick joined her, hands on his hips as he examined the door. He spoke softly. "They don't do things on a small scale, do they?" He gently tapped his knuckles on the door. "That's real gold."

"Mmhmm," Santana replied.

"You could feed a small city with that amount of currency," he added.

Santana brushed a hand across some of the detail of the door, a gleaming trail following in her wake. Gyles staggered behind them, his face pale as his eyes lit up. "You've got to be kidding me."

"Amazing, isn't it?" Santana asked. "That an ancient civilization could create such beauty, such structures. It seems impossible."

"But it's not," Gyles confirmed.

"It's not…" Santana turned her attention to the rest of the door. "The question now is, how do we unlock it?"

To either side of the door was a large hole. Within the holes were thick sets of chains that led to an unknown location. Santana tugged one of the chains but struggled to shift it. "A little help."

Dick came to Santana, reaching his hand to the chain. He pulled, muscles coiled, and managed to build a little momentum to make the chain move.

The door ground open an inch.

Dick tried again, struggling against the chain's stiffness.

"Hey, what about this one?" Gyles asked. Santana crossed to him, taking the chain in both hands. She looked at Dick. They exchanged a nod. Together they pulled.

The chains pulled easier together, the door grinding against the ground as it screeched open. Santana's hairs stood on end as she heard a commotion below her and knew that once again, they were giving away their position.

"It's okay," she reassured herself. "It's cat and mouse. We're the mice, and we only need to stay one step ahead of them."

Although you're also leading them straight to you—and consequently the temple.

The door opened wide enough for them to slip inside. Santana turned, looking for a way to close the door. As she did, something small appeared from the hole, popping out before landing near the door. She had enough time to see the grenade fizzle before the place erupted in smoke.

"Go!" Santana urged, running into the smooth corridors of the temple. Bleached stone and gold trimmed arches had darkened over time, and their feet *clapped* on the ground as they broke away from the hole and the commotion behind them.

They sped past rooms filled with abandoned objects, statues, and furniture crumbled and lost to time. The corridor was long, and by the time they reached the next door, they could see people emerging from the hole behind them.

"Open it!" Santana shouted.

Dick slammed into the door, his shoulder pressing against the stone. The door budged a couple of inches.

Santana helped him, shoving her shoulder against the door. The door slowly peeled open until it was wide enough for Santana to slip through.

"It's stuck," Dick declared.

Santana ducked inside, seeing the fallen stone and rubble behind the door that was blocking the opening. "There's too much stuff here to shift. You'll have to squeeze through."

Dick attempted to slide in, his chest getting stuck between doors. He breathed in, scratching his jacket and chest against the stone. She pulled his arm, helping him through until eventually he was freed and staggered to keep his balance.

Gunshots fired, bullets pinging off the stone.

"Gyles!" Santana roared. She grabbed his broken arm and yanked. Gyles screamed in pain, half his body through the door now.

He looked up into her eyes, pleading with her. "Go, Santana. Go..."

"Not without you," Santana replied, his arm flapping loosely in its socket. "Dick, help."

Dick grabbed a fistful of Gyles' clothes and tugged. Gyles' eyes filled with tears. He grunted as another gunshot exploded. His eyes closed.

"Gyles!" Santana roared. With a final tug, Gyles came through the door. He crashed onto the stone where he lay still.

"Help me close this," Santana commanded.

Dick came to her aid. Together the pair closed the door.

"Find something to block it," Santana stated. Dick busied

himself finding rocks and more loose objects to pile in front of the door. Santana turned her attention to Gyles. She crouched beside him. His chest wasn't rising and falling. Blood pooled around his waist. "Gyles?"

She gently eased him onto his back. Gyles coughed, groaning in pain. There was an open wound by his hip, which stained his t-shirt with blood.

Santana took off her backpack, finding her med-kit. "Stay with us," she instructed, finding a series of gauze and bandages to close the wound.

Dick returned to her side. "Blocked. For now. But if they have dynamite and C4 as they did at the last place, we're fucked."

Santana tore a bit of tape with her teeth and applied the final layer of gauze. "We need to find somewhere to hide him while we hunt for the lock. We can't carry him like this."

She looked up, her breath hitching. In the center of the large room they'd entered was a squared pyramid, stairs taking the corners to lead up to a gleaming golden podium in the center. A shaft of beaming sunlight shone straight down from the ceiling, impossibly so considering that they were far underground.

"It's here…" she whispered.

Something rumbled behind them.

"Santana, let's get moving." Dick nodded to their left where a small room faced them. "In there?"

Santana nodded. Together they helped Gyles into the small room that looked as though it could have been some kind of ancient broom closet.

Or tomb.

"Now what?" Dick asked once they had closed the door and left Gyles with a flask and a power bar.

Santana marveled at the pyramid. "Now, we protect the Temple of the Sun."

"How?" Dick asked. "It's two versus a hundred."

"Only if they all make it through," Santana replied. "First, they have to get us."

Dick gave her a strange look. Santana twisted her bag around, taking out several small items from inside. She held up a small vial of tranquilizer and shook it at him. "I have an idea. It's a little bit radical."

Dick grinned. "I think that's what we need right now."

CHAPTER TWENTY-NINE

The corridor was a hive of activity as Sasha emerged from the ladder.

There was no graceful way to climb, but she didn't care. Her heart buzzed with excitement, her target closing in. Two large golden doors stood wide open, and bodies flooded the tunnel ahead of her, her minions with their weapons, ready to remove all who stood in her way.

"Can you feel it?" she asked the man by her side.

Cameron nodded, his face stern. "Yes, ma'am. It's almost time."

She strode confidently ahead, the bodies parting as she walked between the doors. The temperature dropped a few degrees, the tunnel silencing as she approached. She slowed, taking in the architecture around her, walking the paths that no one had trod in millennia.

She paused halfway down the corridor, two of her order approaching her with rifles in their hands. "The way is barricaded, ma'am."

"Then blow it open," she commanded.

"We're all set." One of them motioned to the clusters of C4

around the door's edge. "All we need is your command."

"Good." Sasha grinned. She spun on her heels, putting distance between herself and the source of the explosion. When she reached the golden arch, she paused. Her father had taught her the safest place to be during an earthquake was beneath the arch of a door. To this day, she held that as truth.

She caught the eye of her minions and nodded. A moment later, they all hurried back, creating enough clearance from the door not to get hurt in the process.

Someone pressed the trigger. The corridor erupted with the sound of the explosion. Hands clapped to ears. Cracks and fractures appeared on the ceiling. Somewhere nearby, rocks fell.

Yet the tunnel remained steadfast, its construction built to last the long years of its existence.

She waited a few moments for the dust to settle. A large hole appeared where the door had once been. "Clear the area," she ordered.

Her men and women rushed around, running into the room. Somewhere inside were her interlopers, and they would be destroyed, dealt with like a cockroach beneath the boot. She smiled at the thought of their extermination, excitement flaring inside her again. Cameron waited patiently beside her.

Until a second explosion came—one she hadn't authorized.

Shouts and screams erupted from inside the room.

Sasha's smile faded.

Santana and Dick sat on the stairs leading up the pyramid, facing the door.

The commotion on the other side was audible, the tension palpable. "How long until they break through?" Santana asked.

"Depends how handy they are with their gadgets." Dick

glanced up at the ceiling. "I'm not sure we should be out in the open."

"We'll be okay." Santana caught him staring at her. "This place has withstood millennia of disruption and changes, and it remains mostly untouched. Say what you will about ancient cultures. They knew how to build things that last. Those walls must be at least a meter thick."

"And if the ceiling caves in anyway?" Dick asks.

"Then I'll go the way of my mother." Santana turned back to the door.

Dick sighed. "I didn't mean…"

"It's fine," Santana replied. "It's always going to be a hazard of the job. There are worse ways to die."

They returned to silence.

"You think Gyles will be okay?" she asked.

"I do." Dick scoffed. "Provided that everything goes to your plan."

Santana crossed her fingers. "Here's hoping." Silence fell on the other side of the door. "It's happening."

They braced themselves. The door erupted into sound and rock, debris shooting in all directions. Voices called with excitement as dust masked the distance between the two factions.

Santana gripped the stairs with white knuckles. Dick shifted beside her.

They waited for the dust to settle. Figures loomed in the cloud, growing clearer with each passing second. Soon several of them stepped through the door.

They paused when they spotted Dick and Santana, smiles growing on their faces. A man with a neat man-bun and a groomed beard aimed his rifle at them. "Found you, at last."

Santana nodded. "Funny that. We still win."

"How do you figure?" the man replied. "You're the ones under fire."

"We got here first," Dick replied. "We win." He turned over his shoulder to the summit of the pyramid. "All we have to do is reach the top first."

"Stay where you are," the man commanded. He snapped his fingers, and twelve guns pointed at them.

Santana and Dick raised their hands.

"Fine. You got us," Santana declared. "Well done. Just...let us see what happens, please. We've come all this way. Tell us we at least get to see the fireworks."

The man eyed them suspiciously. He waved two fingers and the men on either side headed toward them.

Santana grinned.

"Wait! Stop!" Man-bun cried.

It was too late. The two gunmen walked into the tripwire, tensing the line and initiating the trap. Several small explosions rained around their feet from the traps embedded in the cracks in the floor. A fine yellow mist burst into the air, mixed with shards of glass. Many of the men and women clutched small wounds. They breathed in the tranquilizer, falling into a near-instant state of paralysis. Before they could shoot, they were incapacitated.

Those behind the main crowd erupted into shouts. Santana and Dick rose to their feet, their makeshift bombs in each hand. They tossed them toward the doorway, initiating the next wave of toxic gas. When they'd thrown the bombs, they ducked out of sight around the back of the pyramid.

The chaos quieted as those affected fell into a heavy coma. Santana peeked out around the pyramid, watching as the yellow mist settled. A few minutes later, angry cries came from down the corridor.

They crept in cautiously, the remaining dozen sliding through the doors and stepping over the bodies of their comrades. Santana took her tranquilizer gun and unleashed a flurry of darts, knocking out half of their number. Dick took out the rest with a few carefully aimed shots until all that remained were three that they could see.

A shot fired at Santana. She ducked out the way, the bullet missing her nose by inches. Dick reached out and shot. When Santana next lined up her shot, she found only a woman standing in the doorway in a long dark robe, a scythe in her hand. "Enough!" Sasha bellowed.

Santana ducked out of sight.

"We want the same things," Sasha exclaimed. "We both want to see the restoration of magic long forgotten. Why degrade ourselves to such childish games?"

Santana breathed heavily. "No. You're wrong."

"I'm not," Sasha replied, keen confidence in her voice. "I know what you seek, Santana Sokolov. I know the treasures you secretly hunt."

Santana's skin bristled. How did she know her name?

Sasha's footsteps were slow. "I, too, am a motherless daughter. I, too, know the heartache of losing a loved one. Of hunting all your life for a way to erase the pain and accomplish the dreams of those we've lost. This is your chance to make your mother proud. This is my chance, too. Why would we fight and argue over such silly things when together we could achieve greatness?"

"Bullshit," Dick muttered.

Santana looked around the pyramid. Sasha stood at its base with her eyes fixed on the top.

"You don't know what you're talking about," Santana declared.

"I think I do," Sasha replied softly. "Otherwise, you'd have stopped me by now." Her head snapped in Santana's direction. "Tell me you aren't a little bit curious." She drew the dagger from a satchel at her side. "Tell me you don't yearn to know whether the legends are true. Unlimited power from the sun, an endless drought in exchange for one of the most valuable power sources ever created." Sasha turned back to the peak, eyes wide. "All within our reach."

Santana peeled herself from her hiding place and took to the nearest stairs. She ran up until she was in line with Sasha and aimed her pistol in her direction. "Stop."

"Make me," Sasha replied with a smirk. "You might've taken out my men and women, but you could've taken me out ages ago. You chose not to. Why is that?"

She didn't wait for an answer. Sasha continued up the stairs.

"Santana," Dick urged. "Stop her. We've come all this way."

Santana hesitated, her hand shaking. As much as she hated to admit it, Sasha was right. In front of her was a chance to prove the legend true once and for all. Wasn't that what her mother would've wanted? A woman who had spent her life trying to unravel the mysteries of this island? A woman who had died trying to discover the lost secrets of the world.

"Santana," Dick insisted.

Santana climbed the stairs, gun still trained on Sasha. They walked in sync, each taking the stairs together as they neared the top.

When they reached the top, they stopped a short distance from the center plinth. A decorative statue of gold took the center, several limbs and patterns whirling around in a strange formation. In the center was a hollow where a circle sat, a straight line in the center.

The lock and the key...

Sasha's pupils dilated, her smile drunken. She turned to Santana. "It's beautiful, isn't it?"

Santana didn't answer. She didn't need to. Her face said it all.

Sasha cautiously brought the dagger in front of her. Santana remembered the way it felt in her hand, that gentle buzz of electricity. She wanted it back.

Sasha kept her eyes fixed on Santana as she brought the dagger up, aiming for the slot in the center of the structure. She was only a foot away when Santana cracked her whip, the end coiling around Sasha's wrist.

"Ouch!" Sasha cried.

Santana tugged. The dagger flew out of Sasha's hand. She brought the dagger beside her, where she bent low and picked it up. Her hand fit neatly around the handle. "Mine, bitch."

Sasha growled. "You think I'll let you get away that easy?"

Dick appeared behind Santana, gun aimed at Sasha. Sasha tensed.

Santana took a long breath. "It's over, Sasha. Your Order has failed. We'll take this item to a safe home, someplace where you and your kind will never lay their hands on it again—"

A singular gunshot cut her off. Blood exploded, spraying her face in warm crimson. She yelled as the bullet hit her shoulder, clipping the bone. She dropped the dagger. In the chaos, Sasha broke toward them. Santana spun to find Sasha's comrade at the pyramid's base, gun trained on the pair.

"Duck!" she called, shoving Dick down.

They crashed against the floor as another shot fired. Santana spun as laughter came from behind her. When she turned, Sasha had slid the dagger in the slot.

For a heart-stopping moment, nothing happened. The room fell into quiet. Sasha's laughter faded.

"No…" she protested. "No…it can't be…"

Which was when the temple rumbled, and the shaft of light that pooled down from the ceiling intensified, a blinding white light enveloping the interior chamber of the Temple of the Sun.

CHAPTER THIRTY

They stared upward, each shading their faces from the light with their arms.

"What's going on?" Dick shouted, barely audible over the rumble.

Santana had no answer. She couldn't work out where the light was coming from, nor why it was intensifying, washing everything around them in a white glow. A short distance away, she could just make out Sasha beaming into the light.

The rumble continued. The surface beneath her shook. The pyramid's four sides began to peel away, leaving the stairs in place but creating a deadly drop beneath them.

She glanced down into the abyss, finding that light flooded it as well. Her eyes hurt. Her skin burned. She gritted her teeth, trying to make some sense of it all as the distant roar of ancient machinery started whirring.

"What has she done?" Dick called again. Santana staggered forward, holding onto the golden statue for dear life. Dick stood next to her, following suit. Sasha bellowed a laugh, ecstasy flooding her features as she took it all in.

"It's beautiful, isn't it?" she roared, arms spread wide.

"Embrace the light of Inti! The birthing of the holy drought. The gods giveth, and we shall receive." She fell to her knees, tears streaming down her face. "Father…" she muttered. "We've done it."

The whirring of distant machinery grew louder. Santana's heart raced, wondering what the hell they were doing and what she could do about it now. Panels of light exploded around the temple as the temperature climbed.

"Look!" Dick called.

They looked up, straining through the intense light. The ceiling was opening, revealing layers of dirt and rock above, which tumbled and sprayed down around them. The sky came into sight, a foggy azure that was growing brighter with every passing second. The sun was high overhead, and if Santana didn't know better, she could swear it was growing in size, intensifying its rays.

"Shut it off!" Dick roared. "Make it stop!"

"No!" Sasha declared, whirling toward the pair of them. She rose to her feet, lunging for Dick. Santana looked below them for Sasha's comrade but could see only white.

"Get off me," Dick called, wrestling with the crazed Sasha. Santana turned her attention to the dagger, her hand resting above the blade. She knew she must remove it, but what would happen if she didn't? What the hell was going on right now?

"Sokolov!" Dick called.

The pair rolled dangerously close to the edge of the pyramid, Dick on his back, head hanging over the edge of the severe drop. Sasha's hands were around his throat, showcasing a strength that only the crazed could show.

"Santana, please!" Dick called.

Santana's lip curled. In one quick sweep, she pulled the handle of the dagger, sliding it from its bed in the lock, then spun. She spotted something in Sasha's pocket and reached out, quickly hiding the item in the folds of her clothes. Dick cried out.

Santana reared back, then kicked her boot heel at Sasha's ass. Sasha toppled over Dick, reeling down into the depths below.

Santana extended a hand to Dick, her skin feeling as though it was on fire. She helped him to his feet.

"Why's it not stopping?" Dick asked, ducking as a rock tumbled toward him.

"I don't know," Santana exclaimed. "We have to get out of here."

"Agreed." Dick took her hand, leading her toward the nearest stairs.

They raced down, two at a time. The temple continued to shake and rumble around them as debris fell, a few larger chunks falling dangerously close to the pair.

They made it to the bottom, the light still dazzling so brightly they could only see a short distance ahead. They beelined for the chamber where they'd left Gyles, Santana certain she spotted a set of legs sticking out from beneath a large boulder.

Rocks blocked the door to the chamber. Together they nudged and rolled them out of the way until they were able to open the door. Gyles was fast asleep, his face even paler in the light.

Dick threw the man over his shoulder as they made for the exit. They stepped over bodies, a pang of regret hitting Santana's stomach that rubble might bury them all by the morning.

The way out was illuminated equally brightly, light exploding from a thousand unseen sources along the temple's corridor. They sprinted for the ladder, almost crashing down the shaft as the caves around them continued to shake.

"It *has* to stop soon," Santana declared. "We have the dagger."

"We'll figure it out when we're free," Dick exclaimed, leading the way down, Santana struggling with her damaged shoulder.

They hopped the final distance, Dick staggering under the weight of Gyles, who had yet to wake up. Santana took over, leading them along the tunnels, avoiding the dust and debris that shook around them. The farther they got into the natural caverns, the quieter the rumbles grew, the less violent the shakes.

They climbed the slope, eventually reaching the carved stairs leading to the surface. They eased their way out of the waterfall, finding their way to the shore of the lake. Looking behind them, a large column of light shone up and into the sky from a hidden place with the forest at the mountain's edge. They shielded their eyes. "It's shrinking, isn't it?" Santana asked, wondering if it was all wishful thinking.

"It is," Dick confirmed. "It's shrinking."

It was. The column of light reduced slowly, shrinking until all that remained was a series of black ribbons of smoke rising into the sky around the area the light had burned. They made their way to the far shore, resting by the water as they watched the last of the light disappear. They sat there in silence until the sun slipped behind the horizon.

The three fell asleep, weariness finally claiming its victims.

CHAPTER THIRTY-ONE

Night had descended when Santana awoke, a chill sweeping over her skin and filling it with goosebumps.

She sat up, pain throbbing in her shoulder. The wound didn't look great, small flecks of dirt mixed with the dried blood. She dragged her bag toward her and poured on some antiseptic, hissing as it burned. She rose to her feet and roused the others.

Dick groggily sat up. Gyles was harder to wake. It became clear that they would need to work together to escape the throes of the jungle.

They started their long trek a few minutes later after filling their canteens and collecting a bagful of nearby fruits. Santana led them through the trees, aware that they didn't need to keep away from the main thoroughfares now that they'd left the Order behind. They barely spoke as they trekked through the trees, Santana leading the pack, utilizing her whip to keep the critters at bay.

An hour into their trek, they stopped for food and drink. They were all still exhausted, but Santana promised them a safer resting spot soon. The land rose and fell, the stars wheeling above them. Soon enough, the trees thinned slightly, allowing them access to an almost overgrown road lined with half a dozen abandoned vehicles.

They didn't have the heart to smile. They weren't out of the woods yet. Dick helped Gyles into the back of a 4x4 before climbing into the driver's seat. Headlights flooded the dark with light as he reversed and followed Santana's directions back to the city.

The road unfurled like a ribbon. They reached the tree line over an hour later, and Santana couldn't have been more thankful to see civilization. Dick drove to the city in silence, pulling up outside Santana's apartment a little after 2:00 a.m.

They both carried Gyles up the stairs, Santana using her good arm to support him. She unlocked her place, disarming the traps before guiding Gyles to her bedroom.

"What about the couch?" Dick asked.

"He needs proper rest," Santana replied. "He deserves comfort."

They worked together, holding him still as they cleaned his cuts and attended to his wounds. Dick worked on Santana's next as the pair of them sat in her living room, the moon glittering outside her balcony. She sat on the coffee table, back to Dick. He sat on the couch.

"What do you think happened out there?" Dick asked the first real question they'd tossed to each other since escaping the temple.

Santana shook her head. "I honestly don't know. Whatever it was, it was big." She glanced at the dagger in her hands. "How can something so simple release such a reaction?"

"There's magic in the world," Dick muttered. "That's what you told me, right?"

Santana nodded. "You believe?"

"I do now," Dick replied. "I don't know how or why, but I can't deny what we've seen. All those legends and myths of the island...all the strange occurrences in the jungle... I've seen weird things in my time, but I could've sworn that we unlocked a doorway to the gods in there. Inti was shining down on us, unleashing his wrath."

Santana chewed her lip, bracing as Dick worked stitches across her skin. "There are other worlds than these…"

"What's that?"

"Stephen King. The *Dark Tower* series. I don't think he was wrong."

Dick finished, then spread some iodine over the wound. Satisfied, he sat back, fixing Santana with a curious glance. "You should rest up."

"You should, too." She motioned to the bed on the floor.

"Thanks," Dick replied. "I think I should probably head home, though. I'll sleep better in my place. Gyles isn't the only one who needs some proper rest after all that adventure." He nodded at the dagger in Santana's lap. "What're you going to do with that?"

Santana met Dick's gaze, and a smile appeared on her lips. "Give it to *my* client…again. Only, this time I'll be certain that he stores it someplace safer than before. This…" she held the dagger before her, "should not be put into the wrong hands again. Not as long as that temple exists."

"If it still does," Dick replied. "It could have destroyed itself."

Santana considered this. "I guess we'll never know."

"I guess we won't." Dick turned for the door. "It's a shame."

"What's that?"

"So much history destroyed without a trace." He sighed. "Still, that's not my area of expertise, is it?"

Without another word, he left Santana alone in her living room.

Santana waited a few moments, studying the craftsmanship of the blade in her hand. When Dick's footsteps faded, and all that remained were Gyles' gentle snores, she crossed to her backpack she'd left on the kitchen counter. She reached inside and drew out a small parcel covered in cloth. It was heavy, and she grimaced as she dragged it onto the counter.

Peeling the cloth gently away, she unveiled a glowing blue orb, its edges perfectly smooth. It pulsed gently with power, a strange static causing the hairs on her hands to rise. She thought back to the wash of immense light and the crazed woman about to hurl Dick off the edge of the pyramid. She had snatched the orb from Sasha's pocket, and now a sly grin licked her lips.

"Not everything is lost, Johnny Boy," she muttered to herself. "Not everything…"

First, thank you for not only reading this story, but these author notes in the back as well.

For those who don't know me, I'll add an 'About Me' at the bottom of these author notes. For those that do, I'll get right into it.

I'm presently in Frankfurt, Germany (I live in Las Vegas, USA and Cabo San Lucas, Mexico). I'm here for the Frankfurt Bookfair.

Today, our lead of translations Jens Schulze (German), and I walked over to a mall where I could get a PCR Test (COVID test) to travel back to the United States. While coming back, we passed by a Comic / Game shop called T3.

It's packed. I mean, it was floor-to-wall games, miniatures, stacks of games in the middle of the floor (everywhere stacks), and RPG books up against a wall. I wish I had thought to take a picture to drop into these author notes.

So, I'm just about on my way out of the store when I notice my weakness. The treasure in these stores that sparkles and bedazzles my eyes whether I need them (I don't) or not. What could possibly be this eye candy that makes my brain buzz?

Dice.

Specifically, sets of dice you use for RPG games. You know, 4-sided, 6, 8, 10, 12, and 20-sided dice. My dragon (read greedy) side needed to look at the pretty'z. So I did.

Then, almost done with the case on the counter... the gentleman mentions a large orange 'box' he called it. It wasn't a box, it was a standup metal set of drawers where you slid it more pretty'z to ooh and ahh over in the back all by yourself.

So, you know, you don't salivate in public. It's very unbecoming.

Regardless, by the time I went down the row of dice, I found myself about $65.00 poorer.

And yet, I helped out the local economy. That's a good thing, right? That's my story when my wife asks what I did today.

"You know honey, I got the Covid test, had lunch... Helped out the locals a bit. Nothing important."

Now, if the rest of you won't mention this (ever) on social media, I'll be alright.

If you do? Well, if you get no more books because I didn't make it – *that problem is on you.*

Now, for those who have never read a book (or I didn't introduce myself), here is the obligatory 'about me' section ;-)

I wrote my first book *Death Becomes Her* (*The Kurtherian Gambit*) in September/October of 2015 and released it November 2, 2015. I wrote and released the next two books that same month and had three released by the end of November 2015.

So, just under six years ago.

Since then, I've written, collaborated, concepted, and/or created hundreds more in all sorts of genres.

My most successful genre is still my first, Paranormal Sci-Fi, followed quickly by Urban Fantasy. I have multiple pen names I produce under.

Some because I can be a bit crude in my humor at times or raw in my cynicism (Michael Todd). I have one I share with

CONNECT WITH THE AUTHOR

Connect with Michael Anderle

Website: http://lmbpn.com

Email List: http://lmbpn.com/email/

Social Media:

https://www.facebook.com/LMBPNPublishing

https://twitter.com/MichaelAnderle

https://www.instagram.com/lmbpn_publishing/

https://www.bookbub.com/authors/michael-anderle

Martha Carr (Judith Berens, and another (not disclosed) that we use as a marketing test pen name.

In general, I just love to tell stories, and with success comes the opportunity to mix two things I love in my life.

Business and stories.

I've wanted to be an entrepreneur since I was a teenager. I was a very *unsuccessful* entrepreneur (I tried many times) until my publishing company LMBPN signed one author in 2015.

Me.

I was the president of the company, and I was the first author published. Funny how it worked out that way.

It was late 2016 before we had additional authors join me for publishing. Now we have a few dozen authors, a few hundred audiobooks by LMBPN published, a few hundred more licensed by six audio companies, and about a thousand titles in our company.

It's been a busy five plus years.

Have a great week or weekend and talk to you in the next book!

Ad Aeternitatem,

Michael Anderle